Dust and Ashes

Brand of Justice
Book 6

Lisa Phillips

eBook ISBN: 979-8-88552-184-0

Paperback ISBN: 979-8-88552-185-7

Published by: Two Dogs Publishing, LLC. Idaho, USA

Cover Design by: Sasha Almazan and Gene Mollica, GS Cover Design Studio, LLC

Edited by: Christine Callahan, Professional Publishing Services

Chapter One

Friday evening
Cielo Ardiente, Mexico

Hot wind blew the dust off white painted concrete walls down the channel between dilapidated buildings, ruffling Kenna's hair against her face.

Today would be a good day for them to escape.

She lifted the box to the lip of the tailgate. The weight tipped toward her. She gritted her teeth and shoved the box into the back of the semi that had arrived in the dawn hours. They'd been out here for hours loading boxes and crates. Long enough the sun dipped behind the mountains to paint the sky red.

Kenna shifted at the feel of someone at her back. A second later, she heard the word *move* in Spanish from behind her. She got out of the way, but not before the corner of a wooden crate clipped her shoulder. She hissed out a breath. *If they couldn't break me, you certainly won't.*

Elisa dumped her crate on the back of the truck, then

managed to clip Kenna with her elbow moving back to get more boxes. The girl was barely nineteen.

Kenna ran her hands down her screaming forearms but got no relief. Sand and dirt mixed with sweat on her skin. Her mouth tasted like carpet. Her hair lay damp with sweat around her forehead. They'd given her shorts and a shirt, neither of which fit well.

Kenna passed Ana and Lola, two local girls carrying a long crate between them that looked suspiciously like it should hold a grenade or a rocket launcher. The insignia on the side had been sanded off. Military style compound. Ex-military men. If they were smugglers it was more than just black-market weapons.

Whoever it had belonged to was probably looking for their armaments. They'd have no clue it was currently being loaded onto a truck in Cielo Ardiente, an hour south of the US–Mexico border.

At least that was as far as Kenna had been able to gather as to their location in the days since she woke up in the tan building with Jax bleeding.

Don't look over there.

The words had become her mantra.

Don't let them know you care about him.

Don't let them see you're hurt.

She could have all the feelings she wanted once they were out of here. Free of this place, and these people, and the business they had going on.

Kenna grabbed another crate, avoiding Elisa. But not the girl's scathing look. Or the muttered, "No work, no reward."

Not exactly what the girl had said, but close enough. Kenna's Spanish hadn't improved since she got here. Though, she had learned a few choice words. Not helpful. Instead of trying to figure out how to explain that she had no desire to "earn" anything from these guys, she kept her mouth shut.

One of the other girls—the quietest one, Lola—spoke a little English. Enough to translate on occasion, though usually she just kept her mouth shut after refusing to answer Kenna's questions about how they got here. Lola pretended she didn't understand that question.

Kenna gave a second's side glance at the end of the loading bay where the guards stood. Americans. Two of them. Her first clue that this wasn't what she'd assumed it would be.

The guys on the gate were Mexican. Locals couldn't be trusted to not rat you out to the cartel over the hill, so these had been hired from farther away. Lola had told her their accents indicated they were from the south.

None of the girls knew the backgrounds of the four Americans. They'd only known about three of them. Two were currently watching them, holding AR-15s, giving Kenna a military vibe. Then there was the leader—the biggest one. Kenna had seen a fourth these girls hadn't. When they spoke to each other, they moved like a squad. Men who had served together, fought, and bled together. But who had landed down here smuggling weapons.

Barbed wire fence. Four buildings. Six vehicles, two of which were broken down. One had nearly bald tires that risked a flat too much to take the chance. She'd have to be careful which vehicle she stole. The compound had no cover, so no hiding if she was making a run for it. After she got him out from the building he was being held in, Jax might not be able to move fast.

She dumped another box in the truck.

They could maybe hide in the back of a vehicle. She couldn't guarantee they'd stay hidden long enough for the truck to leave before the order was called to lock the whole place down.

Wait until the four military guys drank too much, and chance the hired men being easier to get by than trained US soldiers.

Former ones, or mercenaries maybe? She couldn't figure it out.

The whole thing was a puzzle she had been relentlessly trying to solve since they had been attacked in Washington, DC, and transported in the back of a van all the way here.

Jax injured.

Both of them dehydrated.

Kenna sniffed and only got a nose full of hot air for her troubles. The whole place smelled like sour dirt and sweat. The tang of sewage. She tried to swallow but didn't have the moisture to get rid of the dusty taste in her mouth.

Elisa cried out.

Kenna turned in time to see her shove Lola to the ground and scream a curse.

Elisa flounced away.

Ana dragged the crate to the truck as though determined to do the job no matter what. Even if it was impossible to lift the items, she would strain until someone told her to stop. But was it fear—or something else?

Kenna went to Lola and crouched. "Are you hurt?"

The girl wore a similar shorts and shirt combo that Kenna had been given. Ill fitting, frayed at the edges. Kenna had kept her Converse from when they'd been captured, praying every day that Maizie really had slipped some kind of tracking device into the shoes. The teen tech guru would be working night and day looking for Kenna—she hoped.

Working on a rescue plan.

Sending everyone and anyone who would listen after her and Jax.

And yet, it had been days, and no one had come.

Don't lose hope.

She of all people knew what happened when a captive lost hope. When despair took over and death looked like a way out. That thought made her want to glance at the white building where she knew they were holding him.

She hadn't heard a sound all day.

Jax.

She looked down at Lola, determined not to give away where her thoughts were. What had she been thinking about? Shoes. This girl wore flip-flops. No one was coming for Lola. Did anyone even care? Kenna held out her hands to help the girl up.

Lola ran a finger over the scar on Kenna's left forearm.

Kenna nearly pulled back, a reflex to defend herself. The muscles of her forearm flexed, and pain ricocheted every direction from the spot Lola touched. Kenna sniffed through her nose.

Lola grabbed the inside of Kenna's elbow and pulled herself up. "I'm okay."

"All I see is a whole lot of standing around and not much working." A man's voice thundered down the channel between buildings where vehicles were parked out of sight of the road. Out of the sun. But Kenna knew how hot it got inside.

Lola whipped around. Kenna turned more slowly to face him. Ian Kartom—who they all called Kart.

Broad shoulders, a tapered waist. Cargo pants and a tight T-shirt. A beard. Brown eyes with gold flecks. Attractive by all reasonable measures, but there was something about him that kept people at arms' length. A lethality so tangible she could almost touch it in the air around him.

Elisa sashayed past Kenna to stand close to him. All but offering herself up, probably hoping she'd be retasked with a different assignment—one that didn't involve manual labor. Kenna couldn't even fathom what she might've been through in her life that she made such an advance to a man like this.

"The truck isn't going to load itself."

Lola and Ana both rushed to grab another long crate.

Kenna's arms weren't going to lift much more before her permanently damaged tendons got permanent damage on top of what there already was.

Elisa shot her a scathing look. Like Kenna was trying to be her competition?

Kenna's heart broke that the girl thought as much about the people around her. That she thought she could better her situation by offering up her body to a guy like this, or his friends. Or all of them.

He stared at Kenna. "Won't be long."

"Same threat." She managed to shrug her shoulder. "Different day."

A man's cry tore through the compound.

Kenna didn't have the strength to hold back the flinch. Kart shoved Elisa back and stomped over to stand in front of Kenna. She held herself still while he stared down at her.

Elisa huffed her way past them.

Kenna stared right back at the guy. She picked a spot on his cheek and stared at the pores. If she didn't meet his eyes, surely that indicated indifference. She wasn't looking away, avoiding eye contact, which would come across as defensive. Was this working?

She let out a long breath because she was tired, motioning to Elisa. "Are you ever going to give her the time of day?"

Kart glanced at the three young women, local girls. Elisa, Lola, and Ana.

"Or, you know, pay them for the work they're doing." Kenna shrugged one shoulder again. "That could be good."

"They'll learn how this works."

"Really? Because I'd like to know also." Kenna said. "You work them half to death in the heat, then victimize them. Then what? Send them home to their families?"

"Considering you visited Brian's ranch in Colorado, I'd think you'd know exactly where they go next."

Kenna had connected the dots on that one a day or so after they arrived.

These men here were connected to the operation in Colorado. The threat coming? The sheriff who'd had her and Jax kidnapped from DC and brought here.

And now he was on his way.

Supposedly.

"But Brian's dead," Kenna said, "and the migrant workers he had in the basement are gone. So what's left?"

She'd set those people free in the process of rescuing a young woman. Camila had been pregnant, and she and her boyfriend, Luca, had married in Vegas. Kenna and Jax had been at the wedding—now they were both here.

Another cry rang across the compound, a man in intense pain.

She bit her lip hard where Kart wouldn't be able to see. Forced her body to not move. Every sound from Jax meant he was still alive. *Stay alive.*

Kart sneered. "So you do care about him."

"He's a human being," Kenna fired back. "So, yes. Why wouldn't I when we're in this together?"

"How sweet." He chuckled in the same sinister tone he spoke with. "My cousin will be here soon."

Sheriff Elliot Preston, Brian's brother. The man who'd gone on TV to say he'd survived an assassination attempt... months ago, now. Instead of reporting Kenna's actions to the appropriate authority he'd had her and Jax kidnapped from the US capital and brought all the way down here.

And now he was on his way. *Won't be long.*

"Like I said. Same threat. Different day." Kenna wasn't going to cower. What she was going to do was get Jax and figure out how to escape.

He just needed to hold on. Not lose hope and...

She couldn't think about Bradley. She had to focus, but trauma had a way of impeding clarity of thinking. She'd been considering that a lot, trying to back out of her own mind and assess what was happening. Get some self-awareness. Consider her reactions this time, and how they were different now they would've been.

She'd even tried praying, and it seemed to help her mind settle at least some. But it hadn't changed her situation. She was still at the whim of these men.

"Does the FBI agent care about you as much as you care about him?"

Kenna lifted her chin. "As a valuable human life? Maybe. Who knows?"

Kart chuckled. "We both know it's more than that. But your boyfriend is gonna tell us everything he knows, then he's gonna to disappear."

Which meant they planned to bury him out here in the middle of nowhere in a shallow grave. No one would ever know what happened to Special Agent Oliver Jaxton.

Kind of like another FBI agent she'd known years ago.

Ramon Santiago had been to Quantico at the same time as Kenna. She hadn't seen him much after that—thankfully—but who she'd heard plenty of stories about. He'd gone undercover south of the border and turned dark side. Disappeared. Gone AWOL. Whatever it was written off as, he'd never been seen or heard from again. Whether that was because he was a turncoat or he'd been discovered and killed, she had no idea.

A search had turned up nothing.

Now the guy was a cautionary tale.

Kenna turned to look at the sunset on the horizon, where she wanted to be right now. Away from here—with Jax.

She had little leverage, but she would always be exactly who she was.

The daughter of Malcom Banbury.

She turned back to Kart. "If Jax dies, you die."

He flashed a few teeth. "Is that a threat?"

"It's a promise." Kenna turned away from him and headed for the last of the crates the girls were loading into the back of the truck.

At least she could say she understood these men. More than she understood the FBI these days. But that understanding meant she'd been targeted, Jax had been caught up in it, and he could die.

Because of her choices.

Elisa's glance could've shot daggers, it was so vicious.

"He's all yours," Kenna said.

The girl's expression flashed confusion.

"You made a serious mistake."

Kenna could do nothing to save these girls. However they'd landed here, whether by accepting a job or because they wanted a chance to get out of Mexico and find a better life somewhere else. The choice they'd made might've been a worse decision than staying put.

Or it might've been a choice between two bad situations.

Kenna couldn't help them. She could barely lift a box. Her stomach ached; it had been so long since she ate an actual meal. No matter how hard she'd worked to keep from being vulnerable ever again, she'd never imagined she would be right back in the same situation.

At the mercy of a dangerous man, while the person she cared about was hurt.

Don't lose hope.

If Jax didn't make it...

That sheriff could come. Maybe there wouldn't be anything she could do to stop him from doing whatever he wanted. Kenna had lost control of her life days ago when that explosion flipped the SUV they'd been in.

She had no power here. No way out, and no idea what condition Jax was in unless they brought him to her or let her go see him.

Kenna didn't want to spend another night alone on a dirt floor, wondering what the moment she lived through might encompass. Listening to sounds she didn't want to hear. Or falling into a fitful light sleep full of flashes of what might happen when the sheriff showed up for payback.

"Hey!"

By the time Kenna turned, Benjamin had taken off toward the gate. Anthony stuck to his post, probably about to shoot any of them for doing the same.

The whole compound was surrounded by a chain-link fence. The gatehouse and the two guards were the only thing to block her view of a pickup truck with men in the back, holding weapons.

One of the girls whimpered and ran for her life. Behind Kenna. Away from the gate.

A projectile exploded from the passenger side of the pickup, blew past the gatehouse, and took a section of fence with it before it hit the dirt and exploded.

Kenna ducked, more like a flinch.

The rapport of automatic gunfire exploded like fireworks in the late evening. Flashes of light followed the continuous conversation of back-and-forth bullets. Men ran everywhere—taking cover, then firing to stave off the rush of men coming in.

They were under attack.

She whirled to the building where they were keeping Jax. The door swung open, and three men ran out. He was alone in there.

Now. She had to do this now.

She clocked the fact it was the lid of a crate a split second before Elisa slammed it into Kenna's shoulder.

Chapter Two

Kenna cried out and landed on her hands and knees. No time to figure out the Spanish word for "escape." Would Elisa even want that?

She glanced up long enough to see Elisa rearing back for another go with the crate lid. Kenna pivoted on her knee and swiped out with her leg, taking Elisa's legs out from under her. The girl slammed onto the dirt on her back.

Kenna grabbed the lid and barked, "No." She tossed it aside and shifted to her feet. Her arms might be practically worthless, but her legs worked just fine. "Girl, you have issues."

Kenna couldn't fix the girl's sense of worth, or what she thought she needed from the world. They barely spoke the same language. Right now, she needed to get to Jax and make sure he survived this.

She ran around the back of the truck, then paused behind cover to look around the rear of the building. Most of the fighting was concentrated in front, where the pickup had pulled in. Whoever it was, they had to know they were up against four US-military-trained men and the guys they'd hired.

Kenna had given up trying to count how many there were in this compound working for Kart and his friends, but however many there were, the pickup guys were outnumbered.

She wanted to believe whoever they were would be victorious. But reality usually indicated otherwise compared with wishful thinking. There was about as much chance of Kart and his guys losing this fight as there was of Kenna getting Jax out. And managing to survive dragging him through the desert out of here.

Across the stretch of flat dirt between here and the chain-link fence, Ana ran for freedom. The young woman pumped her arms and legs, moving frantically as fast as she could.

Gunfire erupted.

The girl's body jerked and she fell to the ground.

Lola screamed. Kenna spotted her under the truck, hands clapped over her ears. Hiding.

Instead of doing the same, which might have been a smarter decision, Kenna jumped in the cab of the truck and found the keys on the dash. She fired up the engine as Lola scrambled out from underneath. "Get in!"

The girl ran away.

Kenna gripped the huge steering wheel with both hands and hit the gas. The truck roared out from between the two buildings, and she yanked the wheel to the left. It didn't matter what the odds were for survival. It didn't matter that she could be shot sitting on this side of the truck with only the window for protection. It didn't matter that Jax could very well be dead, or that she'd have to get him up into the truck and get them out of here without anyone catching them in order to escape.

They needed a series of miracles.

She had to try.

Kenna pulled up close to the front door of the building where Jax was being held. The door was still open, but she couldn't see inside. The sun cast long shadows on the ground. The cover of night might help her escape, as long as they could stay alive until then.

She kept the engine running, scooted over to the passenger door, and shoved it wide.

Two seconds later she jumped down and headed inside.

The open room had a chain from the ceiling hanging down, but not far enough that his feet touched the ground. Both shoulders looked dislocated. Blood covered his chest and dripped from his mouth. His eyes were swollen almost completely shut.

She couldn't hold back the cry from her lips as she skidded across the floor toward him.

Get him down. She had to get him down.

Kenna couldn't allow herself to be overwhelmed by the enormity of the task of getting them both out of here. She just had to take it one problem at a time, like finding bolt cutters in the corner and struggling to break the chain.

She squeezed the handles closer to each other.

She wasn't strong enough.

Kenna shook her head against that thought and poured every ounce of strength she had into squeezing the handles so they met at her wrists. She broke one link. The weight of Jax's limp body bent the broken halves open, but he didn't fall.

She cried out her frustration.

An ominous chuckle came to her from the corner of the room, and a man stepped out of the shadows. "Figured you would come here first."

"Where else would I be?"

Kart chuckled again. "I know where I'd like you to be, but we all have our roles to play. We all have orders that keep us alive...and obligations to uphold."

"Like the imperative that says if you kill him, then I kill you?"

His teeth flashed in the dim light. "I'd like to see you try when you don't even seem able to lift your arms. Though, it will be interesting watching you struggle."

It figured a man with no desire to assist his friends in safeguarding his home would take satisfaction from someone else's pain. That was who guys like him were. Predators. This man was close to being an apex predator. At least in this part of the world.

The building rocked. One wall exploded inward sending rubble across the room. She moved to protect Jax from the flying debris, his skin far too slick to keep hold of him under the onslaught. Finally, the chain gave in, rattling through the ring hanging from the ceiling, and he started to fall. She had no strength to catch him, and the two of them collapsed.

Kenna's leg bent awkwardly between her and the floor. Jax lay across her lap, unconscious.

"Tell you what." Kart strode over to them. "If you can get him out of here, I'll let you save him from being buried under this building when it collapses."

He disappeared back into the shadows, leaving her to do this on her own.

Kenna lifted Jax's bound hands over her head so they hung around her neck. She used her hands and feet—but mostly her feet—to scoot back across the slick floor toward the front door, dragging him with her.

She spotted the prick of stars in the sky overhead, trying to focus on them as she made it on to the stoop. She would have to go down the steps and then up into the truck.

A truck that now had flat tires.

Kenna let out a scream of frustration. Jax stirred. He moaned and shifted against her. She wrapped her arms around him and held him close, running her hand down the back of his head. They had come into this situation together, and she was determined they would leave it together—one way or another. If he lost hope and lost his life...she would just have to find a way to end hers as well.

She was going to repeat the past that had nearly destroyed her the first time.

But she wasn't going to be alone.

No way would she survive living when the person with her died. Not when it happened all over again and she had to walk away the sole survivor of a dangerous man who was determined to take lives and steal hope.

Nope. Not happening.

Another explosion rocked the building behind her. The truck shifted as well at the force of the blast.

Kart appeared again. "We can't let the merchandise get damaged."

Did he mean Jax, or her? Whichever it was, he scooped them both up. Squeezing with massive arms, cutting off her air. She held on to Jax as Kart dragged them across the dirt to a building, kicked the door in, and laid Jax on the hallway floor.

Kenna turned to look at him in the light, that white glow from overhead. Before she could start her assessment, Kart dragged her to her feet.

Kenna gasped. "What are you—"

"I don't have time for your rambling. So keep your mouth shut."

She felt his breath hot against her cheek. Kenna struggled against his grip, but he didn't ease even an ounce of pressure on her arm. Just above her elbow. Tight enough hot sparks flashed down to her fingertips. She screamed out the pain and frustration of not knowing if Jax even still had a pulse.

A door slammed open ahead of them.

Kart shifted her far enough aside to lift a pistol and squeeze off two shots into the man's abdomen.

The gun fell before the man did, and Kart shoved her toward him. "Ask who sent him here. And if you pick up that gun, I'll kill you."

The man clutched his stomach, blood all over his shirt. She didn't want to know what his flesh looked like underneath.

She stumbled and set a hand against the wall, twisting back. "What?"

"Ask him," Kart's tone was lethal. "Who sent him here."

She turned more so she could see Jax, who lay on the floor facing the wall. He still hadn't moved. *Don't be dead.*

"Now."

Kenna stumbled to her knees beside the man Kart had shot.

He gritted bloody teeth and said something to her in Spanish.

"I don't speak his language. How do you expect me to ask him anything?" She didn't even want to help put pressure on the wound when it would only be futile. Kart knew how to kill someone, and gut shots were always nasty. But then she didn't get to assess whether someone should live or if they died. It wasn't for her to make that kind of judgment when she had no idea who this guy was.

Maybe this guy was a local freedom fighter.

Or someone who made the wrong choice, like Lola. As opposed to someone like Elisa who seemed bound and determined to better herself in all the worst ways—like somehow becoming Kart's girlfriend, or whatever she thought she was doing.

"Figure it out."

Two gunshots went off behind her. Kenna flinched.

The guy on the floor bleeding muttered something he seemed to think was hilarious. Blood bubbled between his lips.

She winced. "Who do you work for?"

This was hardly the kind of questioning she usually did with people. But then, this was a far cry from anything she'd ever done as a private investigator. Or as an FBI agent before that, a short but renowned career that ended after a serial killer kidnapped her and her partner—who also happened to be her boyfriend at the time and the father of the baby she had been carrying.

Bradley had lost hope and ended his life.

She couldn't lose another man she cared about. She was only just beginning to have deep feelings for, and wanted to see where it could go.

Which would be nowhere...if she didn't get them out of here.

She shook the man's shoulders. "Who do you work for?"

He stared at her with glassy eyes. He wouldn't last much longer. She had seen enough people die in front of her to know that.

She'd need medical supplies to get answers. "You want me to save his life so you can question him and end up taking it when his body gives out? Get me a first aid kit or *something*."

"Fun as that sounds, we don't have time." Kart walked to her and said over her shoulder, "Héctor Álvarez Navarro."

Kenna had heard that name. El Falcón was notorious in this part of Mexico. That was who Kart thought had sent these men? She twisted around. "You're going up against the Falcon?"

Maybe he wasn't as stable as she thought.

"Now I definitely want to get Jax and get out of here." She shuddered.

The man on the floor muttered something. His eyes rolled back in his head, and his last breath puffed from between his lips.

"He's dead."

Kart hauled her up by her elbow. "No kidding."

Before she could say anything to the contrary, he dragged her the opposite direction from Jax. "If he dies—"

Kart cut her off. "Yeah, I heard you the first time."

The door at the far end of the hall slammed open. But it wasn't a gunman. Kart lowered his weapon and Benjamin stepped inside. "They winged Anthony, but I think we've got them on the run."

Two men knocked him aside and raced inside. Guys who had been working around the compound in buildings she had never seen the inside of. No telling what they did in those. She only knew that she could hear deliveries and pickups at all hours of the night. One time she had even thought she heard a helicopter arrive and depart.

Kenna planted her feet and straightened, lifting her chin. "If you let me go, I can make sure Jax stays alive for whatever questions you still need to ask."

Benjamin looked at Kart, yet another indication that the big man was the one in charge.

Kart motioned with his head. "Go get the fed, Ben." And dragged her with him.

Kenna tried to keep up. She tripped over her other foot and nearly went down, slamming her shoulder against the wall.

Men ran in and out of the structure while gunfire continued outside. The building shook, and dust rained down from the ceiling.

He dragged her past an open door. She saw an extended room with long tables covered with drugs being packaged. A couple of fireproof safes. People, women mostly, she had never seen.

No one even looked at her. They kept going as though nothing was happening. Certainly not a gun battle outside.

Men with automatic weapons stood around the edges of the room. Each person packaging drugs or counting money wore only underwear, their hair pulled back and masks over their mouths and noses.

"Is that what Elisa is trying to get in on?" Kenna stumbled but caught herself before she went down. "What other parts of the market have you cornered?" If El Falcón was raiding Kart's compound, it most likely was because Kart's drug smuggling business was cutting into Navarro cartel profits.

A whole lot more of this situation made sense now.

And yet he wasn't actively protecting his business? Instead, Kart was leaving it to those men and the guys outside. He was here with her, making sure she got somewhere. Because his cousin, that sheriff from Colorado she had never met—but had seen on TV—was on his way?

She wanted to offer him a concession in exchange for her freedom, but that would sound a little too much like Elisa coming from her lips. She cared about Jax being free a whole lot more than she cared about herself and whatever fate was in store for her. Could she go through with that bargain?

As they continued through the huge building, she spotted the doorway that led downstairs, to the cell where they put her in the early hours and during the heat of the day.

Her head swam.

He was shutting her back down there.

She struggled against his grip on her. "I need to see Jax. I need to know if he's okay."

A local man rounded the hall in front of them. One of Kart's men, who started when he spotted the boss coming toward him. He blustered. "I was just...checking on things."

Kart lifted his gun and shot the man in the head.

Kenna flinched and turned away. Far enough she spotted a man behind them creeping down the hallway. Dark hair, jeans, and a shirt. Beat-up dusty running shoes. A revolver in one hand, and a pistol in the other he'd most likely retrieved off a body or from somewhere else in this compound. If he wanted to kill Kart, she wasn't going to stop him.

She lifted her gaze to his face and swallowed a gasp. Maybe she was unconscious. That could at least account for why it seemed like her past had been manifested in front of her, the thought she'd had about that FBI agent earlier. Like a waking dream because she had just a while ago remembered him.

The agent she knew in Quantico.

An undercover who had disappeared, never to be seen again.

He was here.

Chapter Three

"I heard you beat him."

Kenna pulled on her polo shirt and sat on the edge of the twin bed to put on her boots. She grinned at her roommate. "You bet I did."

Cecilia Warren, a Nebraska native, tipped her head back and laughed. Her red hair swung from a ponytail. Freckles dotted her pale skin and rosy cheeks. She was barely five two and had flipped a six-foot man onto his back yesterday—before ultimately being defeated.

Kenna hadn't tapped out. "He might think he's all that, but it felt good to give him a run for his money. You know...for the sake of making the FBI better."

Cecilia nodded, a grin stretching her mouth wide. "Right. That's why." She laughed.

Kenna hadn't been entirely joking. If these macho guys thought they were all that, and she showed them they could be wrong on occasion, maybe they'd strive to be better—or make less assumptions about women. "I can try, anyway."

Kenna finished lacing her boots and stood. She glanced over her shoulder at the drawer where she'd tucked away a photo of her father. Taken the day he'd been sworn in as an agent with the FBI. Years before her birth. He quit right around her sixth birthday to become the private investigator he'd been for years, before he turned his journals into books, which were then turned into movies.

One of the guys had hidden a movie poster under her pillow.

Another sang a famous theme song every time she walked by.

They all thought she was here to follow in his footsteps and try to do the same thing. Like she only wanted the glory her father had when it was all based on the ways he'd embellished their lives?

No thanks.

Kenna was only interested in following his true legacy— the one that brought her here to FBI training. It might sustain her, and it might not. They'd questioned if the drive to make him proud would keep her on the straight and narrow as an agent, or if she would eventually lose her grasp because the focus was on a memory that would fade with the coming years.

You don't know me, and you never knew him.

No one did.

Cecilia nudged her. "There he is."

They walked in silence past the recruit from Arizona, Ramon Santiago. No one else spoke to him.

The guy had an edge that didn't seem to fit with the Bureau—but maybe they wanted all types.

Women who could pass for Sunday school teachers like

Cecilia. Guys like Ramon who could slip easily into a Hispanic gang nearly anywhere. One of the recruits had suggested Kenna might easily blend in at a strip club, so she'd added a small dose of laxative to his coffee—just enough to get his stomach rumbling all day during class.

Cecilia continued, "I heard he was under suspicion as a kid when a series of animals went missing in the town where he lived."

"Which is where?" Kenna glanced over, rolling her eyes. "Because I have no idea where to even start looking. Has he even told anyone where he grew up? Or who he is?"

"Maybe it's some kind of special recruitment. Like he's here as a test to see if the rest of us are paying attention to what's going on around us."

"So file a report with your concerns."

"You really think I should?" Cecilia said.

"It's that or sleep with the instructor so you can ask." After *another* comment from one of the male recruits, it had become a running joke.

"Right. Between the studying and classes, working out, and the chronic lack of sleep...I'll get right on seducing someone in charge to satisfy my curiosity."

Kenna chuckled, which turned into a yawn.

"Coffee time."

"Always." Kenna nudged Cecilia ahead of her into the dining hall. The line nearly reached the door, so they hung back.

Ramon edged past them and headed for the water station. Instead of getting a cup, the guy cupped his hands under the running stream from the fountain and lifted the water to his mouth a few times. Kenna could hear the slurping across the room, drawing attention from a few people already eating.

Someone behind Kenna muttered a comment about the

guy that she wouldn't repeat in front of children or older folks out of respect for their sensibilities.

Cecilia shot Kenna a look that clearly said, *I told you so.*

"Not using a cup?" Kenna paused. "He's clearly a criminal mastermind."

Cecilia snorted, then her light skin flushed a violent pink.

Kenna smiled with her roommate and watched Ramon head to a table, where he sat and watched the room from the corner. The guy was entirely too tuned in to every single person. In a way she often found herself, purely because that was what her father had taught her.

"Whoever he is," Cecilia said, "I want him posted far away from where I'm assigned."

Twelve weeks later, both Kenna and Cecilia were sworn in as FBI agents. Her friend's parents and siblings traveled to the East Coast to see the ceremony.

Kenna had no one in the audience there just to watch her.

Though, a white-haired man in a suit entered partway through the ceremony. After she received her badge, he stepped quietly out the back.

She'd never seen him before or since.

Ramon Santiago was also sworn in as an agent that day, and Kenna never saw him again.

She and Cecilia had speculated about his fate via email several times since. Until the mystery lost its luster. Like her drive to honor her father's career by wearing a badge of her own had turned to a drive to be the best agent she could be.

Then the news had broken.

FBI Agent Goes Rogue

Chapter Four

The door opened, casting light from the hall into the room. Two men strode in, carrying someone between them. They dumped Jax on the floor. He didn't move.

Kenna swallowed a cry and started to scramble across the floor to him, pushing out all the thinking she'd been doing about that guy from the hallway.

After Kart had shot at him, the man she knew had run off.

Ramon Santiago was here—but gone now. Kind of like the way he'd been in her life years ago: there and then absent. Now he was back. She could almost believe that stress had her see someone who hadn't been there. After all, it had been years, and it made no sense that she'd seen him.

First, she'd remembered him. Now she saw him?

Maybe she was crazy, like how she looked scrabbling across the floor on her hands and knees.

One of the men moved and pointed a gun at her. "Stay

where you are." That was Benjamin, who had a white bandage on his upper arm.

She shifted to lean back against the wall.

A slender man strode in wearing linen pants and a white shirt with the sleeves rolled up. His dark features were capped by silver hair. In any other situation he would have a kind smile, but right now it was lethal. Like the smear of blood beside one of his shirt buttons. He asked her in English, "What injuries do you have?"

Kenna stayed where she was, leaning against the wall with her legs out straight in front of her. He could plainly see the blood, but she pointed at Jax. "Him first."

Benjamin snorted.

Kart wasn't in here for her to remind him of their agreement—that if Jax died, she would kill him. As leader of this group, he was responsible for what happened here in this compound. Kenna was angry enough to abandon all sense of what was right and wrong and simply start shooting.

Just as soon as she got her hands on a gun.

"Help Jax first." He was far more hurt than she was.

The doctor set one of those leather medical bags beside her and knelt, completely ignoring her statement. "Anything I should be aware of?" He motioned to her.

"I'm not taking my clothes off, so don't worry about what you can't see."

"Shame." Benjamin scoffed. "I was looking forward to it."

The doctor glanced over his shoulder.

Benjamin shut his mouth.

She wanted to talk to this doctor, probably some local that they paid, but she couldn't ask him any questions with Benjamin and Anthony listening in. So that killed the idea he might be able to help her. Or that she could use him to escape.

He put a blood pressure cuff on her arm.

Kenna mostly ignored his checking her vitals, because the only vital thing right now was that she get Jax and get them both out of here.

She closed her eyes. *I've said it before. Seems like a constant refrain. We need Your help.*

Was there precedent for nagging God so much that He ignored her, or would it help? She didn't know but chose to hope—otherwise, she had nothing.

"Unless you have some injury I can't see, you seem to have come through tonight's events unscathed."

She opened her eyes and saw his attention on her forearms, and the twin scars. "What I've survived, and how *scathed* I am, is none of your business."

"Fair enough."

"Now help Jax." She pointed at him, wanting with everything that was in her to crawl over and roll him to his back. But they would see the desperation in every inch of her movements. They would know how deeply she cared for him, and men like this would use that against her.

It was enough that Kart had been clued in, finding her trying to save him. But that could be written off as partners—the bond of captives together. Friendship. Basic respect for another life that was at risk. He might've done enough research to know how her life intersected with Jax's.

But knowing her heart?

No. No one was allowed in that she didn't let in. And that only happened when she trusted a person enough to let her guard down. It would never be more than a handful of people, and it wasn't something she needed to grow out of. She was wired to have a small circle.

"Fine." Benjamin walked out, leaving just the doctor and Anthony. Too many people in this small room when all she wanted was to sit alone with Jax and get him to wake up.

The doctor rolled him to his back, put ointment on the cuts on Jax's chest, and covered several of them with bandages. He felt around Jax's head and didn't indicate he'd found anything. Maybe he was just great at keeping his thoughts to himself.

"Your friend is strong."

Kenna already knew that. Everyone had a breaking point. Would Jax's be physical, or mental? She needed him to wake up so she could check in with him. Make sure he hadn't lost his hope.

The way Bradley had.

Kenna sniffed back the burn of tears. Jax might eventually succumb to the fear, and there would be nothing she could do to convince him things would be okay if he lost hope.

Benjamin came back in and said to Anthony, "You were right. She's gone."

The doctor tensed very slightly, tiny enough that if Kenna hadn't been looking at him she'd have missed the sudden flex of his shoulders. A reaction to what the two men at the door said.

Anthony swore. "Ran off."

"Or they took her with her when they peeled out," Benjamin said. "We don't know she disappeared."

"You looked everywhere?"

Benjamin nodded. "Kart has them tearing apart storage just to check."

Anthony blew out a breath.

Kenna filed all that away. "Are you talking about Lola? I can help find her."

It might be Elisa. Ana had been shot in the forecourt, but they couldn't find Lola. Or someone else? She didn't want to stand right now, but if she found a missing person, she could get them to owe her a favor she'd be able to cash in on. Right?

"It's actually what I do. Finding missing people." She shrugged like it was no big deal. "I don't know if you knew that."

Anthony glanced at Benjamin. "Get her to find the mules?"

"Or she takes Lola's place." Benjamin seemed to think that was funny.

"So that's what they're here for." And now they only had one, instead of three. It made sense now why the girls had been working on loading that truck, not in the room with all the other locals cutting and packaging drugs. They had a different job. *Mules.*

Benjamin shrugged. "There's a guy in Seattle that likes his drugs delivered personally."

And they asked no questions about what happened to the girls after they arrived. Was that how it worked? Kenna swallowed. "It's good to have multiple streams of income."

Benjamin tipped his head back and laughed as he walked out. "Now she's getting it!"

The doctor glanced at her, then capped a needle and returned it to his bag.

Anthony stared.

A minute later they were all gone, and the door shut. Darkness descended on the room, and she only heard the sound of her own breath as she inhaled and exhaled.

Kenna used her feet to pedal herself in a slide across the floor. No one needed to know that her arms were practically useless. Between everything today, she needed some serious recovery time. She couldn't lift her arm enough to run a hand over the outside of her shoulder where Elisa had hit her with that crate lid.

"Jax." She collapsed onto the floor beside him, just enough strength to turn his head to her so she could scan his face. Her hand slipped to his shoulder so she left it there, able to feel the rise and fall of his chest. Thank God his shoulders hadn't actually been dislocated, but he was still a mess. "Jax."

Tears slid from the corner of her eye onto the floor.

She sniffed, but more fell. "Don't give up. You have to hold on. We both do. You've got to believe we'll get rescued."

Because if they didn't have faith they'd get out of this, what did they have?

He was a fed. FBI special agents had been killed at the same time they were taken. There was no way it hadn't elicited a full-blown manhunt to get their agent back.

So how long would it take for them to come in like that pickup truck? Or with huge SUVs and a helicopter. They'd have to mount a rescue to recover him.

She'd been half expecting it since they both woke up here. But so far...nothing.

Jax still had his injury from the accident. The one that had slowly bled for days. Now it was a broken scab, surrounded by so many other abrasions and cuts she couldn't imagine how much pain he would be in when he woke up.

If he woke up.

No. She wasn't going to do that. "We *will* get out of here. Years from now, we'll be sitting at a coffee shop, remembering the time we were captives in Mexico." She tried to smile, but it slipped. "We might even laugh about it, right?"

The time they had been held by four military guys, threatened with the arrival of a sheriff from Colorado who wanted revenge. When they'd struggled against the fear and pain and found a way to escape.

When she nearly got him out the night a rival cartel attacked.

That had been their best shot so far. That pickup truck

had rolled in and caused enough mayhem it might have enabled her to sneak him out. But she hadn't managed it.

If she could get them to do it again—or get the guys here to go to the cartel and cause mayhem over there—she would have an even better chance. She wouldn't need to risk the FBI finding them after it was too late.

As it was, there were far too many ways this could go wrong before a rescue. Or an escape. But she couldn't not try just because the odds weren't good. The fact she couldn't think of a time when she'd faced worse and succeeded wasn't the point. Surviving alone wasn't what she wanted. Not again.

She and Jax were getting out of this together.

Or not at all.

The door lock clicked, and it opened. She hadn't even heard it lock, but they never left her to roam. If she was allowed to walk around the compound without oversight she'd have blown this place to kingdom come and destroyed their business already. And they likely knew that.

"Come with me." Kart stood there, silhouetted by the light. "Now."

Kenna tucked her arms against her front, almost folding them. She tucked her feet under her and rolled to a stand in one move without putting her hands on the floor. Something Jax had taught her. Finding strength in other areas to account for the weaknesses she had—building muscle in her legs for when her arms refused to work.

Her arms were a weakness she could try and cover by tucking her hands into her pockets. As a bonus, it made her look all casual instead of scared to death and at the end of her rope.

As she passed him and stepped out into the hall, he sniffed. "You need a shower."

"Do I? Weird."

He held a gun by his side, apparently confident she wouldn't attack him. Or certain that if she did try then he could overpower her.

Which was, of course, completely true.

He walked her down the hall to what looked like an office...on a military base. Metal file cabinet, metal desk. "Sit." He shut the door and rounded the desk.

She settled in the chair in front of the desk. "Got a job for me?"

He settled in the chair behind it. "Actually, yes. That attack was the Navarro cartel, and we need you to return one of their dead—with a message."

Like a bomb stuck in the dead guy's chest cavity, or a strongly worded note? "What kind of message?"

"One you're going to hand-deliver before you return to us."

"Because you need me here—and alive—when the sheriff shows up?"

The skin around his eyes flexed. "I don't need you to comment. Just listen, shut up, and do as I say."

She pressed her lips together.

He wore dusty clothes in a way that kept things buttoned up, no matter that he'd fought for his compound just a short time ago. He might've retucked his shirt, but that was all it took to put his appearance back together. His hair was short enough he didn't have to do anything to it.

He still held on to that military decorum.

But with no flags on the wall. No photos, or commendations. Nothing that indicated he'd been in a squad with the three guys outside. Kicked out of the army, maybe? It was that or they'd gone AWOL, and that wasn't easy with four men in the group. They moved like a team, borne of hours of training.

Kart, Anthony, Benjamin...what was the fourth guy's name? She couldn't think if she'd heard it.

Maybe they'd all been reported as killed in action as a cover to start a new life south of the border.

She'd asked Kart once why they chose to live here.

Down here I can do anything I want. He'd meant it as a threat to her, but she took it both ways. He needed to be outside the law.

She stared at him.

"You will be here when my cousin arrives." He stared right back. "I keep my word."

"Good for you."

Given the look in his eyes, if they'd been within arm's reach he'd have cuffed her for being snarky.

She wasn't going to apologize. "When do I leave?"

Kart leaned back in his chair. "Benjamin will take you as far as their ranch. You take the truck through the gate, deliver the message, and then leave."

"Like...drive the truck back out, or run away in a hail of gunfire?"

"Can't say how they'll react to the message. So let's be prepared for anything."

What she needed was to get inside this "ranch" and get to a phone. Or convince the head of the Navarro cartel to retaliate back at Kart in such a way it created enough chaos she could escape with Jax. Could she pull that off? Make some other kind of deal. Or figure out a way to call for help.

She knew which she would prefer.

"You're thinking too much." Kart shook his head. "Drive the truck in, and when El Falcón sees his man, you make sure he understands what happens when people come at me. And then you leave."

Risky move, putting her in danger like that. But she

couldn't argue there was too much chance she might get killed, or he might not let her do it.

And this could be her only chance.

"Fine. Great." Kenna stood. "Let's do this."

His throaty chuckle reached her. She didn't like the sound of that at all. "Anything happens, I slit your friend's throat. I don't care what he might tell me about the FBI's operation. I'll bleed him out in the dirt."

She turned back to him. "And I'll burn this place to the ground if you do."

The words were already out before she realized it was true. She would do that—she was angry enough to not care at all.

Regardless of the loss of innocent life, if Jax was taken from her, Kenna would have to fight the need to destroy *all of them.* Maybe few would blame her for it. Or she would spend the rest of her life in a Mexican prison.

If she could take out both Kart's operation and the cartel, then it would be even better.

"I like a woman with spirit." Kart laughed all the way to the door. Then his amusement disappeared. "You think Navarro will offer you a chance? Unlikely. I'm your best shot at staying alive."

He shoved her through the door.

Chapter Five

Saturday, before dawn

Kenna had lost count of how many days it had been since she saw the world outside the compound. Or how it felt to be free. She climbed out of the pickup truck inside the gated ranch. In the middle of nowhere it seemed to have popped up on the hillside. Like an oasis surrounded by trees and green grass with the sprinklers running. Unlike the dirt and rundown buildings of Kart's place, this was someone's home.

She wouldn't be here long enough to enjoy it even if she wanted to. Not when Jax was still back at the compound, and she had no idea what was happening to him. She didn't like the fact that she had to leave him. It made her antsy.

Kenna stood very still, not even closing the driver's side door behind her. She counted four men within sight. Three guards and a man she'd guess was the cartel leader, Héctor Álvarez Navarro.

She spread her hands wide. "I'm not carrying any weapons."

Who knew if they even spoke English.

"That doesn't mean we won't kill you where you stand." The man she thought was Navarro had dark hair, tanned skin more than the natural color of the people around him, and bright white teeth. Tanning bed maybe, or a pool out back? The guy had enough money he wore it like a second skin, not just in his features that had been lifted and tightened but also in the clothing he wore. Even the shoes on his feet, and rings on his fingers.

She watched him walk between two of his men toward her.

His dark eyes took her in. "Do you know who I am?"

Who he was? A rich guy who spoke English with the Texas twang. But Kenna didn't think that was what he was talking about. "The head of the Navarro cartel?" she said. "Though, that's just a guess."

"And you are...?"

Kart hadn't given her any instructions as to whether she should give this man her name or stay anonymous. He also hadn't wired her up, which meant unless there was a bug in the truck, he couldn't hear anything she said.

"My name is Kenna Banbury. Your friends over the hill sent me with a message." She motioned to the bed of the truck.

"You are right, Kenna Banbury. This is my home." He tested her name like he wanted to see how it tasted on his lips. "I am Héctor Álvarez Navarro."

"It's nice to meet you, Hector."

"You work for these American men?"

Kenna must have made a face—too stressed out to hide her thoughts from her expression.

Hector chuckled. "I see you do not." He motioned to one of his men, who pulled back the tarp in the bed of the truck.

The smell registered first. The rotten scent of a deceased human, this one lying in pieces in the back of the truck.

"I see." He turned from the truck bed and took a couple of steps toward her. Measured movements. This guy could dance. And he'd do it until you were dizzy—then he would stab you in the heart and leave you bleeding out on the dance floor.

Not good.

"In case you understand the reference," Kenna said, "this is probably some kind of Trojan horse situation."

She had no idea what Kart and his friends were planning along with her delivering a dead guy back to Navarro, but it couldn't be anything good. Any retaliation had to be swift. Preferably when the enemy was recuperating from their attack. She'd begun reading Genesis a few weeks ago and got far enough to have learned that retaliating when your enemy was incapacitated would turn out in most cases to be extremely effective.

Was that why she felt this anger burning hot in her? Some kind of Old Testament justice mingling with Kenna's own brand of justice. Creating a kind of soup inside her that was now boiling because she felt like there was no way out of this situation.

She was determined to create a way out. No matter what.

Héctor Álvarez Navarro eyed her. "Beware of Greeks bearing gifts?"

So he did know what a Trojan horse was. "Exactly."

"And you are the expendable messenger I am not supposed to shoot?"

"I won't stop you, but I do have an issue with it."

Not that she wanted to survive just because Kart needed her alive so he could turn her over to his cousin. It might be better for both her and Jax if they didn't make it out of this situation alive. Though, she could do without being tortured first.

Kenna shuddered.

"You look like you could use a drink."

Kenna knew a few Spanish words and said, "Agua."

He nodded as though bestowing a great gift. A king in his own kingdom. He gave orders to his men in rapid-fire Spanish, and several moved away across the gardens and around the house. If she could reach the trees, she might be able to find some cover. But with only desert around them, she would only be hiding until she was discovered.

Not a long-term solution.

They walked in silence down the front path, bricks set into concrete that were nice change from the sand and dust. Bushes. Tall pots with perfusions of flowers spilling out whose scent wafted up to her nose.

"Wow." It slipped out before she could call it back.

"I enjoy the finer things." He glanced over, studying her face before he looked at the rest of her. Apparently, he wasn't all too impressed with dirty Kenna covered in dust and sweat. No surprise there.

Considering the last thing she wanted was to appear attractive to the leader of a cartel, she was as grateful as she was pretty much willing to consider whether she had the stomach to play this scenario that way. Even to save Jax's life. She would much rather get a gun and kill every single person in this lovely home before she offered up that in exchange for freedom.

"Elisa picked the wrong house."

He glanced over. "Excuse me?"

Maybe he knew something about Lola. "When your men returned home from their well-crafted attack on the American compound, did they have a young girl with them?"

He chuckled. "Would that I could say yes."

"They didn't take any captives?"

"They brought back only what they were instructed to bring."

She wanted to ask what they had been after, but the last thing she needed was to get in the middle of this turf war. At least, that's what she was assuming this whole business was about. "That's a shame. She went missing from their compound, and I was hoping to find her."

"The only woman I know that is missing is my love. But she was taken from me months ago and never returned, despite my attempts to get her back." He stopped at the thick wood front door and glanced at her. "I know those Americans are responsible." He practically spat the words at her. "And they will pay."

Now she knew what Navarro wanted.

Information about the woman he lost could be the currency she traded for her freedom.

Before she could figure out how to work the conversation around to him using her to get the information in exchange for her and Jax being free, he stepped inside.

A young woman in a flowered dress and sandals, long hair down to her elbows, stood in the entryway with a tray. On top were a bottle of wine, a bottle of sparkling water, and two glasses—one of which had been filled.

He handed the water to Kenna.

She twisted the cap. Even with all the strength she had in her, she couldn't fight the condensation to get enough grip to take the lid off. She sighed.

Navarro took the bottle from her and uncapped it.

"Gracias."

He dipped his head very slightly and took the wine glass. "Let's go to the deck."

From the view she got walking through the house to the back, Kenna could say with complete certainty that Elisa definitely picked the wrong house.

She had finished the bottle by the time they stepped through the French doors, where another young girl took it from her and disappeared. Kenna stared out at the pool and the gardens. "It's so peaceful." She couldn't hear much but the buzz of insects in the trickle of water.

Horses grazed on the hill behind the house.

A red barn with a wide-open door. Several other buildings.

This seemed to be a working ranch, and if there was any illegal business happening at this location, then it occurred completely out of sight, where not even surveillance could detect it.

To go suddenly from a dismembered body in the back of the truck to this view, with the sunset easing down the sky and setting the world aglow, she couldn't help but notice the stark contrast. Like the compound to this ranch. A contrast as evident comparing this man standing in front of her now to the person he became when it was necessary to take a life. Or the difference between Kart and Navarro.

"I'm glad you are able to appreciate it as much as I do." He sipped his drink. "So you can imagine my displeasure when those Americans moved in over the ridge. Or when they send a gift that is nothing but another attempt to undermine me."

"Do you know what they are going to do?" Kenna asked.

"I am prepared for anything," Navarro replied.

Across the other end of the pool, an elderly woman walked along with a little boy probably not more than three years old. She held his hand, and they headed for a small pond in the corner of the garden.

Navarro's son?

And he had lost his bride. He still cared about what happened to her. He needed a mother for his son.

One of his men stepped out of the house, strode over, and spoke quietly in Navarro's ear. His gaze came to her, and he waited until the man had stepped back to take up a guard position before he said, "She is Kenna Banbury."

So they knew who she was now.

They'd run her name to see if she'd been lying—and maybe her picture as well—and discovered her history. Even a summary would give them enough to get their heads spinning.

Now was the chance to make him an offer he couldn't refuse.

"If you've looked me up, then you know I can help you find—"

The pool house exploded.

The old woman screamed, and the child broke away from her to run toward the house. Navarro spun to his man and barked orders. He didn't even finish getting the words out before the barn exploded.

Kenna jumped back and clipped the table with her hip but managed to keep from falling.

Smoke filled the air. Flames licked at the debris of the pool house, sparks jumping to nearby bushes.

Navarro was on the ground, blinking. *You weren't ready for that.*

Kenna rushed past him into the house. Two men stood inside the door. She ducked to the right, down the hallway, and tried to find a landline phone. Or someone's discarded cell.

Someone yelled behind her.

She grabbed the first door handle and ducked inside. The room was lined with bookcases interrupted by what looked like a shrine—but was probably an altar given the tall candles and the photos she didn't have time to stop and look at.

There was a desk at the far end. Velvet chairs she would have enjoyed curling up in and falling asleep if she weren't completely filthy. Kenna snatched the phone from its base on the desk and listened for a second.

Dial tone. She hammered in the number Maizie had given her and listened to it ring.

Another explosion rocked the building.

The American military guys were going all out in their quest for vengeance. Did they realize what had been stolen? She had no idea what it might be. For all she knew it could have been a person, or a ton of product. She didn't care what their squabble was over. This was her shot to call for help.

But no one answered the phone.

She heard a small whimper. Kenna gripped the phone and rounded the desk, stretching the cord with her so she could look underneath while she listened to it continue to ring.

The child who had run inside crouched under the desk, holding his knees to his chest. Tears ran down his face.

She held up the fingers of her free hand. "Okay."

The call connected, and a man said, "Ken—"

Stairns.

It cut off.

Kenna whirled around.

Navarro stood on the other side of the desk, one finger on the receiver holding it down. Kenna dropped the phone, and it clattered against the desk.

The kid whimpered.

Navarro realized the child was under the desk.

Kenna backed up but stumbled and landed in the chair. No energy. No fight. No way out.

No hope.

She stared at Navarro, looking at the lethal intention in his eyes.

Then she felt the tiny hand touch her knee. She flinched. Another hand touched her other knee, then grasped at the skin there.

A child-sized knee dug into her thigh, and the kid slammed against her, curling up in her lap.

Kenna gasped. "Okay."

Navarro's jaw flexed.

The kid clung to her. Kenna's arms shifted reflexively, wrapping around the child so she could hold him safe. "It's okay."

The door flung open again so hard it slammed against the wall and bounced back. Several men raced in. Navarro held up a hand, and they rushed to a stop.

The door to Kenna's left opened, and the old woman who'd been watching the boy raced in, blood on her forehead.

Navarro pulled a gun, pointed it at the woman, and squeezed the trigger. The kid flinched against Kenna, thankfully with his face turned away from the bloodshed. She held on tighter, smoothing her hand up and down the shirt over his back.

"Hector!" Ramon Santiago raced in, shoving men aside. She watched as he clocked the situation in two seconds. Followed quickly by the fact it was Kenna sitting behind the desk holding who she guessed was Hector's son.

Navarro handed the gun to Ramon. He said something in Spanish, then strode around the desk and gathered the boy from Kenna's arms. Navarro carried him from the room. The rest of his men except for one went with him.

Ramon Santiago stared at her. "It is you." He stood facing

her across the desk. Folded his arms in a way she could still see the gun.

Kenna didn't have the strength for banter or anything else. "I need to get back to the compound." When help came, she wanted to be standing right next to Jax so they could be rescued together.

"You think Navarro is going to let you walk free after what just happened?"

"You tell me. You're the one who has apparently been working for him all this time." She managed to shrug one shoulder. "I'm a captive."

"So it's true." Ramon stared at her, ten years had given him lines around his eyes and a worn aspect to his demeanor. Though that was no surprise, given the life he had been living. "The Americans have an FBI agent in their compound? But that surely can't be you. You haven't been one for years."

So the cartel had heard word of what was going on in Kart's compound. "You know my story?"

Ramon's expression hardened. "I've kept apprised of what it was necessary to know. But you only popped back up on my radar when you killed the FBI director in Vegas."

Why she felt the need to say, "It was justified," Kenna wasn't sure. She didn't want to contemplate it over much. She would chalk it up to exhaustion instead. The fact that nostalgia maybe made her want to defend herself. She sighed. "So what do we do now?"

Ramon stared at her.

For a man who had betrayed his country and gone to the dark side, he certainly seemed content with his decision. Or maybe the former undercover agent was extremely competent at hiding what was on his mind.

Had he been playing this part for years?

Kenna said, "If you need help, and I need help, then

maybe we can work together and figure something out that will benefit both of us."

"Like you grabbing Navarro's kid during a raid to make the point that you could hurt him where it counts whenever you want?"

"I don't think that's how I convince any of you to give me a shot at getting Oliver Jaxton free of Kart and his friends."

The skin around Ramon's eyes flexed. "I've never heard of Oliver Jaxton."

"Your loss. He's a great guy," Kenna said. "The kind of agent who always does the right thing and would never betray the oath he took to uphold the law with fidelity, bravery, and integrity." She paused a second. "Unlike us."

Ramon chuckled. "Navarro didn't think you were going to hurt the kid."

"Navarro has no clue what I'm capable of." Kenna had to admit something, though. "But I could use his help. And in return maybe I can figure out what happened to his bride."

Ramon turned and wandered to the altar, staring at the pictures tucked between flickering candles. Hiding his expression from her because he couldn't hold back his reaction to that? For some reason talk about the missing woman affected him deeply.

Was the same true of all of Navarro's men?

"Who was she?"

If they had that kind of loyalty for one woman, there wasn't much they wouldn't do for the man they worked for. Another stark contrast—if she considered Kart and his brothers in arms. They might be loyal to one another, but she had detected entirely too much independence.

Where Navarro's men would live and die for him, their team was strong only up until one of them considered themselves above the others. Or decided to challenge Kart for leadership.

"What happened to her, Ramon?" As much as she would like to continue sitting in this chair, Kenna would have to get up at some point. And when she did, she was going to need a plan. A way to get Jax and get out.

Just making a run for it as fast as possible didn't give her a lot of room to account for issues that might crop up—probably right in front of her, blocking her way to the gate.

"She disappeared months ago." Ramon squeezed the bridge of his nose. "One day she was here, and the next morning she was gone."

Kenna shifted and tried to stand. "I'm going to need more than that if I'm going to find her."

Chapter Six

Navarro strode back in. He said something to Ramon in Spanish, then turned to her. "Get out of my chair."

Any response she might've given disappeared when Ramon rounded the table and dragged her out of the chair by her elbow. He hauled her back to stand in front of Navarro. There was no time to ask if Navarro knew who Ramon really was.

Then again, he was alive—and not like Jax hung on to life. So maybe the cartel leader didn't know who Ramon had been in his previous life. Or was he deep undercover, and the "gone rogue" thing was only a fake to keep his true motives secret?

She glanced between the two men and realized they looked more upset than angry.

"Everything okay outside?" Kenna didn't like the idea that anyone had lost their life. No matter what side they were on, a life was a life.

Keep telling yourself that.

At least it would remind her she had morals. So far she had lived her life according to the law. Kart might think that down here was the Wild West. He believed he could do whatever he wanted and be outside of the gaze of the US government. But that wouldn't last long, surely. Now that she had made that call, it was only a matter of time before this whole area was descended on by local law enforcement and their US counterparts, or some kind of international cooperative task-force. Something good, like Homeland Security or the DEA.

Navarro studied her, and the skin around his eyes flexed. Confused by her question?

"Is anyone hurt?" Kenna asked. She didn't mind being nothing like anyone he'd ever met before. But she didn't want to be enough of an anomaly that she drew his attention. That would lead to being here one second longer than necessary when Kenna was determined to get out as fast as possible. "Are all of your people safe?"

Ramon made a chuckle-like sound, as though he didn't want to laugh outright in front of the man who pulled his strings.

Navarro said, "Those Americans are going to have to work harder if they want to injure me."

"And your son?" Kenna paused. "He's okay now?"

"His nanny has recently found herself in need of alternate employment." He lifted his chin. "But my *nephew* is fine, thank you."

"That's good." The kid had seemed pretty scared.

Kenna was the last person who'd have thought she had any kind of maternal instinct. It wasn't like she spent that much time around children. Except the few that she rescued —which hadn't happened much lately. Or her friends' kids.

She didn't need Navarro to offer her a nannying/bodyguard position.

"I should get going."

Navarro lifted one eyebrow.

"There's a friend of mine back at the American's

compound, and if I don't return, they're going to kill him." She glanced at Ramon to see if she could tell from his face whether he cared or not that there was an FBI agent in danger.

Neither Ramon nor Navarro said anything. It was more what they didn't say than what they did. They likely wanted revenge against Kart and his friends for their man's violent death. But if they did, it wasn't something they were planning on explaining to her anytime soon.

Were these men going to say anything at all? Or would they wait until she said more than she'd planned and gave something away she shouldn't?

Navarro probably believed that there would never be a world in which he was required to explain himself to anyone. Least of all her.

"Did they manage to get in?"

Navarro shook his head. "Just you. The Trojan horse."

"Did they destroy any product?" She had no idea what he even made or stored here.

"These Americans only buzz at my door like flies."

Kenna figured that explosions were a bit more than flies hitting the window. "So...just irritating?"

"I keep my business tight," Navarro said. "Something these Americans have yet to learn."

"If you let me make a call to the FBI, I can have the problem of those Americans taken care of." At least, she was pretty sure she could.

"She was making a call when I came in here." And with that, Ramon threw her under the bus, selling her out even though she could have written a report when they were both at Quantico explaining what she'd seen of his instability.

But she hadn't, because both Kenna and Clarissa had preferred to avoid the limelight of being singled out—especially when it only looked like they were attempting to sabotage his success in FBI training. It would've looked far too petty to complain about him.

Navarro only chuckled. "We shall see about that."

"Still, we don't want to be living under a microscope," Ramon said. "So if the FBI does show up, we'll know who brought them here."

She wondered if he believed he was still working undercover—maybe this was some kind of years long mission for him. Could it be such a level of need to know that the reports and news articles indicated he'd turned to the dark side?

It wasn't completely out of the question that a man sent in undercover had been discovered, then flipped the entire script and turned to work for his enemy and double-cross his government in order to continue the mission.

So which was it?

Navarro frowned. "Get her out of here. She has a response to deliver."

"Door." Ramon shoved her, and she figured at the last minute that he meant for her to be the one to open the door.

Kenna pushed down the handle with her fist, far enough it unlatched and swung open.

A scream echoed down the hallway. The sound of a man in intense pain. Similar to what she'd been listening to for days—except this one sounded so much worse. All of Jax's torture distilled into one moment.

Ramon chuckled. "Message received."

She glanced over her shoulder at wild dark curls around his face in a halo. His beard had been overwhelmed by silver strands in places. "What happened to you?"

He shoved her into the hallway.

Navarro followed them outside, where the pickup truck

had been moved from the gate up to the driveway in front of the house.

The engine was running.

"You're really just kicking me out?" Kenna turned to look at Navarro. "I can help you find the woman you lost. I can bring her back to you."

Ramon tensed.

Navarro closed the gap between them, making Kenna back up. Her hips slammed against the side of the pickup truck, and he moved way close to her. Enough she could feel his hot breath on her face. She heard the unmistakable sound of a knife being pulled from its sheath and then the prick of the blade tip against her neck.

Kenna's stomach clenched. "I find people who are lost. It's what I *have* to do, not just a job."

His dark eyes scanned her face. Then he took a step back and motioned someone forward. A man strode toward them carrying a potato sack leaking red liquid that dripped onto the ground. Ramon took the bag and placed it on the front seat.

Navarro said, "As I said earlier, you are going to deliver a message from me."

And that was exactly what she'd come here to do for Kart. "I usually charge money to be a go-between."

No one laughed.

"He'll want me to come back to him with information I discovered from inside your house." While Kart and his friends had been blowing up outbuildings and generally causing mayhem — but for what?

Navarro said, "Tell Ian Kartom that I don't keep my valuables under my pillow. If he wants the mine, he can stop stealing from me and offer a deal."

Ramon shoved her in the driver's seat and slammed the door so hard the pickup rattled.

Time to go.

Kenna turned the truck down the drive and headed for the gate. Her hands shook, but she gripped the wheel as much as she could.

If Maizie had even received that call, or Stairns since the answer had come from a male voice, her friends would be sending help to the wrong place. There was no way to tell her she hadn't phoned from the place where Jax was being hurt. Not to mention that in making the call she had now also exposed that phone number to a cartel. At least it wasn't a physical phone at a location that would now be compromised, putting Maizie in danger. Rather it was one of Maizie's cloud-based phone numbers that would alert the teen Kenna had called.

She didn't need Navarro to go after her friends.

About seventeen years old as far as Kenna—or anyone else —could tell, the girl had lived enough trauma in her lifetime that she needed to stick to spa days, vacations, and anything else that would give her a stress-free life. She deserved it now that the man who had victimized her since the day she was born was dead.

Because Kenna had killed him.

Maizie currently lived in Kenna's father's Airstream in the backyard of her former boss and his wife. Safe. Cared for. Protected so she could heal in her own time, with the help of Stairns' wife, who was a therapist or counselor or whichever. Kenna didn't know the difference, and it didn't matter. Elizabeth knew how to help, and that was all Kenna needed to know.

The tires crunched the gravel under the pickup truck.

Sweat rolled down the sides of her face. The smell coming from the bag on the passenger seat made the bottled water threaten to come back up.

She grabbed the handle for the window and rolled it down a couple of inches to get some airflow.

Kenna knew what she was capable of when faced with the worst kind of person. Most folks wouldn't quibble about her methods when pushed to the extreme, but that wasn't the kind of person Kenna wanted to be all the time. Those were the exceptions.

She'd made an oath to uphold the law, and then the FBI had forced her out. She wasn't about to end up like Kart and his friends, living outside the law just because she had no tether to the civilized side of humanity.

She crested a ridge and spotted two men as they stood up on either side of the road, coming out of ditches they'd been lying in. All three wore military surplus clothing, camouflage paint on their faces, and backward ball caps over their hair.

If she hadn't been studying their every move, looking for weaknesses since she arrived in this country, she might not have been able to tell it was them under the disguises. Kart and Benjamin.

Kart flagged her down.

Kenna eased off the gas and pressed down the brake.

As soon as she stopped, he pulled the passenger door open and spotted the bag. "What is this?"

"Your message from Navarro."

Kenna didn't let go of the steering wheel. She was about to hit the gas and just keep driving until the fuel ran out, but how would that help Jax? There were still armed guards at the compound. They would get word she was on her way to get him, and they'd be ready for her when she showed up to bust him out. There was no way she was going to leave him and escape herself.

That would be the ultimate betrayal.

Kart shifted. "What did he say?"

"I don't think Navarro was too impressed with your attempt to weaken his operation."

From what he'd said to her, it seemed like Navarro didn't even keep any of his business dealings at the ranch. That place looked more like it was only his home, and not where he would keep narcotics or anything else he was smuggling—or any*one*.

Kart handed the bag to Benjamin, then climbed in the back seat. He slid over so Benjamin could get in beside him, after tossing the potato sack onto the dirt.

The door slammed.

"Go." Kart hammered the back of her seat with his fist.

She hit the gas and set off again, toward the compound.

"What did he say to you?"

Kenna could still feel the prick of Navarro's knife on her neck. "It could be worth Jax's freedom for all you know."

"Unlikely."

No, but worth a try. "If you want the mine, you can stop stealing from him and offer a deal."

"He really said that?" Kart chuckled. "Well, I'll be."

She gripped the steering wheel. "I guess attacking each other wasn't worth it after all."

"Maybe not, but it was fun."

She pressed her lips together. Better that than say something else and wind up being injured or killed.

"Well then, I guess we'll need to overlook the fact he cut off Anthony's hands and sent them back to me. We can have a sit-down with the guy and see if we can work something out with the mine."

She couldn't resist saying, "What is it?"

"Only one of the largest undiscovered lithium mines on the continent."

"Huh." She'd have preferred it to be some kind of ancient

culture's buried treasure, but apparently that wasn't going to be a thing today. Recently she'd gone after a cult with ties that went back to medieval times. Generations of people following in the same footsteps, creating terror and teaching those who came after them to do the same.

This couldn't be an Indiana Jones thing?

Kart said, "What were you saying earlier about diversifying?"

"Right." Kenna rolled her eyes because he couldn't see her face. "Makes perfect sense."

The lithium mine would have to be a serious windfall in the making if both Navarro and Kart were arguing over control of it.

She pulled into the compound as armed guards watched her drive down the lane. The place had suffered some damage, and there were men hauling debris already. Clearing the road between two buildings.

"Over there." Kart patted her shoulder and pointed at the loading bay.

She managed to contain the flinch. Her nerves had started to fray right away, and now she was reaching critical mass.

Something had to give, or Kenna didn't know what kind of state she would end up in.

As she climbed out the front seat, a couple of guys ushered Elisa and two other girls Kenna had seen in the room cutting and packaging drugs out of the building toward the truck. All three young women looked sick, pale, and sweating. One clutched her stomach.

Behind them was a Caucasian man. The fourth member of the team, who she hadn't had any contact with and didn't plan to. Every part of the guy screamed something lethal. She was pretty sure he was the one who had been torturing Jax.

Kart lifted his fist, and the man bumped it. "See you in a

few days, Walk." Then he patted Elisa's stomach, a grin on his face, and watched while she was loaded into the back seat of the pickup truck.

Drug mules.

"Later, Hoss." The man slid in the driver seat.

The three girls were shoved in the back. Another guy, equally lethal but a local, got in the passenger seat. The five of them left as fast as Kenna had peeled out of the drive-through with her milkshake the first time she had her license. Just because she could.

Kart had found replacements for Lola and Ana, girls he could use. Victimizing the broken and afraid all so he could make money.

"I want to see Jax." She wasn't going to back down about it.

He smirked. "It doesn't change anything."

It wouldn't even make her feel better, either. But she had to see if he was still breathing. Wanted to pray he would be awake today. The way he had been the first few days they were here.

Instead, Kart grabbed elbow. "Let's go. We need a place to hold this meeting."

"Why am I involved?" Kenna wanted to stay quiet, but she just couldn't. "I should be here, waiting for the sheriff. Not going to a meeting."

Kart glanced at her, the smirk back on his face. "Turns out there's a use for you after all."

Chapter Seven

Kenna sat in the back of the car between two locals in Kart's employ. Gunmen with wandering eyes, but they'd allowed her to shower. She didn't know whose dress this was. It fit reasonably well, falling to her mid-thigh and keeping her cool. She'd opted to keep her Converse just for some sense of normalcy in this chaos.

Not only in case Maizie had doctored the heel of one and could track her.

Kart drove. Benjamin sat on the passenger side, occasionally smirking at her wet hair. No makeup. All so they could head into town and meet with Navarro.

She'd tried to check on Jax, but they refused to let her back in that room. They'd shut her up in a storage closet all night, and she'd slept on the bare floor. Listening to female screams from across the compound. Staring at the ceiling. Praying she didn't lose hope.

Keep him safe, God.

She didn't want to be the person who only turned to God when she had nothing else and ignored Him anytime she could take care of things herself. If she decided to believe, it would change everything for her and not just some things.

The car bumped over a rut in the road and onto the blacktop that led into town.

She closed her eyes and tried to push away everything but what she needed to focus on. Thinking about her need for survival meant a chronic level of panic. Calm was the name of the game. Control she didn't have, except over her reactions and emotions. These men didn't get to tell her what to think, or how to feel. She might not have power in anything else right now, but she had that.

Nothing was more important than saving Jax.

Not even her need for vengeance.

The distant sound of traffic, the bustle of humanity that occupied hamlets of people where life moved at a steady pace as they went about their business. Kenna wasn't the kind of person to reach for connection. She preferred the peace of solitude and knowing she was cared about by people she cared for in return.

Until now.

Now it seemed like she needed someone—anyone—to notice her.

She opened her eyes and soaked in the sight of houses. People walked the sidewalk, past cars parked at the curb. She spotted a storefront. A school. In the center of town, a church reached up to the sky as if it possessed the same yearning inside her.

Kart pulled over at the curb down the street from a café on the corner, milling with a few people. Honest, small-town folk. This place would be nice to visit on any other day. Even if some cast furtive glances at them and walked quickly, that was the same as it would be anywhere when Kenna had these men for company.

Kart pushed his door open. "Let's go."

Kenna stayed where she was until he reached in the back door and dragged her out by her elbow. She walked the fine line between defiance and a refusal to cooperate. Her leverage over delivering those messages back and forth to the Navarro cartel had dissipated overnight, and she was back to a commodity they could use to get business done, until such a time as Sheriff Preston from Colorado showed up.

Kenna needed to not be around when that happened.

Her feet hit the ground and she stood out of the car.

"Stay here." Kart closed the door. She took a moment to lean against the back quarter panel while he scanned and held his phone to his ear. After a minute he said, "Copy that," and stowed his phone. "Let's move."

The group of four men and Kenna headed to the café on the corner and a couple of tables that had been pulled together. A harried waitress came out, the shadow of fear in her eyes. She spoke in Spanish, and one of Kart's guards replied.

The chair had a wood seat and a woven backrest, the upper frame of which dug into her shoulder blades. Kenna welcomed the discomfort that would help keep her aware and alert.

Kart sat beside her, watching the street.

Two minutes later they had a serving of coffee and mugs deposited in front of them on a tray with sugar cubes in a bowl and no cream or milk.

Not waiting for orders, Kenna poured herself a cup. Kart swiped it before she could take a sip, so Kenna poured another one. She remembered when she'd visited Jax at the FBI office in Salt Lake City months ago and the agents she used to work with did the same thing. That slice of normalcy gave her enough to hold on in the next moment.

Navarro crossed the street, surrounded by at least six men. Traffic stopped for him. The morning sun glinted off the shades he wore.

"Gotta hand it to the guy," Kenna said. "He might be bad, but he looks good doing it."

Plus his nephew was *super* cute. She wasn't going to mention the child to Kart, though. She had no idea if he knew Navarro had a family, and if it was up to her at all, he wasn't ever going to find out. A child shouldn't be a target.

Resolve crested inside her, pushing out the fear that had been constant.

Thank You, God.

He'd given her something else to anchor to in the middle of all this chaos to draw strength from—the innocence of a child. A light moment before everything real came crashing back in.

"Kartom." Navarro pulled out a chair and sat across the table from them.

Kenna and Kart were on one side, surrounded by his people who were there to watch his back. Navarro occupied the other side, his men protecting him.

Would this end in peace, or bloodshed?

She didn't much care what happened to their respective businesses, except what was in her power to break down and destroy. What Kenna cared about were the innocent people who would get caught in the crossfire.

"Navarro." Kart took a sip of his coffee and set the cup down.

Kenna glanced at the cars that eased by slowly, watching their conversation. The locals had to know who Navarro was, but maybe they didn't know Kart. Like the grocery store owner in a dirty apron who moved to stand on his front stoop and watched them.

A couple of doors down, past a shop that had been boarded up, she spotted a priest and studied him for a moment. She had met a priest in Albuquerque and this guy reminded her of him, though it was too far to see more than just the basic similarities of graying hair and that white collar with his black shirt and pants. Short sleeves, and dark-skinned arms.

It was simply his age and his uniform that made him familiar. That need she had for connection right now.

The priest stood in a doorway, inset back from the street, and a gray-haired man approached. From the back he almost looked like Stairns.

Kenna watched until her eyes burned, and she had to blink. Straining to see who it really was, while at the same time she couldn't let anyone around her know she might've seen a friend.

Had Stairns really come down here?

Maybe he'd been in the area for days. Since she and Jax had been kidnapped. He could've been trying to find her this whole time and then figuring out a way to rescue them both.

Is this it, God?

She could cause some kind of diversion as soon as they got back to the compound. Let Stairns help her get free.

The priest motioned all the way over to where Kenna sat with these men. At least, that was the direction he waved. The man he spoke to—Stairns, or not—didn't turn back to look. Did he know?

Kenna's stomach clenched. The coffee made it so she wasn't quite so hungry, but she hadn't eaten much beyond a couple of protein bars and half of a stale peanut butter and jelly sandwich in days. Kart's chair scraped the concrete. He stood at the same time Navarro did, both men practically spitting fire. She'd completely tuned out their conversation.

What was going on?

Kenna poured herself some more coffee, trying to act like she was stone-cold and cared about nothing. "If you kill each other here and now, it would solve a lot of my problems, so feel free to shoot each other in the street."

Navarro shot her a glance. "You find people."

Kenna said nothing.

"It's not a bad idea." Kart put both hands on the table, his body leaned toward his enemy. Nothing but males posturing so they appeared strong in front of each other.

Whatever they were talking about, she wasn't interested.

"I have no reason to help either of you." She didn't even want to be here. No one was making sure Jax survived. They also weren't back at the compound interrogating him so that was at least something, but it wasn't much.

Navarro glanced at Kart, then they both sat. "You find people, and your friend and I have the same problem."

Not Kenna's friend.

Kart said, "Missing product."

"You're talking about people." She glared at him. "Right? Just so we're clear what kind of scum both of you are." She waved a finger between them. "The kind of people who prey on innocent lives to make money. Who consider a person to be property."

Kart's eyes flashed as he chuckled. "So high and mighty."

"I've never broken the law the way you both do. And I am far from broke, so it's not like I need the money."

Kart huffed. "How is the view from up there on your pedestal?"

Navarro frowned. Maybe not understanding the expression?

"It's great, thanks." Kenna wanted to ask for a glass of ice water, since the coffee was hot. The temperature out here made heat shimmer up from the asphalt road. Sweat ran down her back only part due to the heat, but more the fact she sat in the center of a circle of lethal men.

If Stairns really was here, he'd probably wait for a good time to grab her. Right now would be the worst possible time.

Kart leaned toward her. "You want to live? You figure out what's happening at both our places. You bring us the person who is undermining our operations."

Kenna wasn't going to assume God was giving her this hot anger that gave her an ounce of bravado. Might be her frustration, but it also might be a prayer she had prayed that enabled her to say, "You want me to figure out who is stealing from you? Then you let Jax go free." And she said it without even flinching.

Kart chuckled.

"So you do have an FBI agent in your compound." Navarro leaned back in his chair.

Kart said, "You want him, give me the mine."

Kenna's stomach clenched. "My friend isn't your bargaining chip."

"Everyone is a pawn in someone else's game," Kart said. "Even me."

Navarro said, "Speak for yourself."

"Yeah?" Kart fired back. "Is that how you feel about Alejandro? He's got no hold over you?" Kart paused. "We all owe a debt to someone."

Kenna chose who she owed, and who might feel like they owed her. But that debt was paid in support and compassion. A currency neither of these men understood. Though, she prayed Navarro's nephew did as he grew up and managed to hold on to it.

They really wanted her to solve their problem?

"How do either of you know I won't favor the other?" She

set her cup on the table and waited while a truck rattled past them. When the street had quieted again, she said, "Or do you believe it was a third party, not one of you stealing from the other and then retaliating?"

Kart dug out his phone.

Navarro sat completely still.

Kart showed him the screen. "Do you have this girl? Did your men take her from my house?"

The picture was Lola.

Navarro shook his head. "Where is my bride?" His throat bobbed, just a tiny hint of his emotional state and nothing more. "Did you take her from me?"

Kart lifted one hand and looked around. "To do so would have meant war. Why would I take her?"

"To destroy me. Why else?"

"But you didn't?" Kenna turned in her chair to face Kart.

He simply shook his head.

"So someone else is interfering with your businesses." Who hated them both?

"Not one of my men," Navarro said. "They would never betray me like this."

Kart's jaw flexed. "Mine wouldn't dare."

"Okay," Kenna said. "It's good we got that settled. Let Jax go free, and I'll figure out what's going on."

She had to shift in the seat, in lieu of getting up and running, which would only result in her death and Jax's. Everything in her wanted to flee, but she couldn't. She might manage to save herself, but it would cost Jax his life. Still, the edges of her composure were about to fray.

The heat. The lack of rest. No peace. Little food. Not much water.

This couldn't go on much longer before she would lose it completely.

"You figure it out, and I'll set him free." Kart sat back in his chair.

"No deal." Kenna shook her head.

Navarro studied the two of them.

She wasn't going to bother explaining to Kart that she would do everything in her power to save Jax's life—but she also had no intention of being here when that sheriff showed up. No way could she afford to subject herself to whatever his plan for revenge would be.

"Perhaps you'd like to reconsider," Navarro said. "I can make it worth your while."

They had to know by now. "The only thing I care about is Jax." Even if she had to face the sheriff. If Jax had been set free and he was alive, what did it matter what happened to her? Surely he'd mount a rescue of her if it came to that. Things might not end in pain and death.

Navarro went back to studying her.

"Fine." Kart huffed. "If that's all you want, I'll set the fed free. You find Navarro's girl and whoever is stealing from both of us, and he gives me the mine. Since I was so gracious to share my asset."

Navarro barked a humorless laugh. "Only when she is brought back to me do you get the mine."

"Deal." Kart turned to Kenna. "That means you've got until Elliot shows up to do this."

She lifted her chin. "When is he coming?" She needed a timeframe.

Kart leaned close again. "Soon."

"I need a more specific timeframe, so I know what I have to work with."

"He's on his way but running into some setbacks getting coverage in his county."

So he'd been delayed. "Meanwhile I have to track people

who by nature aren't traceable. Great." She looked around, trying to see that guy who looked like Stairns.

Her former boss turned betrayer turned volunteer employee might still be around. Watching. Waiting for a good time to mount a rescue. She spotted the priest he'd been talking to by the front doors of the church up the street, now speaking to an elderly woman.

Apparently she needed to find Navarro's bride.

Hopefully the woman had run off and escaped like Kenna wanted to.

Most people trafficked were targeted because there was no one in their lives who would be concerned if they went missing. Not some middle-class, suburban kid who would spark a public outcry and media attention. That was way too risky. And there were plenty of children and young people in the world that were vulnerable and cut off from support.

Navarro reached into the inside pocket of his jacket. He slid a photo across the table. "Find her." He stood. "You can have whatever you want."

Kenna stared at the image of Navarro and a young Hispanic woman.

Never mind that she didn't look as enamored with Hector as he clearly was with her. The woman was gone now, living free of him in peace and safe with a good man who loved her.

And Kenna knew *exactly* where she was.

Chapter Eight

Navarro swiped the photo from the table and stood, taking it with him. "I look forward to hearing about your progress."

Kenna was about to snap.

Now that she knew who the "bride" was, she had no intention of doing this. But instead of keeping quiet and playing along, it was as though her mind couldn't process anything. Just panic.

"You expect me to solve your problem?" Both of them did, not just Navarro.

"It's what you do. Solve mysteries." Navarro stared down at her.

"And you destroy children—kids like your nephew."

Kart shifted in his seat, making Kenna wonder if she'd just told him something he didn't know.

Then she remembered she had planned to *not* tell him. *Oops.*

He said, "You really think you have a choice in this?"

"Of course, I have a choice." Everyone had choices about what they did. Even if refusal meant death.

"So you're choosing to die rather than do a simple job?"

She twisted around to Kart. Part of her wanted to find the humor in this, but it was more tragic than funny. "I'm supposed to turn a blind eye?"

"There's that high horse again."

Navarro said, "It's in your best interest to broker this peace treaty."

Kenna glanced at him.

"Or more people will die than is necessary." He waved at Kart. "We will continue to be rivals and destroy each other. Innocents could be caught in the crossfire."

She could ask them to set free every captive they currently had and halt all business just to satisfy her need to feel like she helped them. But life was never that simple, and it was unlikely they would voluntarily lose money just to satisfy her. "No children."

Neither of them said anything.

"If I see even one single child, or a teenager. Anyone under the age of eighteen. In either of your operations"—she took a breath—"I'm done."

"You want paperwork?" Kart snorted.

"I could do nothing."

He shifted, and she couldn't stop herself flinching. "But you won't. Because you know what will happen."

"I expect to hear from you." Navarro walked away with his men.

Ramon wasn't among them.

Kart didn't get up, and neither did Kenna. She bit the inside of her lip between her teeth, where no one would see. *Camila.* Before Kart could say anything, she pushed her chair back. "I want to go in the church. Get some guidance."

She also wanted to run.

Look for Stairns.

Scream at the sky.

Shove all these armed men away and try to escape—which would likely result in her being shot.

Kart grasped her forearm. The snap of pain that whipped through her arm broke a piece of something inside her she'd been trying to keep contained for days. She screamed out all the pain and frustration in his face until tears ran from the corners of her eyes.

He let go. Not a reaction but a slow and measured move. Assessing her.

Ascertaining that pain was very real.

She hoped he felt bad for all he'd put her through. That somewhere deep down inside him there was a spark of empathy. She doubted it would lead to him letting her go—but maybe he'd feel bad about handing her over to his cousin.

A car marked with a *Policia* decal slowed in front of them. The driver glanced at them as he rolled by, window down. Kart lifted two fingers. The driver continued.

"Friend of yours?" She had to clear her throat, and that question didn't sound like she had any bravado left. Which was absolutely true.

"He's good for a poker game and a bottle of whiskey." So Kart had an agreement with the local police department? "I don't trust anyone, but it pays to know the people around you."

She shifted in her chair. "In case he makes trouble for you, you'll know how to hit back at him and make it hurt?"

He hauled her to her feet. "Now you're getting it."

Kenna nearly tripped. She wouldn't have bothered catching herself but didn't want to wind up bleeding. The bustle of humanity—and freedom—around her wasn't comforting. It was more like torture. Being so close to losing them in a back alley when she made a run for it with all the strength her legs could muster.

But then what would Jax do?

She'd only be leaving him to his fate while she saved herself.

They sandwiched her in the back seat again, with Kart beside her this time while one of the others drove. Kenna didn't care who. She had a thirty-minute car ride to gather some semblance of strength with which to face the next fight.

The one where she had to find a woman. Or at least pretend to.

Months ago she'd infiltrated a ranch belonging to Sheriff Elliot Preston's brother. Along with a young migrant worker, she'd found a group of captives the brother had been using to work his property. She'd set them free, and they had killed Brian Preston. A few of them had headed to find the rest of the siblings next, including Elliot, bent on revenge.

Weeks later Elliot had been on TV talking about surviving an assassination attempt. But why be so public about it if he intended to kidnap Kenna and get his revenge?

Maybe the attack happened in a way he hadn't been able to hide, and he'd doubled down by going public.

All the while plotting to come after her.

The young migrant worker, Luca, had married the woman he returned for.

Camila.

Navarro's girlfriend. A woman who'd been pregnant last time Kenna saw her—with the cartel leader's baby? Perhaps he was more concerned with retrieving another heir than the woman carrying the baby. Or he genuinely cared about her.

But she'd been in Colorado, and a captive. Did that mean Kart had sold her off through one of his channels to get back at

Navarro? Or someone else used his routes to get her to Colorado.

She could hardly ask Kart if Camila had been trafficked to America without tipping her hand and letting them all know she knew *exactly* where the girl was.   .

Well...not exactly.

Maizie could probably use her tech know-how to find where Luca and Camila had settled. But Kenna couldn't say without that information. And that was how it would stay if she had anything to say about it. That way no one could compel her to tell them where the two had gone.

Luca and Camila and their baby would be safe.

It was all that mattered.

A phone chimed three times in succession. Benjamin, in the front seat, said, "Elliot's foreman wants a delivery when the sheriff returns to Colorado."

Kenna tried to figure out what that meant.

The sheriff was coming here, and when he went back, he wanted a "delivery." Could be a lot of things. It didn't necessarily mean...

"Round up half a dozen who want a better life in America." Kart glanced at her. "Adults."

Someone snorted. "Right."

She didn't know if they were reacting to the misbelief— the hope—these people would have for a better life. Or her request they not be children.

"Adults who can work."

Benjamin said, "I'll call the doc and set up..." His voice trailed off, and he swore.

Kart leaned in front of her to look between the front seats. "They dead?"

The driver slowed.

She peered out the windshield. The gate had been broken

open, and the men who'd been on guard at the compound now lay sprawled in the dirt. Bullet wounds. Blood everywhere. Multiple shots, until the shooter could be certain the person was dead.

The gate had been rammed at high speed with something big and heavy enough to bend the gate. It had happened fast and hard.

"Navarro." Benjamin swore again. "He did this while we were in town!"

The driver hit the gas and raced to the forecourt between buildings. The semi had left, but she didn't know when. Kenna sat completely still while they jumped out and ran around yelling.

Another attack.

But Navarro's men, or someone else? Ramon hadn't been at the meeting. Maybe this was his doing.

One of Kart's guys, a local, ducked his head in the open door to her left. "You know what happened?" He spoke in broken accented English.

She shot him a look to encapsulate her answer, then faced front again and closed her eyes.

Protect us.

She had no idea what went on here, or what was about to happen. This could be the start of a deadly battle between Kart and Navarro that swelled into bloodshed and all-out war. And meant she would have the opportunity to escape.

Help us.

Prayer still felt awkward, but she had become more used to it. Desperation was a good teacher.

She opened her eyes and spotted the keys still in the ignition.

Freedom.

But not for Jax.

She might be able to... Had to...

Kenna grabbed the front seats. She moaned against the pain but hauled herself through to the front. She got her long legs bent, folded into the driver's side. Door open. All the doors were open.

She twisted the key.

A punishing grip wrapped around her arm and dragged her out of the car onto the ground. Her hip slammed the dirt, and she lay there without the strength to move.

"I told you." Kart stood over her. "You aren't going anywhere."

Kenna stared at his boots, her mind an eerie kind of calm she didn't like. It would lead to her losing hope. Having nothing to grasp onto.

"You knew he would be gone."

She blinked and looked up at him.

"Who did you tell?"

"What?" She managed to choke out the word.

"You timed it well. I'll give you that. They came in hard, ignored the operation entirely, and got your boy out."

"Jax..."

Kart chuckled, a dark sound. "He's gone."

Kenna sucked in a breath. The one hand she had bracing herself up with gave out, and she slammed onto the ground. Her face hit the dirt. Pain slammed through her head, and she coughed against the dirt.

He's gone.

Kart hauled her up.

Kenna felt something inside her crack. She screamed and thrashed, saying words but not understanding what even came out of her mouth.

Her awareness blurred.

Pain sparked in her side. Then in her head. Someone

restrained her. She fought with every ounce of strength she had, practically feral. Nearly zero control over herself, and what little she did have she gave up to instinct.

The world spun around her, and she hit the ground.

The floor.

Inside.

Everything went black. Kenna blinked and rolled over. Just a dark room with no windows and no door. She lay on her back, staring at the ceiling, each breath coming fast. Adrenaline raced through her as her chest rose and fell in rapid succession.

Help.

Jax was gone. They'd come in and rescued him while she wasn't here. It had to have been the FBI. Who else would just leave her here?

Hot tears gathered in her eyes, sliding back to her hair. She didn't bother holding back but cried out every ounce of fear. Pain. Abandonment.

It wasn't supposed to be like this.

She shouldn't need anyone, but she'd let them in. Stairns. Maizie.

Jax.

Now she knew she hadn't seen Stairns in town. It was all just wishful thinking—like the idea of anyone coming to rescue her. Maybe they didn't care at all. Or they figured she could get herself out of anything.

But she couldn't.

Kenna rolled over to her side and curled up, tucking her knees to her chest. She couldn't even wrap her arms around herself. She wasn't strong enough to do that. Her arms were useless. Her legs felt like noodles. Every part of her thrummed with pain.

She wanted to throw up, but there was nothing in her stomach.

Jax was gone.

He was free, and she never would be. With no strength to fight what was coming she couldn't save her own life. She hadn't saved his. This was it.

The end.

Kenna closed her eyes.

I guess You aren't going to do anything.

God might've saved Jax—probably because he was a good guy—but she was still here. After years saving the lost and forgotten...it was her now.

Lost.

Forgotten.

The door cracked open, and light spilled on the backs of her closed eyelids. Her actions had brought her here, and there was nothing she could do about it.

"Are you done?"

She rolled onto her back and said nothing. Kenna took a long breath and held it. He could drag her around, do whatever he wanted, and then kill her when he was finished—or leave her so his cousin could do the same.

She had no strength to stop them.

And no one was coming to rescue her.

"So you *didn't* plan that." Kart leaned against the door frame. "You had no idea. And before you ask, yes, he's really gone."

As if she was going to ask that. Kenna doubted she could voice anything. Her throat burned. She'd probably screamed herself to laryngitis.

"Now you can tell me how you recognized that photo of Navarro's girlfriend."

Kenna's body flinched. It hurt, and she couldn't hold back the moan. Her voice sounded rough and raw.

"That's what I thought." Kart came over and crouched. "Tell me where she is, and you get this." He held up a needle.

Kenna said nothing. She didn't even have the energy to try and formulate a lie. She couldn't have sat up even if he threatened to kill her. She'd probably have opted for a bullet.

Maybe what was in the syringe would kill her.

She eyed it.

"Tell me what I want to know."

She shook her head.

"Then you don't get pain meds."

"I don't—" Her voice cracked. She swallowed against the burn in her throat. "Don't know where she is." She sounded like she'd had a cold for two weeks, and strep throat on top of that.

"But you've met her." He waved the syringe.

"I can't find her." She had no way to track Luca and Camila. And if she could, she wouldn't tell him or anyone. She didn't save people only to expose them to another threat. They deserved to live free and happy, together.

In a way she knew now that she never would.

"Tomorrow you can tell me the rest of the story." Kart jabbed the syringe in the fleshy part of her upper arm.

Hot pain from the needle stab made her grit her teeth.

He pressed the plunger in and pulled the needle out roughly. "You'll need your strength back for what's coming."

Warmth swept over her.

Kenna's eyes fluttered closed, and everything sucked down into the floor as she lost consciousness.

Chapter Nine

"Come on." Kart led her out the side door to where a UTV—a side-by-side—had been parked.

Kenna didn't want to admit to anyone, least of all him, that she felt better today than she had yesterday. Plus, he'd actually given her another cup of coffee this morning. She could almost say she felt human. But without knowing whether Jax was okay or not, even if he was free, she still had no grasp on what would happen next. Or what any part of her future might hold.

Except the impending arrival of Sheriff Elliot Preston from Colorado.

Kart drove the UTV across the compound, still in disarray from the attack. What she'd been able to gather indicated some kind of strategic strike that completely ignored the locked down room in the main building where drugs were cut and packaged. None of those people had even seen whoever had breached the gates and killed the guards.

A few other people had been killed as well, those who'd been guarding Jax.

A rescue operation.

They had known exactly where to go to find him, and they had struck during one of the only times when Kenna wasn't in the compound.

She couldn't believe that whoever came in to get him didn't also care about her. Then again, maybe that was exactly what happened. She wasn't exactly in good standing with the FBI, considering the last time she saw any agent was the day they were kidnapped and the rest of the SUV's occupants had been killed. The time before that was the night in Vegas when she had killed the FBI director.

Not exactly a stellar resume.

If she were still in the FBI, she probably wouldn't be interested in saving her life either.

Kenna shielded her eyes from the wind and the sun. "Where are we going?" she asked. Even though there was a decent chance the answer to the question might be out into the desert so he could kill her, she still needed to ask. If only to get her out of the downward spiral of her own thoughts.

Kart yelled back over the noise of the engine, "Over there." He waved at the horizon, toward a couple more men and another vehicle like this one. Plus a dirt bike.

When he cut the engine, she waited for him to usher her out. Compliance was a means to an end—not the statement she wanted to make. If she pushed back repeatedly, they would only retaliate by taking her life.

Which meant she would never know if Jax had made it out alive. Even if it saved her from Elliot.

Kenna had to work a combination of playing the game and looking for the first chance to get free. Even so, there was a tiny niggle at the back of her mind over what had been in that syringe. Given how well it worked and how much better she felt after healing sleep, she would probably get to a point where she needed more.

Enough to get her through.

Or enough to hook her on the effects of the drug until she got to a place where she couldn't live without it.

She liked to believe that she didn't need anyone, or anything. The fact was that Kenna wasn't so far removed from the people she took down. She would kill, and had, when it became necessary. There wasn't more than a fine line between her familiarity with taking lives and some of the people she went after.

If she had to take more pain meds in order to do that, so her arm injuries didn't hinder her, would she? If it came down to saving a life that would otherwise be lost, was she the kind of person who would allow herself to battle an addiction just to do it?

Saving victims had become a compulsion over the years. A way to experience the freedom she had after the death of her partner—the man she had loved.

That kind of obsessive drive could lead her down a dark path if she wasn't careful.

Kart said, "Let's go."

Kenna stuck her hands in the pockets of the clean shorts Kart had given her. She also had on a new T-shirt and a pair of boots, and they'd found a rubber band she had used to get her hair off her face. Tying back the scraggly mess helped almost as much as coffee did.

All the better to escape.

As she and Kart approached the others, she spotted something in the desert beyond the vehicles. Kenna walked in a wide circle around the men, giving them plenty of space. Not so she could run off—or even feel like she might be free for a second—but to get a good angle as she circled the dead young woman who lay in the sand.

Lola wore the same clothes she had when Kenna saw her

last. Blood covered the front of the shirt, tugged up slightly to reveal the dark skin of her lower back and the end of whatever wound she had been given. Her body lay twisted at an odd angle, almost as though she had been running and fell in the dirt. Her hair sprawled out on the ground, matted and tangled. Sightless eyes wide open.

A fly landed on her cheek.

"Who did it?" one of the men asked in thickly accented English.

Kenna kept studying the body. Absorbing everything she could, the way she did with any scene she came across.

"Hey, I said, 'Who did it?'"

Kenna blinked and glanced over at the men. "You're asking me?"

"You're that famous investigator." The local man waved at the young woman's dead body. "So who killed her?"

Kart stood there, saying nothing, waiting to see what she would do.

"Do you seriously think that's how murder investigations work? Generally evidence is taken, and there's a whole lot of processing—which can take weeks. Knocking on doors, asking lots of questions." Kenna straightened, her hands still in her pockets, giving her an air of feeling casual even if what was happening on the inside was nothing like that. "Right now, I can tell you with reasonable certainty that yes, she is dead."

One of them barked a laugh, and another shoved at him.

She glanced at Kart. "Did you call the police department?" She didn't want to say "your buddy" if the others didn't know he had friends in the local law enforcement community. "Did you report this so they can go inform the next of kin and properly bury the body?"

"It doesn't work like that out here."

Kenna frowned.

One of the men said, "We dispose of them ourselves." He shrugged. "Most times the families don't care."

Kenna swallowed back bile. It was only that way because that was the kind of victim they preyed on. The ones whose lives wouldn't be missed.

Maybe only a few months ago she might have been one of those people. She might have had a friend or two to wonder where she ended up from time to time. But no one would have noticed her disappearance.

Now?

She had to believe that Maizie and Stairns wouldn't rest until they found her. If she couldn't get herself out of this before the sheriff turned up.

"Before we do bury her," Kart said, "you're going to figure out who did this one."

Kenna stared at him. "I'm not a magician."

"This is part of our deal. It's how they get lost." Kart shrugged. "If you don't work on this, then Benjamin can find something else for you to do. I'm sure you won't like what it is."

Great. They had worked their way to the part of the conversation where things dissolved into threats back and forth. "Do you have anything like an evidence collection kit?"

They all stared at her.

She wasn't going to bother asking for lab equipment. They already knew who the girl was, or at least that no one cared to identify her. Which meant it was doubtful her identity played into the reason she had been killed. Still, it was possible.

Something Kart had said stuck with her. *This one.*

"So she's not the first?" Kenna said.

Their expressions were enough of an answer.

"How many others have you found like this?" If she got details, then she might be able to figure out a pattern.

After she'd escaped.

"A few." Kart wandered over to stand by her. "Since we got here, which was four years ago... before you ask."

She stared at him. "So there is a serial killer in the area."

"Let's not make some news story out of this so you get your face on TV again." Kart shifted, lethality in his movements. Everything he was amounted to a threat. There was nothing passive about the man at all. "That's not what's happening here. We aren't going to draw attention to ourselves, are we?"

She had zero problems drawing attention to herself.

Whether she wanted to or not usually, right now it would come in very handy.

Kenna could string them along while she figured out an escape. "Anyone who has committed a series of murders, whether or not they had good reason or if they have any kind of pattern, is a serial killer. So if this is something that's happened before, then you've got one in your midst."

"So figure out who it is, and I'll be able to put a stop to it."

The part Kenna hated the most right now was that she wanted to do what he said. Not because he'd asked her to, or the impending threat of what was going to happen to her when the sheriff got here. It was more the fact that if she didn't figure it out, then Lola and all the other victims would go unavenged.

Assuming Kart intended on shutting down the killer. As opposed to shaking the person's hand. She had no idea what he would do with the person when she found them—if she found them. She also didn't want to ask, or she'd end up an accessory to yet another crime.

All because she'd volunteered to go to Washington, DC, to testify over what had happened with the FBI director.

Maybe Elliott Preston and his men would have found her anywhere and brought her to Mexico. She was the one who had taken a flight. It put her back on the radar when she showed up to meet with the FBI.

Actions that could have led to Jax's death. But she thanked God he'd been rescued, then prayed that he was all right.

Kart shifted. "Well?"

"How do you dispose of them?" Kenna said.

He frowned. "Why?"

"Just tell me. Do you destroy the bodies, or bury them?"

"I don't think you want to be exhuming anyone. And none of my men is going to pick up a shovel for you."

Kenna sighed. "What if I need information from their remains that will answer questions I have?"

"We don't bury them. We burn them."

Great.

Kenna wandered around the scene, mostly to give herself a chance to think this through.

Could she use the situation to get free, or get a message out?

That was it. She turned to Kart. "You should call the priest from town and have him come out here and perform last rites before you...dispose of her."

"Why?"

She wandered back over to him. "Because if there was ever an ounce of a decent person somewhere inside you, then you have to respect the fact that this young woman's life ended and maybe you don't share her beliefs, but she saw the world a particular way. And we should honor that even if no one ever cared about her while she was alive."

"Is this a hill you want to die on?"

Kenna folded her arms, noting the twinge of pain in her forearms. The drugs he had given her last night, and then again this morning, were wearing off now, and it was barely noon. "We need to get her out of the sun. Vultures are already circling overhead."

Did he realize that asking her to question everyone he worked with meant they would all begin to see each other in a different light? She could incite suspicion and then destruction from within, and there would be nothing he could do to stop her. It would be satisfying, in a vindictive kind of way.

"You get the priest out here to say what he needs to say, and I'll figure out who did this." Kenna dismissed him, turning away back to the body. She crouched beside Lola and tugged up the shirt so she could see the wound on the victim's back. The girl had many scars that had healed over a long period of time.

Not what had ended her life.

Neither was the W that had been carved into her lower back. A brand, but not the wound that killed her.

Kenna rolled Lola onto her back, revealing a series of knife entry points on her front side, one of which landed over her heart.

I might not be able to find out who did this to you before I leave here. But I can try.

As far as she was concerned, all the men here were suspects. Even Ramon.

She crouched for as long as she could. "Do any of you see a knife around here anywhere?"

While they turned and looked around on the ground, she assessed each of them. It seemed customary to carry a knife sheathed on the belt. She could take some measurements from the body, but without something to compare it to, she might not be able to find a match. And it would be crude at best. Unless the wounds were from a distinctive-sized blade. Or with some kind of unique serration.

No one found the murder weapon.

The other men loaded the body onto their UTV, and Kart drove her back in theirs toward the compound. When he had shut off the engine in the forecourt between two buildings, she said, "Who is it that found her?"

"It wasn't him that killed her. He goes and meets with his woman on the road to the west." Kart snorted. "He says she can't go more than a few days without seeing him."

"So you're going to vouch for this guy?"

"And you're going to ask everyone who they are willing to rat out?"

"You're the one who wants this murder solved." Kenna shrugged. "It's either that, or you're looking for me to pin the blame on one of Navarro's men. So which is it? Do you want me to find out who did this so you can get rid of the problem causing you a loss margin on your bottom line? Because clearly you don't care about the merchandise. I guess that means you only care about the money."

"I must. Otherwise, I would have killed you already." He stared at her. "But I have to keep you around so I can get paid."

Interesting. "How much? I'll give you double to let me go right now."

He tipped his head back and laughed.

"It wasn't a joke. You think I'm being anything other than deadly serious? We're talking about my life." And her sanity, and whatever it would cost her when Elliott did whatever he was going to do before he killed her.

Kenna didn't even want to think about that.

"My cousin isn't a man you cross. Not even for double."

Chapter Ten

Kenna leaned against the wall, the sole of one shoe on the wall. Watching. Across the room the priest from the town of Cielo Ardiente spoke softly in Spanish. Delivering last rites for Lola. Praying over the girl.

Kenna didn't know a whole lot about Catholicism, but she did understand that this was an important part of the end of someone's life. She wanted to do what she could whether she got a shot at getting a message out or not. As with anything, it was about what she had the ability to control.

Right now that control was about the freedom she had to make the right choice for a dead girl.

And for her own survival.

It hadn't been her choice to investigate this for Kart and Navarro. More like something to occupy her until the sheriff came. Until she found a way to get out *before* his arrival. However, as always the thing God had put inside her, forged in everything she'd been through, the part of her that needed to find peace for others didn't exactly allow her to let this go.

Especially not with a letter carved into the victim's lower back.

Multiple murders.

No one to investigate it but her.

She wanted to let it go and worry only about getting out, but the compulsion to find the person responsible was like a living thing inside her.

The priest finished up and moved across the room to her. He wore a robe over his street clothes and held a Bible between his hands.

Did you see my friend in town? she wanted to ask, but Kart and two of his men were in the room with them. Instead, Kenna said, "Do you know if she has family?"

The priest studied her with a passive expression. "Not many have loved ones to care for them down here."

The sadness of it all washed over her. She pushed out a long breath, still not steady enough to let go of the wall, but she could at least stand on her own two feet.

"You're not what I thought you'd be."

Kenna started to ask what he meant, but Kart spoke over her. "Did you bring what I asked for?"

The priest reached into his pocket and pulled out a vial. "The doctor said this should do what you need."

So much for finding a way to give him a message to take into town. There was no way to ask him if she could use his cell phone, or somehow explain who Stairns might have been. Surely Jax had told whoever rescued him that they needed to come back and get Kenna.

She'd overheard a conversation between two guards. They had no intention of letting her outside the gates anytime soon. Kart had doubled the guard, and everyone was on high alert just in case someone tried to rescue her. Or attack again.

She never would have thought when she decided to go to Washington, DC, to testify that it would end up with her here.

How could she have even imagined this would come from it?

She'd tried to do the right thing. To stand up and tell the truth but manage to protect Maizie at the same time. She'd known it was what God wanted her to do rather than continue to hide under the radar and avoid the entire issue.

And it ended like this?

From her point of view, she had tried to do the right thing and it had all gone down in flames. One attempt to stand up and tell the truth...and the result was a giant failure.

Kart turned to her, and she realized that while her thoughts had been drifting, he had prepared another syringe. She took a tiny step back as he smirked. "I didn't figure you'd want something from downstairs."

She stared at the syringe. Then him. Aware the entire time that the priest was watching them. "So you're doing me a *favor*?" That made no sense. Why give her some kind of concession while also victimizing her? It might be about lulling her into a false sense of security, or deep down in there he had a heart. Though, she very much doubted that.

More likely it was just that the sheriff wanted her healthy. And aware of what was happening, rather than suffering from the effects of illegal narcotics. Anything they gave her from "downstairs" could cause an overdose. Falling back on traditional medicine from a doctor meant he could get the dosage right and she would be healthier when the sheriff got here than she was right now.

Kart stuck the needle in her upper arm. Kenna hissed.

He knew that she had seen Camila. That Kenna might even know where the girl had gone—and where she was now. Someone had used his trafficking operation to get the girl to Colorado. But why do that when it was only for the sake of handing her over to be just another worker, and Navarro had no idea that'd happened?

She blinked and realized the priest had gone.

Along with her chance to get him to take a message with him back to town.

She twisted around to face Kart.

"What have you figured out so far about this case?" he asked.

Kenna snorted. "It's hardly a case. You probably just want me distracted so I don't try to escape."

"Honestly, I was more worried about you trying to kill yourself."

"What do you care if you lose merchandise every once in a while? It can't be more than an annoyance unless they matter. Or whoever killed Lola hurt someone you care about."

"Emotions never did anyone any favors." He shrugged. "They just twist you up in knots, or make you react in a way that isn't smart." He walked her outside, where the sun beat down on them. Bright enough she had to blink against the harsh light of day.

Kenna kept going, out into the middle of the area behind the buildings. Between them and the fence in front of her. Then kept walking with no thought of where she was headed or what would happen when she got there.

Attempting to get over the fence wouldn't work when she could barely lift her arms, let alone climb with them. She would only get shot for her trouble. What was the point in showing these men just how weak she was?

She turned around and realized Kart hadn't come with her. She stood there alone and stared back at him, trying to figure out why it seemed like he cared.

More likely he didn't. But occupying her with this task—

even just trying to figure out why he gave it to her—kept her off guard and distracted from what was really going on.

She glanced at the edges of the buildings and spotted more than one armed guard with their eyes on her. Kart. Benjamin. More were on the front gate that she couldn't see on the other side. No way out. No chance to escape.

And no one coming to rescue her.

Kart strode toward her. "You want me to chase and capture you?"

Not a threat that he would kill her if she tried to escape. That was interesting. "You're not allowed to shoot me?"

"I never said that." Kart lifted his chin.

"But you let your cousin tell you what to do?" She scoffed. "I thought *you* were the one in charge here."

His right cross came out of nowhere.

She managed to jerk her head around. Still, his punch hammered her jaw, and she ended up on her hands and knees on the ground.

Someone called out, "Are the two of you done with your spat?"

Kart hauled Kenna to her feet.

She realized Ramon had arrived at some point. Now he stood over by the buildings holding a man, his face beat up. Hands tied together behind his back. "We need to see what this guy knows."

Kart dragged Kenna back over to where Ramon stood. "And you need us to find information for you?" Kart snorted. As though he thought Ramon wasn't capable of getting information by himself.

Why was Navarro's man back all of a sudden?

He'd been here during the raid, and then gone.

Kenna's head swam, and she fought to gather her thoughts.

"This is about the spirit of cooperation." Ramon studied Kart with a dark look in his eyes. "And working together, rather than wasting money destroying each other. That's why I brought you this." He dragged the man in front of him, and the guy fell to his knees. "He has information."

Kart turned to her. "Then I guess it's time for Kenna to get to work."

Ramon walked the bound man. Kart dragged Kenna behind them down into the basement of the main building. To a cell previously used for something like this, given the mess on the floor.

Ramon wrinkled his nose and muttered something in Spanish.

Kart said, "I figured I would set the mood for our friend here. So he understands what will happen if he doesn't tell us what we want to know." He let go of her and exited the room, returning a minute later with a wooden chair, which he set in the middle of the room.

Ramon sat the bound man in the chair.

"I have things to see to," Kart said. "But I'll be back." He shut the door.

Kenna closed her eyes and blew out a long breath. She heard Ramon move toward her. When she opened her eyes, he stopped right in front of her, so he could look down at her. She frowned. "What?"

Ramon twisted her upper arm around so he could look at it.

She hissed.

"Do you even know what they gave you?" He laughed.

She wanted to quip back that whatever it was made her feel better, but just didn't have the energy to formulate something witty. Not when she had bigger priorities. "Can I use your phone?"

Ramon shook his head. "They made me leave my weapons and my cell phone at the gate when they let me in here."

Great.

"Who do you need to call, anyway? The FBI doesn't care about you. They already got their man out."

Her stomach lurched. "So it was them?"

She wasn't sure who else it could have been. But she was a US citizen, and a person of interest to the FBI regarding the death of their director. Why wouldn't they have waited and extracted both her and Jax at the same time?

Ramon shrugged. "I figured it would curry favor with them if I told them where their guy was. So I left a message that Jax was here, and they came and got him out."

Kenna sucked in a breath through her nose.

"But you're like me." Ramon shrugged. "They don't care about people like us." He touched her chin, turning her head one way and then the other. "That punch he gave you is going to leave a bruise. But I don't suppose he'll give you an ice pack when he gives you another dose of narcotics."

"I need you to figure out how to take me with you when you leave here." She had to get out or she wasn't going to last much longer.

"I doubt I can make that happen."

"Which means you aren't even going to try?" Kenna leaned against the wall. "Why should I help any of you? I'm just hanging out here waiting for some guy I've never met to do whatever...I don't even know." She didn't care one bit about Elliot Preston.

"I thought you were all about bringing justice." Ramon paused. "Isn't that who you are now?"

"I need to get out of here." He said nothing, and Kenna stared up at him. "What happened to you?"

If he didn't tell her, then why should she give him answers to his questions? She had no obligation to tell him anything about her. She didn't owe any of these people anything, least of all her help with their problems. But they still all thought they knew her.

They didn't.

Kenna studied his blank expression. "You were undercover, and your handler lost track of you. Now you're here working for Navarro. Did he make you a better offer than the federal government?"

Ramon snorted. "Like that would've been hard."

"Maybe the pay working for a cartel is better. But what about the fact you've been branded a criminal, and you're an accessory to a list of federal crimes perpetrated in more than one country? You'll never be able to escape the consequences of the choices you've made."

"And you're such a saint?"

Kenna stared at him.

"Let's just do what we have to do." He turned to the man in the chair, whose head lolled so that his chin touched his chest. Ramon grabbed a handful of the man's hair and tipped his head back.

Blood bubbled from between the man's lips.

"He doesn't have long left." Kenna moved to stand closer. "Who is he?"

"One of Navarro's delivery guys. A local." Ramon studied the man's face, one eye swollen nearly shut. The other one glassy and unable to focus. "He was out driving and saw the killer dump the body in the desert." He patted the man's cheek and spoke in Spanish.

The guy sucked in a breath through his nose and blinked his one eye, finding a semblance of focus on the two of them. He muttered something, a series of mumbled words.

"We need to know what time it was, and we need a full description of the person."

Ramon glanced at her. "I thought you weren't interested in solving this case?"

She could try to have no emotion, the way Kart seemed to think served him better than the alternative. Kenna could pretend she didn't care about a single victim with no one to seek justice for her. She could pretend she didn't prefer having something to take her mind off what was going on around her.

But all of that would be a lie.

She didn't know why her drive to seek the truth often also felt a lot like empathy for the victims. If she had been given a choice, she would have opted to do this without the anger and the grief over the senseless way so many people's lives ended.

She stuck her hands in her pockets. "We also need to know if he saw anyone else."

"So we work together," he said. "Like we did back at Quantico."

It took Kenna a second to figure out what he was referring to.

But she remembered.

Chapter Eleven

NINE YEARS AGO
QUANTICO, VIRGINIA

Special Agent Santiago entered the room first, and Kenna strode in right behind him. She had the paper file with the "suspect" background. The man on the other side of the table was an agent from the behavioral analysis unit, specially tasked with playing the suspect in this scenario.

Kenna dropped the file on the table. She waited a second, then grinned. "I've always wanted to do that. Plus, it makes a cool sound when it slaps the table."

The suspect blinked.

She'd successfully already caught him off guard. He definitely hadn't expected her to say that. "We found your burial ground. Every single body that you concealed in that field. We have all of them." Kenna touched both palms to the table and leaned forward. "It's over, Emerson."

His gaze shifted to Ramon, then back to her. "Probably just a bunch of animal bones. That's all those cadaver dogs ever find, and then you guys write it up like it's a missing person."

"Is that right?" Kenna pushed off the table and straightened.

She and Ramon had dressed the part of full-fledged agents. Their task was to get this suspect to tell them who his accomplice was.

They weren't supposed to compare notes with any of the other trainee agents, but her roommate Cecilia had told her that the exercise involved throwing them a curveball at some point.

She was ready.

The suspect sat back in his chair, a smirk on his face.

Ramon opened the file and spread the gruesome photos across the table. "We know you buried these people. What we *don't* know is who you're working with."

"No?" The suspect chuckled. "That's a shame."

So he wasn't going to deny that he had a partner. She figured he would use some tactic that pitted her against Ramon. She decided to do the same thing between him and his "partner" with a snide comment. "Well, it's not like you could have pulled that off on your own."

Under the photos was a full history that had been put together on their suspect. His entire background—for the sake of the exercise.

"Domestic battery," she began, then read down the list. "More than one bar fight. A couple of speeding tickets and driving without insurance. You don't strike me as a guy with their creativity it takes to pull off something like this." But the history they had been given for this exercise spoke of a guy who absolutely would choose to target women—especially if the accomplice convinced him that he could get away with it.

The suspect lifted his chin. "I know who you are, Kenna Banbury."

She shrugged. "Okay, so you can read a newspaper. Or you can watch the news. You're just proving my point."

"You're not the kind of guy with the brains to come up with something like this," Ramon pointed out. "After all, you're sitting here."

"And if you're not careful," Kenna added, "you're going to be the one taking the rap for all of it." Maybe that was what he wanted. To feel like he was the big man. Even if that meant serving multiple life sentences, he would be known in the public eye as the one who dreamed up the entire escapade. "If you tell us who brought you in, we can speak to the US Attorney and try to get you a deal."

The suspect barked a laugh. "You think I'm going to roll over? I don't play dead."

"You do realize that you were only brought into this. So when the heat turns on, you're the one who gets cooked." She pointed at him.

The suspect glanced between them.

Kenna realized this was where it would come.

She knew she was right when he said, "You won't find enough evidence to tie me to these people."

"We already have." She shrugged one shoulder. "And why are you so convinced that we can't pin all of this on you?"

He eyed her. "Maybe I have inside knowledge of what you need to make a case." More likely it had been told to him —the man he was pretending to be for the training exercise.

She continued, "Or whoever you are working with watches a lot of true crime shows. Or reads books. Even a modicum of above average intelligence coupled with access to the internet would tell you what you need to know. It's really not that hard."

"Is that how your dad got away with all those crimes?" Here it came. "Pinning them on other people when he was the one who was the killer. That must be how you know so much about accomplices."

So he was going to play that card?

"Is that the best you can come up with?" She stared at him. "It's a shame you didn't think of all this first." She waved at the photos on the table. "Then someone else could have been the patsy instead of you. It's almost sad, really."

Ramon snorted. "Tell us who recruited you. Because whoever they were, they were only manipulating you into doing what they said."

The suspect looked at Ramon. "Why are you doing this to me? You said you'd help me if I got caught."

Kenna glanced over at Special Agent Santiago. Sure, the guy had an edge to him. But pinning him as the one who was the killer's accomplice? The tactic was divide and conquer.

And Kenna wasn't going to let that happen.

A muscle flicked in Ramon's jaw. He didn't know how to fight off being undermined?

Kenna gathered the photos back into the file. "All you've got is accusations that we are involved personally? Do you realize how statistically unlikely that is?"

The suspect's expression faltered.

Ramon stood stiff, and said nothing.

"I'll be sure and inform the US Attorney that you will say just about anything to try and get out of this. You aren't going to see any kind of a deal." She stepped back from the table. "Enjoy prison, Mr. Miller."

Chapter Twelve

"Cargo pants," Kenna said. "That's it?"

Ramon leaned against the wall next to her, half his attention on the man in the chair. "I guess it tells us whoever he saw dumping the body was probably one of the Americans. Everyone around here wears jeans."

"It's pretty thin."

She was still grasping for control of the situation. Whether that meant refusing to cooperate, or allowing herself to slip into that comfortable spot where she was investigating a murder, didn't much matter. Though, complying did seem to be better for her health.

Kenna lifted two fingers and touched her cheek bone where Kart had slammed his fist into her face. She pushed out a long breath, not just because taking as long as she could to do this might play in her favor with whatever happened next.

Ramon shrugged one shoulder. "Light hair could be

blond, or it could be a light brown. That rules out any of the locals, or you and I."

"I don't think I was ever on the suspect list."

Ramon seemed as interested in solving this case as she should be. Maybe for old time's sake he wanted to feel like an investigator again, and not the man he had chosen to become.

A guy on the run from the feds and the law who worked for a dangerous cartel.

"Why did you do it?" Kenna had to ask, and maybe at some point he'd tell her. If she asked enough times.

The same reason she found herself naturally slipping back into the mode of investigator herself—whether or not she wore a badge.

"You were undercover." She studied him. "Did you take the money they offered you? Turn on your oath and because you decided it was more lucrative to be one of the bad guys?"

"There's good and bad in all of us." Ramon glanced aside. "The Bureau teaches us to view ourselves as the good ones, and everyone who breaks the law is a bad guy. So that we see it all in black-and-white, like those blind scales of justice."

"And that's a bad thing?" she said. "We should be impartial when we investigate."

"Is that what you do? Taking the law into your own hands, working cases as a private investigator so you can do what you want and go wherever you want, and you don't have to answer to the federal government?"

And yet, she had been on her way to testify. "None of us is ever in a place where we don't answer to the federal government. That's the choice we make as citizens, to come under the power of the authority over us."

"So you be a good little girl, and they take care of you?" He shook his head. "You and I both know you're kidding yourself if you think that." Ramon must've told them to come get Jax, and either neglected to tell them about her or told them to show up when he knew she wouldn't be here.

"Honestly?" Kenna paused. "Yeah, when you get kidnapped and taken to a foreign country, you kind of expect your government to come and rescue you. But you screwed that up for me, didn't you?"

He shrugged. "They could have made sure you would be here as well. But it seems like all they did was rescue their golden boy."

She hoped they considered Jax to be that. She didn't want her association with him to lead to him being blackballed as a special agent. She knew he'd already turned down a promotion—or been denied it. She might have already cost him far too much in terms of advancement in the Bureau. But all that office politics stuff was for a time when she wasn't a captive in a foreign country.

"Do you want me to blame you for the fact that I'm still here, or do you want to figure out a way we can both get out of this?" She had no idea what Ramon's endgame might be. Maybe he had zero problems with what he did and who he was now.

"Navarro sent me here to help you guys figure out who is undermining his and Kart's operations. He wants Camila back."

She studied his blank expression. "And that's it? You just do what you're told?"

"What do you want from me? I made my choices, and there's nothing I can do to change what happened." He seemed sincere. "It is what it is."

"Why don't you tell me what happened, and I'll see if I can't help you change things?" She had to at least offer.

He shook his head. "You know there's something about me. Some kind of edge. It's always been there. So I become a cop, and every time I turn around, the finger is getting pointed at me for being the most likely to be dirty. Even at Quantico I fit this type, the profile."

"But it never amounted to anything," she said. "And then it became an asset."

"Because I went undercover?" He shot her a look. "You think that's what I wanted to do?"

"So you got typecasted whether you liked it or not?"

Ramon shrugged one shoulder. "No one asked me what assignment I wanted."

"So you didn't you tell them you didn't want to be undercover?"

He snorted. "No one would have believed I was some straightlaced FBI agent. Maybe it never would have worked." Maybe he'd given up trying. Or he'd been through too much to believe it would've worked. "Kind of like the daughter of Malcom Banbury staying under the radar, working the job, and never getting her name splashed in the public eye."

Kenna stiffened. She'd given up trying to convince people that she never purposely drew attention to herself.

"So you understand." He paused. "Choices are made for us, whether we like it or not."

"But I can choose how I react to it. How I feel about it, and what I decide to do next is up to me." She wanted more control than she had, especially at a time like this. But maybe even that was an illusion. It would be difficult to keep from succumbing to the fear and losing the last scrap of hope that she had.

"When I found you in Navarro's office, I guess your call made it through."

She flinched. "What do you mean?"

"An older guy visited the ranch. Passed your picture around and asked about you. I pegged him as a fed before Navarro did. We ran him, but he's retired."

Her stomach flipped. "Stairns."

Ramon nodded. "That was his name."

"Did you tell him where I am?" If she could've lifted her arms, she would have grabbed his shirt. Two grasping handfuls, betraying precisely how much desperation she had inside her.

"Navarro told him you were helping us with a problem."

"You should have told him where to find me." If anyone could bust in here, it was Stairns and whatever army he found to help him. "I need to get out of here, Ramon. You have to get a message to—"

"You don't have to convince me. If you want to get out of here, just give me the number and I'll make the call for you."

"You'll have to memorize it."

Before she could even begin to get the number out, the door opened.

"Let's go," Kart said. "Both of you."

Kenna buried her reaction. Kart couldn't know what was between her and Ramon, the shared history they had. If he knew, then she had no doubt he would use it against them. Maybe she could find a pen and a piece of paper, and he could take the number to contact Maizie—and hopefully Stairns—with him.

Kart held a gun down by his side. He instructed them to go ahead of him, through the building to the office she had talked to him in before. Instead of being empty, a uniformed local man sat in a chair drinking from a stoneware mug.

Ramon glanced back at her. "That's the local police

chief." Before she could respond, he said, "And he speaks good English."

"That I do." He set his mug on the desk. The uniform he wore had dark pants and a white short-sleeved shirt, bars on his shoulders. A hat lay on the desk beside the mug. When he reached for it, the muscles in his forearms flexed. "I brought everything I have on the cases I haven't been able to solve." He stood and walked toward Kart. "I expect to see you in a few days."

Kart shook his hand. "I'll bring your payment."

The police chief stiffened, apparently not expecting the American to say that. He glanced back at Kenna and Ramon. Because Kart had just informed her and Navarro's man that he was receiving payments from the Americans.

She doubted that had been a slip on Kart's behalf. More likely it was intentional so the police chief would know that at any moment Kart could make trouble for him. Unless he cooperated. This entire situation was nothing but a series of underhanded deals and threats.

Kart closed the door to the office, shutting the three of them inside. "The files are on the desk, Kenna. Turns out he's had a series of unexplained deaths and hasn't found the person responsible."

"And I'm supposed to solve those as well?" She shot him a look. "Why would I voluntarily do that, when there's absolutely nothing in it for me?"

"I can make it worth your while."

"But you're still going to hand me over to your cousin. So how is that worth my while?" She figured it was a losing battle trying to get him to change his mind and welch on the deal with Elliot. It seemed to her that he was far more afraid of the consequences of that. Maybe he was even scared of his cousin.

Ramon said, "Navarro can make it worth your while."

She turned to him. "Is your boss offering to kidnap me from here and take me to his ranch?" She wasn't sure that would amount to a better deal. "Because I'll take it."

If there was a chance she wouldn't have to face the sheriff, it was better to take those odds than do nothing.

Kart chuckled. "Are we going to barter with her and each other over who gets to take Kenna with them?" His body language signaled frustration as he rounded the desk and sat in his chair. "And don't bother trying to leave. There are two men outside this door who won't hesitate to shoot either of you in the leg."

Ramon said, "Navarro is expecting me back as soon as I'm done interrogating the asset I brought you."

"What did that guy tell you?" Kart asked.

Ramon reiterated the details about cargo pants and light-colored hair. "Are you prepared for the fact that it's one of your men undermining this business and creating a war between you and the Navarro cartel?"

Kart stared at the two of them as they faced him across his desk.

"How well do you know the men you've brought into your circle?" Kenna shrugged. "Is there a chance that one of them could be a killer?"

Kart barked a laugh. "You honestly think there's a chance one of them isn't the person behind the deaths?"

"So you already know they'll betray you. Isn't that nice." She stuck her hands in her pockets, trying to look casual and take the weight off her forearms. She didn't have much left in the way of reserves. The fight she'd been able to gather so far had waned. Low enough she doubted she would even be able to struggle against his tight grip on her arm at this point.

Let alone figure out how to escape.

"Now that you know it's one of your guys, I'll leave you two to figure out which one it is." Ramon lifted his chin. "I'll be needing my gun and my phone back."

Kart only stared at him. "You think I'm just going to let one of Navarro's men leave with information, and insider knowledge of this compound?"

"You think my boss doesn't already have someone inside your operation feeding him back information?" Ramon shifted his weight from one foot to the other. "Asking me to do the same would be redundant. And you knew that when you let me in here."

Kart lifted a cell phone from the desk and made a call. When the person picked up, he said, "Navarro has a man inside this compound. One of the locals." He hung up and tossed the phone on the desk.

Kenna itched to pick it up and stick it in her pocket so she could make a call later.

Please let me have the chance to do that.

She needed God to be on her side. After all, she didn't have anyone else to help her in this situation. She couldn't do anything for herself to escape. She needed God to bring things together and provide her a way out or bring her friends to rescue her.

Peace settled inside her, in a way she hadn't felt for days.

I need Your help.

Because she had nothing else.

A tiny note of distrust deep inside her wondered how long that peace would last. And if it would change the situation. Maybe it was only supposed to be reassurance, until the timing was right, and God saved her.

But for now, nothing had changed. Except her reaction to the situation—the one that she could control. Was the peace from her, or a gift God was giving her?

And why did she have to be so suspicious of it in the first place? She didn't need to doubt. That was a bad idea with faith, though it could also be understandable.

Kenna couldn't get her thoughts straight about anything right now. All she had was that familiar fire of angry desperation that wanted to get out of here. That wanted to grab the phone from the desk and bash Kart's head in with it.

Even if she had the strength, it would ruin her chance to call for help.

And what would it prove to anyone—or herself—except that she was no better than these people?

The kind of person responsible for bringing down a good man, an FBI agent.

Drawing him in when if it wasn't for her, he'd have never been anywhere near this.

Ramon lifted his chin. "I'll be sure to tell Navarro that you treated me well, and that you're going to take care of the problem." He glanced at her, something like sympathy in his eyes, then back to Kart. "He'll be glad to know things will be resolved."

Kart sat silently for a second, staring at them. Then he shook his head. "You aren't going anywhere, Santiago. There's too much risk of you contacting someone who can take Kenna from me. No one leaves until the sheriff gets here, and I can wrap up my business."

He would be rid of her then.

In the meantime, he wasn't taking any chances that Kenna would be able to escape.

Kart continued, "The chief saw you, whole and healthy. The priest. The doctor. If anyone asks, Navarro will hear that you're here and you seem fine."

Kenna's stomach clenched.

Ramon shifted. "You can't keep me—"

"Enough," Kart barked so loudly Kenna flinched. "I won't be changing my mind, and you won't be leaving. So why don't the two of you put your heads together and figure out how many people this guy has killed, and who in my compound is doing it."

Chapter Thirteen

After delivering his order, Kart had Ramon and Kenna escorted back to the room where she had last seen Jax. Under armed guard. Holding the files the police chief had left.

Kenna had already tried the lock on the door twice since Kart shut them in.

There was no way to get out of here.

She paced to the window, through which she could see next to nothing but the sky. The music playing in the distance that she might otherwise have enjoyed now became a hated thing she would associate with this sense of desperation and hopelessness for the rest of her life.

Whether that was a matter of days, or decades.

Ramon sat on the floor with his back to the wall. "Are you going to pace the entire time?"

"How are you so calm? It's like you don't even care that we can't get out of here."

He lifted the pile of files from the floor and opened the first one. "You need to put a lid on all of this." He motioned to her. "It's not doing you any favors displaying to anyone who even glances your direction what's going on inside you. You're like this roiling mass of tension right now."

"There's no one in here but you. Why not show it now?"

"Because it's exhausting just watching you." He sighed. "Figure it out."

She would rather kick the door than do that. The sense of calm that had settled on her in Kart's office was gone now. If it had ever been real.

"Why don't you help me go through these files instead?" he suggested.

But she couldn't let go of something Kart had said. "Tell me what you know about the doctor and the priest. Are they really going to tell people that we're fine here, and there's nothing wrong with me?" Hot tears burned in her eyes. "I need to get out."

"You and me both," he said. "And who knows what people will say. Or if they'll even get asked."

She shook her head. "You don't understand. That sheriff guy who is on his way? I can't be here when he gets here. I won't survive it."

His impending arrival had kept her alive and mostly unharmed so far. Because Kart had been ordered not to touch her, and not to let anyone else do so either. It had kept her in one piece so far—but that wouldn't last much longer. Mentally she was coming completely unraveled.

He stared at the files and didn't answer her question.

"At least tell me you have a way to get back to Navarro," she pressed.

"You think he cares about me enough to mount a rescue?" He shot her a look. "He's interested in money and family, and that's it. Too bad for me that I'm neither."

"So you're expendable." She paced toward him. "But that

doesn't mean Navarro won't come looking for you. He'll want to know what happened."

"He only cares about his nephew." Ramon sighed. "He was hoping for an heir. That's why he wants to find his bride so badly. He believes she was pregnant when she disappeared."

She wasn't going to tell anyone here how that was correct.

"But now that she's gone," Kenna said, "you can secure your position as the one who will take over everything. Is that what the plan is? You become invaluable to him and maybe he'll let you take over."

Ramon shrugged one shoulder. "Navarro doesn't need me. There are ten guys lining up behind me to take my place, and all of them have ideas about how he can make more money than he is. Or how he can find her."

"He never will."

His chin snapped up. "Where is she?"

Kenna winced. "So you can use the information to trade your way out of here and back to Navarro?" She slid her back down the wall and sat on the floor across from him. "If you do that, then you're going to be taking me with you."

Ramon shook his head. "You're only saying whatever you need to so you can try and get out of this. We all have to live with the consequences of our choices, Kenna. Even you."

"And if I told you that the sheriff who is on his way here wants retaliation because I set Navarro's woman free?" She stared at him. "What then?"

His eyes narrowed. "You don't know where she is."

"I can tell him how to find her." Of course, it wouldn't work because she would give him completely wrong information.

She had no intention of selling Camila back to Navarro in exchange for her freedom. As much as she wanted to get out of here, Kenna refused to ever be the kind of person who destroyed someone else just so she could survive.

Ramon looked back down at the files. "There's nothing we can do right now, and no way to contact anyone. So why don't you help me look through all this. That way, when Kart asks what we've been doing we'll give him something to show for it."

"You think I care one little bit about that?"

"Reading these will help give your mind something to do while it puzzles over how to get out of here in the background."

Kenna understood how creative thinking worked, but she didn't have enough presence of mind to occupy her thoughts in the hope that her subconscious would come up with an answer. Wasn't that what she'd been doing since she got here? Puzzling over how she ended up brokering a deal between two warring groups and how she was now being tasked with catching a person who had kidnapped and killed multiple women.

"I don't even care anymore," she muttered.

"So you've given up," Ramon said. "You don't have it in you to fight back. You're waiting for someone else to rescue you." He tossed a file across the floor to her. "What if they never do? What if you're abandoned in the very place your nightmares come from and no one will ever come and get you out?"

She stared at him. "You were undercover." It wasn't like he'd been captured by a serial killer. So what was he talking about?

"Tell me," Ramon said. "What did my handler report in about all the times I tried to call her and I got no answer? Or about the attempts I made to contact the office, but I was told that my credentials were no longer valid?"

"Someone sold you out?" She frowned. "Why would they do that?"

Ramon snorted. "You think I haven't been trying to figure that out ever since?"

"Why haven't you just left? You could have gone home and set everything straight." She lifted the file and held it close, as if paper and card stock could provide a defensible barrier against anything at all. "You could have told your side of the story and been given a fair shake."

"Meanwhile, my handler is promoted and given a cushy corner office in the city of her choice."

"She lost an asset. Why did she get promoted?"

Ramon shrugged one shoulder. "You tell me. I haven't been able to figure that out."

"Does it have anything to do with Navarro, or Kart and his operation?"

"The undercover operation wasn't anywhere near here. When I realized I'd been sold out as a federal agent, I put the call out for extraction. But no one came, so I had to run."

"Why didn't they kill you?" Surely if they figured out a man among them was a federal agent, they would have ended his life and buried him where no one would ever find him. Then again, that hadn't happened to Jax as soon as the men here had put together precisely who he was.

Kenna had no idea why they'd taken both of them, instead of just her.

Or if they'd known all along who Jax was.

In the moment she had simply been grateful that she wasn't alone. Kind of like now, where she was given a somewhat friendly face. Then again, being captive with another man was in a way that torture of its own. *The place of your nightmares.* That was what Ramon had said.

She frowned. "What did they do?"

Ramon studied the file in front of him. "You don't want to know. But when they were done, they traded me to another cartel. Then another. I was lost in the shuffle, then managed to persuade Navarro that it was in his best interest for me to work *for* him rather than be captive. I earned my place here in a way the FBI never allowed me to do. Because they never completely trusted that I wouldn't turn on them. When my handler wrote the report that I had gone off the reservation and become a turncoat, do you really think anyone was surprised? More like it was a self-fulfilling prophecy."

"I was surprised to hear it." But he was right, because part of her had also been unsurprised to learn that he'd turned. "I do understand. And I would help you get your standing back if that's what you want to do."

He shook his head. "You think I care? The FBI never did me any favors. Why tell them there's poisoned fruit on the tree? They'll never believe it anyway."

"I would." Kenna could use that to convince others. "We could get what we needed to prove it to everyone else."

"I think you're saying whatever you need to say just so you can try and get out of here." Ramon glanced over at her. "And then the minute you get free, you'll make a run for it and leave me holding the bag."

"I don't do that," she said. "I don't hang people out to dry."

"Then I know you'll never tell Navarro where to find Camila." Ramon tossed the file aside and picked up the next one. "You only save people and try to be a champion for justice, but there's none to be found down here. There's nothing but the dust and ashes of what you thought your life would be. And there's nothing you can do about it. So as soon as you realize that, the sooner we can try to figure out how to make it through the rest of the day."

"So that's it? You aren't even going to try?" She wanted to

shake him. But how would that possibly persuade him to help her? It would all be based on faith, and she didn't think he had it in him to trust anyone, least of all someone who hadn't stuck their neck out to help him.

Back in that interview room during the exercise they'd been teamed up on at Quantico, she might have diverted the course of things away from him. But it wouldn't hold weight with Ramon now. She had nothing to offer him that he couldn't get himself.

"I haven't lived this long by being dumb," he said. "I can keep myself alive."

"Until you can't."

"At which point I'll be too dead to care."

Kenna wasn't worried about the part where her life would be taken from her. She was more worried about what might happen before that.

And how much pain she would have to suffer.

Elliott Preston wanted revenge for the death of his brother. Wondering how he would extract that from her was stealing the last threads of sanity she had left.

Kenna grabbed the edge of the file and tried to tear it. She didn't have enough strength to rip the card. She pulled out the first piece paper and shredded it into pieces, flinging them all over the place. Tearing apart page after page until there was nothing left of the file. She scrunched it between her hands and crumpled it, tossing it aside.

"You feel better now?"

"No, I don't!" she screamed. After that she only had the strength to slump back against the wall. Her eyes fluttered closed, and all the energy in her seemed to dissipate into the floor beneath her. "I need to get out of here."

It wasn't the first time she'd contemplated ending her life the way Bradley had. Making the choice to leave this world behind and face whatever was next because she couldn't stand the idea of even one more second of the torture that her life had become.

He had lost hope and used what was around him to end his life. In the process he had given Kenna a way to escape.

Right now she had nothing.

Heavy footsteps in the hallway drew her eyes open. The light shifted beneath the door. She heard the lock rattle, then the door swung open and Benjamin strode in.

He dragged her up by her hair. "You thought you could pit us against each other, and I wouldn't hit back at you? Well, guess what. Turns out *you're* the one who has been killing people. Time to take a pound of flesh out of your hide."

Kenna managed to get her feet under her.

A weapon. She needed a weapon.

Ramon said something, the sound like yelling but she couldn't make out even one syllable over the pounding in her ears. She gasped for air. The pain in her scalp felt like he was ripping her hair from the root.

Ramon slammed into the two of them, knocking Kenna's head against the wall.

She blinked and tried to get her equilibrium back. A weapon. A phone. Surely Benjamin had one of those on him, and she might be able to get it before someone came in here. She tried to speak, but no words would form on her lips.

The door stood open beyond Benjamin and Ramon.

If anyone was coming here, maybe she could get out before they showed up.

Kenna pushed off the wall, past the tangle of the two men fighting. She stumbled toward the door and slammed against the frame.

One of them grunted behind her.

Ramon knew where she stood, and she could say the same

about him. He would do what he could. Meanwhile, there was nothing else she could do but make a break for it. This could be the answer she had been asking for since she got here.

Her way out.

Kenna looked out into the hallway but couldn't see anyone. There were stairs at both ends, and it was a gamble choosing between them when she had no idea who might be coming down.

She raced for the door to her right. Her legs dragged, her feet nearly tripping her with each sluggish movement. Did she even have the energy to get to a vehicle and try to blow through the gate out of here? Maybe she should try for a phone.

A gunshot exploded behind her.

Ramon's cry rang out over the eruption of ringing in her ears.

Tears rolled down Kenna's cheeks. She couldn't turn back, no matter what. She had to get out of here. Once she did that, she could put things right for both of them.

She saw no one all the way to Kart's office and couldn't resist the temptation to check inside. It was far less likely that he would still be in here than that she would actually manage to get all the way outside the compound without being discovered.

His phone lay on the desk.

Kenna dialed the number while she slumped onto the surface of the desk, hopefully out of sight for long enough to...

"Hello? Kenna, is that you?"

Her head pounded. Tears rolled down her face. "Maizie, I need help."

Chapter Fourteen

Kenna fell awkwardly and let out a yelp. Her arm gave out and she landed on her side, her butt on the floor. Then her head.

"Kenna?" Maizie sounded far away. "Kenna, are you there?"

She grasped the phone and held it to her ear, her temple against flooring that didn't smell good. She tried not to sniff. "I'm here."

"We're in town. I'm at the hotel if anything happens and you end up on your own. I'm in Cielo Ardiente at the little motel on the north side of town." Maizie rattled off a couple of cross streets, and some landmarks.

"I can't get out, Maze."

The teen whimpered. "We know. That's why Stairns is getting you out. He's coming tonight, so just hang on."

Kenna wanted to hang up right then so Maizie wouldn't have to hear the pain in her tone. So the girl could get some relief. God knew Kenna needed some as well. This situation seemed determined to be never ending, despite anyone's attempts to resolve it.

She wanted to argue that it wouldn't work. That Stairns would need an army if he wanted to get her out. Or did he think that coming in as one guy, under cover of night, meant he'd be able to sneak in and out easier?

The words wouldn't form.

And even if they did, she wasn't about to put that worry on a seventeen-year-old with her own trauma, which had lasted far longer than Kenna's few days. And been a whole lot more torturous, both physically and mentally. She didn't know how Maizie managed to stay standing after living that life. Or how she was even sane.

Kenna had lost Jax to rescue, and she was just about feral over the whole thing.

"You just have to hang on, Kenna. It won't be long." Maizie sniffed.

"I'm sorry."

"For what?" Maizie paused. "You didn't do any of this. We know about the sheriff coming from Colorado, and who those guys are. Are you sure you're okay? Have they..."

"No one touched me." Except grabbing her, shoving her around. And that punch. Maizie didn't need that information when Kenna knew what she was really asking.

Maizie whimpered.

The door slammed open.

Kenna thumbed down the volume and held the phone tight, keeping completely still. *Just leave.* Whoever it was could think there was no one in here. And maybe they would shut the door, never discovering her presence in here.

God, You could do that.

She'd heard sermons of Bible stories where God hid people out of sight, so they weren't discovered by their enemies.

The door didn't close again. "I always tuck my chair in."

Kart's boots hit the floor as he strode over. At least it wasn't Benjamin. She hoped he was dead, rather than Ramon.

Kenna hung up the phone and tucked it in her pocket. "You think I'm hiding down here?" She still didn't move. "I was running, and I fell."

Kart came into view over the desk. He lifted his gun and pointed it at her. "Get up."

She tried to sit up. "You don't need to haul me to my feet. But you might need to give me a second, okay?"

He held the gun on her.

Kenna managed to rock enough motion so she could get her legs to straighten. The strength she'd purposely built that kept her upright through so much made it so she could find her feet now.

When she was standing, she stared him down. Shrugged. "The door was open, and I ran."

He wasn't going to blame her for that was he? Surely he couldn't fault her if he thought it was only instinct that drove her here.

"Benjamin was going to kill me. Ramon stopped him." So really she'd done Kart a favor by surviving. Elliot would be mad otherwise.

"And now Benjamin is dead," Kart said. "And Ramon has a hole in his shoulder to show for it."

She tried not to let her feelings show on her face.

"Is that really what happened, Kenna?"

"Benjamin unlocked the door. He accused me of being the reason you guys are all pointing fingers at each other over the Lola thing. But all I did was point out the evidence, which is exactly what you asked me to do." All of which was the truth.

She didn't need to lie when it might jeopardize whatever rescue could be in the works.

Kart studied her. "So it's every man for himself, now?"

She didn't think he'd work any other way. Wasn't that what all these guys did?

Kenna said, "Anthony didn't feel the love of the team when you left him to have his hands cut off and delivered back to you." The guy was no doubt dead now, and if she ever had to see another pair of severed hands in her lifetime it would be entirely too soon. Once was too many. "Is Ramon okay?"

Kart stared at her.

"You said he got shot."

"And you ran away and came here. To find a phone?" He looked around. "Guess you're out of luck since it's not where I left it." He motioned with his gun at the door. "Let's go."

She went first to the door. "Benjamin would've killed me. Or damaged the merchandise."

"Go to the main hall."

She'd only gone there a couple of times when they'd deigned to give her half a sandwich. "That way?" She pointed right.

"Left."

"Oh, okay." She headed left and stepped from the dim hallway to the expansive hall. Probably an old meeting place. She didn't want to think about the group who built this compound or why they wanted basement holding rooms. Holding cells.

Probably a group like the one she'd met in northern Washington. It was only a short time ago but felt like much longer. She felt that way about her time with Bradley, making years feel like decades.

Even more recently, that time with Jax unconscious seemed like weeks ago. Or when she'd found him in the other building hanging from that chain. Being alone had a way of warping everything. Or maybe not alone. But on her own.

Facing down the darkness by herself.

Not her favorite thing to do, but it happened more often than not in her line of work. It was the road she had chosen, or the inevitable end of the path she was on.

If she wanted to avoid the terrors most people only sought out in their entertainment, she would've found a different job. Like at a bowling alley, or a movie theater.

Benjamin was stretched out on a long table. He stared at the ceiling, no light in his eyes. Blood covered his chest. He was gone.

Ramon lay on top of a table, writhing while two men worked on him.

"What are you doing?" She shoved one man away.

The other had pliers in Ramon's shoulder.

She yelled, "Stop!"

He didn't. "Gotta get the bullet out."

"You're hurting him more!"

The men all ignored her.

She looked at each one in turn. No care registered on any of their faces. Not even grief for their dead friend. "What do you think Navarro will do when he finds out you let one of his men get shot?"

Kart stared at her with that same impassive lethality. Like nothing fazed him—except the threat of failing to do what Elliot wanted. "I guess we should let Navarro's man die, then? Rather than attempt to save his life."

Before she could argue with that, the man with the pliers said, "Got it." Metal clanged against metal, then he peeled open a packet of gauze.

Kenna snatched it from him. "I'll do it." She pressed it on the wound.

Ramon jerked. His eyes fluttered open.

"Just me." She turned to Kart. "Did you call the doctor?"

"Why?" The other man cleaned off his hands with a wet wipe. "I fixed him up."

She looked over her shoulder at Kart.

"So it's true, then." Kart lifted his chin. "He is a fed."

"No, he isn't, and neither am I." She kept applying pressure on the bandage, using what strength she had—which amounted to a lot of elbows and leaning.

"But he was, right? Like you."

Kenna didn't have time to get into this. "Someone needs to stitch him up, and I don't know how to do it. So call the doctor."

Kart said, "Everyone out."

"They killed Benjamin." The man who'd removed the bullet finished wiping his hands and tossed the bloody wipe at her.

She wrinkled her nose and let it fall.

He said, "I wanna watch you kill them."

"Get out!" Kenna shouted. She needed them *all* out. All she wanted right now was that solitary despair. She could recall the conversation with Maizie, take some time to run it all down in her mind again. They were on their way.

Stairns was coming.

She would be broken out of here—tonight. Rescued.

All she had to do was hang on a little longer, and someone would get her. She had held out for long enough, not gone too insane, and survived to see this day.

Ramon shifted under the press of her hands. His blood had already soaked through the bandage. They'd pulled out the bullet but left the wound open.

She looked around. "I need a clean piece of gauze. Or a towel."

Kart moved to the far side of the table.

Her knees pressed painfully against the bench seat, but she ignored it. If she let go of the pressure she had on Ramon's wound, he could bleed out. "Give me something I can use." She motioned with her head.

"You're different." Kart stared at her. "Something happened."

"Yeah, Benjamin tried to *kill me*...and he shot my friend. That isn't enough?" Her breaths came fast. She had to keep it together.

"Maybe." The skin around Kart's eyes flexed. "Maybe not. I haven't seen that fire in you in a few days."

She needed a good explanation, or he'd realize she'd made a call. She had hope again. "I hate everything about this, and everything hurts."

"So basically you're just an adult."

Except that not all adults had suffered two severed tendons. "Well, it *sucks*."

His chest shook with what might've been a laugh. He swiped a bandage from the surprisingly well-stocked medical bag and handed it over.

"You've had this bag the whole time, and you didn't let me help Jax once?" She exchanged the bandage for the towel. "What a jerk."

"Yeah, something changed."

She could feel him studying her and refused to let anything out.

"You think you figured out a way out." He paused. "Or you..." He strode around and dragged her back, shoving her toward the neighboring table. He shoved her hands on the table and kicked her feet apart like he'd been a cop for years.

Kenna yelped. "What are you—"

He patted her down, not sparing one single inch of her.

Unsurprisingly, he found the phone. "Shame. I wanted to explore longer than that." He patted her butt. "Maybe later."

Maybe later she would elbow him in the face and break his nose.

She knew which way she wanted it to go, and it wouldn't involve more groping. Kenna spun back to Ramon and pressed down on the towel. "Call the doctor."

He shifted behind her, and she tensed. "I'd rather dial this number in the recently called list... Yeah, hello there, girlie. Who are you?"

Kenna twisted around, wrenching the muscles in her forearms. She had to keep pressure on the gunshot wound but also confront him. "Don't talk to him, Maizie! Don't say anything!" She yelled it as loud as she could.

Kart's eyes narrowed. "Maizie, huh? You sound a little young to mount a rescue operation. So who are you? Kenna's...sister? Daughter?"

"My family is none of your business!"

His teeth flashed. "That's what I thought." He held the phone to his ear but stepped closer to her. "But guess what? You should've called for help instead of checking in with family, Kenna. You could've gotten out of here, but instead you'll die in this desert when Elliot comes for you."

She heard Maizie say something through the phone but couldn't make out the words.

Kenna said, "Hang up. Leave her out of this."

Kart chuckled. "Is that right, kid? 'Cause I don't think so." He paused. "I guess we'll see about—" He stiffened.

What was Maizie...

"You drain my bank accounts and you're dead, girl. And I'll kill Kenna. I don't do threats, so you can trust me, that's the stone-cold truth." He whirled around and jogged to the door.

"If I get to my computer and you've—" He disappeared through the door.

Kenna glanced around. Moaned. "Maizie."

There was no one else in here with her, just Benjamin—who was dead—and Ramon. Her former colleague had lost enough blood that his face had paled, his skin nearly translucent.

"Hang on, Ramon. I'm going to get you out of here."

An explosion rocked the building.

Kenna sucked in a gasp and had to cough it out. Ramon was out, completely unconscious. She didn't want to let off pressure on his wound, but she was the only one in here with him and Benjamin—who she really hoped was actually dead and not just out of it.

"Come on." Whoever was here...

Kenna shuddered.

Focus.

She patted Ramon's pockets but found nothing. Which stood to reason if they'd taken his things when he came into the compound.

Another explosion rattled the building, shaking the windows. Dust rained down from the ceiling.

Kenna lifted Ramon's hand and laid it on the towel. As soon as she let go, it would likely slip off, but she needed a phone or a weapon. Preferably both. She raced over to Benjamin's body and checked his pulse first. The injury on the side of his forehead was nasty. She found no sign of life. *I guess you finished him for good, Ramon.*

Gunfire rattled outside, a steady hammering of shots in quick succession. It sounded like war outside the window, but she couldn't worry about what was happening. Or whether it really was Stairns. Could he really be here? If he was, then he needed to help her get Ramon out.

She wasn't about to leave one of Navarro's men in this compound.

Kenna found a knife on Benjamin's belt. She folded the blade out of the handle. The door flung open, and she pointed it at the men who poured in. As if a knife was a match to a gun.

"Come." The first man waved her with him. "*Vamanos.*"

Another one of them lifted Ramon over his shoulder.

"Careful." Kenna followed them to the door. "His shoulder."

The man who'd ordered her to come with them looked at her with a note of confusion in his expression. He didn't speak enough English? She pointed at his gun. Then at her shoulder. Then said, "Ramon."

He nodded. "Come."

She went ahead of him, part of a huddle. They backtracked through a couple of hallways before emerging outside. The men were already loading Ramon into a van.

Kenna climbed in the back.

She was either being kidnapped by Navarro, or this really was the rescue operation she wanted to believe it might be.

The van door slid closed and set off. Everyone rocked with the sudden movement. Each building in the compound was decimated. They'd laid waste to the whole place.

She gasped. "Is everyone dead?"

No one answered.

A second later, the building she'd been in exploded.

"There were people in the basement," she pointed out. Including some who were innocent of the crimes Kart and his friends committed. "You just killed them all."

The van raced through the broken front gate, and she spotted a line of people walking down the dirt road. They turned one by one as the van passed them, each one haggard and covered in soot. Navarro's men had set them free, then blown the building.

Kenna had to know if they had killed everyone. "What about Kart?"

Someone said, "Está muerto."

She hoped he really was dead.

They drove in silence for twenty minutes before the van pulled over. She spotted a rusty pickup ahead, and one man in the driver's seat. The door slid open, and one of Navarro's men waved her out. "Come."

She climbed out past the man who liked that single-word order. "Gracias."

He grinned, then the van was gone in a cloud of dust.

Stairns climbed out of the pickup truck. He looked her up and down and winced. "Hospital."

For once, Kenna didn't argue.

Chapter Fifteen

By the time she spotted it, Kenna wasn't so sure. She gripped the door handle. "You know, I might not need to see a doctor."

Stairns pulled into the hospital parking lot, the building a squat two stories that couldn't be much larger than a medical center in the US. Probably because they were so far from a big city. "I have a place inside where you can wash up and change your clothes."

"Okay. But why can't I do that at the hotel?" They were still in Cielo Ardiente. Part of her had expected him to drive to an airport, or straight to the border. But Maizie had said she was in town at a hotel.

So why the hospital?

Stairns shoved the rattling pickup into park and cut the engine. "Because Jax is here, and I figured you'd want to see him."

She gaped. "Still? Why haven't they taken him back to the US already?"

"They decided it was too risky to move him with his

wounds. They want to wait until he's more stable before they transport him back home. Something about a head injury."

Her stomach lurched. "So the hospital is crawling with FBI agents?"

"I don't want Maizie seeing you until you wash up and change."

Kenna wanted to fire back something sarcastic about how terrible he apparently thought she looked, but just couldn't bring herself to form the words. It would be a while before she'd be able to quip back about anything.

"All I need is sleep." But if Jax really was here, then she definitely wanted to see him. Could she leave the country knowing Jax was still here, with his health undetermined? She ran her fingers along the handle.

"Let's just find out how he is." Stairns shoved his door open. "And if you happen to run into a doctor, then no harm, no foul."

She climbed out, saying nothing. If he wanted to push it, that was up to him. The fact was that her skin itched in a way that made her want to stop and scratch everything. "I need a shower." But she knew it wasn't that. "And some chips and queso."

They walked together to the front doors.

Stairns glanced over. "You're going to want to go easy on the spicy foods. Maybe stick to something plain at first and see how your body does with it. You look like you've lost more than a few pounds."

She saw the question in his expression but didn't offer him an answer. She wanted to not say anything at all and keep her own confidence, at least for a little while.

She'd have to talk through everything that happened. Run it all down for them, so they knew what she'd been through.

Maybe Elizabeth had an appointment for her—since Stairns' wife seemed to be doing a great job with Maizie.

Stairns spoke in Spanish to the older woman behind the desk who nodded and waved toward the hall. Kenna frowned. He must have seen her expression, because he said, "I speak enough Spanish to get by. Don't lose your mind."

"How very...progressive."

He snorted. "That's about as progressive as an old codger like me gets. But truth is, it was for a vacation Elizabeth and I took right after I retired. While you were in the hospital, back when you got shot. And it came in handy coming down here to get you, so I guess it was worth it in more than one way."

She followed his lead to a kitchen type break room, and through that to a bathroom.

Stairns said, "I'll wait out here. Obviously. But I just want you to know I'm not going anywhere."

Kenna turned back, one hand on the door handle while she leaned her shoulder against the frame on the other side.

A litany of questions ran through her mind. How he had permission for them to be here. How he got her out. What deal he'd made with Navarro.

All that came out was, "Stairns."

He waited.

She didn't say anything, wondering if she even could. No words seemed to want to come from her mouth even if she'd known what to say right now.

"You don't ever have to thank me for anything. I've already told you that."

Burning-hot tears gathered in Kenna's eyes. She clicked the door shut before they could fall and splashed cold water on her face, gasping against the need to cry. A lump built in her throat. She swallowed it down, splashing more water.

Drinking some and ignoring the fact she probably was crying whether she wanted to admit it or not.

It wasn't like anyone would blame her. Even if she had been raised to believe tears were a sign of weakness, they were still a perfectly understandable reaction. Instead of disparaging them, she chose to acknowledge how she felt. That way she could decide whether the feelings she had were true or not.

There was nothing to be afraid of in this bathroom. There was nothing to be afraid of in the break room—it was just Stairns, and Kenna was grateful.

She was safe, and this was only a byproduct of the fear. The relief of being rescued. A way for her nervous system to bleed off the adrenaline of stress and process the fact she was free now.

Jax was alive.

Both of them were safe.

Kenna stripped, dug in the backpack Stairns had given her, and found a washcloth, soap, and a full set of clean clothes. Maizie must have packed it for her. She tied up her hair and cleaned off, scrubbing her skin for probably longer than she needed to. And making a puddle of soapy water on the floor.

When she was changed, Kenna stuffed everything back in the backpack and took it with her. "We should probably burn all this."

He grasped it and slung the strap over his shoulder. "Elevator."

Kenna found it, knowing he was giving her the chance to lead the way so she could feel as if she had some semblance of control over anything in this situation. So she could experience the freedom she had now, even if only in a small way.

Kenna hit the button for the second floor.

When the doors opened upstairs, she glanced both ways and spotted a couple of FBI agents outside one of the rooms. Jax had a protective detail keeping guard over him, and she wanted to get their badge numbers. Have Maizie run their names. She'd know if they were the kind of agents who cared enough to do a good job of protecting him.

Both acknowledged Kenna and Stairns on approach. They shifted toward her, and she said, "So they know who I am?"

But they still left her with Kart and rescued their agent.

"Gentlemen." Stairns tugged something from his pocket, which he handed over.

She glanced at him. "What's that?"

"Our IDs."

"You have two minutes." The agent handed both cards back to Stairns. "No more."

"I appreciate it," Stairns said.

The agent made a face. "Only because I owe you." He shot Kenna a look. "Make it fast."

She wanted to say something to either of their agents about the fact they had for all intents and purposes left her to rot in that compound—even if she hadn't been there when they showed up to get their agent back.

What would the public think when Kenna made everyone who cared to listen aware that the FBI had abandoned a US citizen in a foreign country, knowing full well they were in danger? That they saved only their man and not her?

But she didn't have time to get into that right now.

Kenna shoved the door open and closed it quickly behind her. She didn't want anyone to see her reaction.

Jax lay in the hospital bed, hooked up to all kinds of wires. He had a tube in his throat. She wasn't sure if the machine was breathing for him or just helping him get enough oxygen.

Bags of medicine hung from a stand. Monitors recorded every beat of his heart.

She swiped at the moisture on her cheeks and moved to stand beside the bed.

Kenna took his hand, entwining her fingers with his. She sniffed back the rush of tears and leaned down to touch her forehead to his. "I'm sorry."

He wouldn't have been hurt if it wasn't for her. He would never have been dragged into this. And while she knew without a doubt that he would never be mad at her for the fact he was captured and tortured, that didn't stop her from wishing he never had been.

She wanted to be altruistic and walk out of his life. Leave. Because he was clearly better off without her.

It was the right thing to do.

Jax should go back to the US and back to his life. He should heal and forget all about her.

She was going to let him be rather than dig her heels in and stay in this room. But she also wasn't about to never see him again. Kenna only had a few people in her life. She'd fought through the fear of others being hurt because of her—or her being the one who hurt them. She'd come to the point where she could accept her need for a small group of people who cared about her.

Right now she could honestly say she was too selfish to let him go.

If he didn't make it, then she would have her answer. But if he did survive and he got through this—if he healed and returned to his life—would that be the answer that the future was about them being together?

Kenna thumbed away the tears that fell on his cheek.

She laid a kiss on his forehead, almost glad he was unconscious so he didn't have to see her carrying on like this.

There was only one thing she wanted to say to him right now.

Kenna held both sides of his head gently in her hands and touched her forehead to his. "Don't leave me."

If he died...

The door opened. "Time's up."

She straightened and rounded the bed, her chin up as she passed the agent. Whatever he thought about her she didn't care. "Take care of him."

"Why does that sound like a threat?"

She didn't turn back, just strode to the hall and Stairns. "Because it is."

He waited until they were back in the pickup before he said, "You good?"

"I will be when he's up and moving around." And far from her.

"Fair enough." He drove across town, past the coffee shop where she and Kart had sat down with Navarro.

Kenna wanted to ask a million questions about how Stairns had managed to convince the cartel leader to attack the compound. If it was only about getting Ramon back, or whether there was more to it.

She didn't want to believe he might have given up Camila's location. Stairns might not even have the young woman on his radar as being part of this, and just because he betrayed her once didn't mean he would do it again. Not even to save her life. And absolutely not if he knew Camila was pregnant.

Stairns had daughters and grandchildren. There was no way he would put an innocent life in danger—unborn or otherwise.

He pulled up behind the hotel and used a key card to open a back door. The place was older but had some ornate aspects to the décor. "Two sixteen." He glanced at her.

"Should I add a night or two to our reservation, or are we checking out right now?"

Kenna stopped outside the elevator and turned to him. "I don't want to be anywhere near here. But I also don't want to leave until I know Jax is going as well."

Stairns nodded. "I'll keep it open-ended." He handed her a key card. "I'm next door."

Her hand shook, but she managed to jab the button for the second floor. The elevator rattled as it rose, and she located their room at the end of the hall close to the exit door. So they would have multiple exits if necessary?

She inserted the key card, but the door opened before she could pull it out.

A teenage bundle of blond hair slammed into her. Kenna rocked back two steps and held on tight while Maizie gasped and squeezed her middle. Then she leaned back. "You're not hurt, are you? Am I hurting you?"

Kenna shook her head. "Let's go inside so you're not out here any longer than you need to be." She grabbed the key card and let the door shut behind her. Maizie needed to stay as far below the radar as possible.

"I can't believe you're really here." The seventeen-year-old stared at her with those huge blue eyes that had seen way too much, and suffered far more than anyone ever should. "Are you sure you're okay?"

"I need a cheeseburger." Kenna strode to the bed with the unrumpled covers and slumped down on top, dragging over a pillow. Then she realized she was still wearing her boots. She groaned and unlaced them enough so she could kick them away. She peeled off the socks and stretched out flat on the bed. "And fries." She let out a long breath. "And a strawberry milkshake."

But for now she would settle for the longest nap ever.

"I'm sure we can find you some real food."

Kenna only had the strength to smile.

Maizie shuffled, moving around. "Yeah, she is." Kenna heard her come over. "Ryson wants to talk to you."

Kenna cracked open one eye.

Maizie nearly smiled, but not quite. Had the girl ever done it?

Kenna managed to wave her hand. She put the phone to her ear. "Yeah?"

"It's good to hear your voice." His low rumble settled in her chest. "I was about to get on a plane."

Ryson. "I'm good." She swallowed against the lump in her throat. "Stairns and Maizie made sure of it."

The teen settled beside her on the bed. Kenna handed her back the phone, then her awareness floated as she listened to the end of the conversation.

And everything drifted away.

Chapter Sixteen

"How are you feeling?" Stairns touched her forehead with the back of his hand.

Kenna pushed it away. "Why are you being weird?"

Maizie sat at the small round table, typing on her laptop. She glanced over to watch as Stairns stood up. For a second it looked like he might sit on the edge of the second bed, but he didn't. A good thing, considering it was Maizie's and he made a point to not invade her personal space. It was enough that he was in the room—and had been since right after Kenna woke up twenty minutes ago.

Neither of them had offered her a cup of coffee.

"Fine." He ran a hand through his short gray hair and leaned against the wall, often doing so because reclining poses made him look less imposing. Though for a stocky former Marine, imposing pretty much encompassed who he was. "I tracked down the doctor in town, and he told me what Kart gave you. It's not available in the US. It's a synthetic pain med, and it's highly addictive."

Stairns dug into his pocket. "He also gave me this. Regular narcotics." He tossed the tiny pill bottle next to her.

Kenna let it land on the blanket without trying to catch it. "Great." She made a face, rolling her eyes for Maizie's sake so the girl wouldn't worry so much. "What's the plan for today?"

Since she had been abducted from Washington, DC, Kenna hadn't been keeping track of what day of the week it was.

Maizie lifted her hands from the keyboard and twisted around in the chair. "You slept for eighteen hours."

"Naps are my superpower," Kenna said.

Maizie stared at her. "I thought that was cheese."

She shook her head. "Cheese is a super*food*. Because we all know corporations are lying to us about what's healthy and what isn't just so they can make money."

Maizie, almost smiling, came and sat on the bed beside Kenna, shoulder to shoulder with her. The trust it took for the teen to seek out physical contact with anyone made Kenna remain very still, not wanting to disturb it.

Stairns looked at his watch like he didn't notice. "I can call the doctor to schedule a visit. Or we can go back to the hospital."

Kenna saw something in his expression. "But..."

"You need to tell me how you could tell there was something else." Maizie glanced at her. "Because I didn't know there was more just then."

"The two of you are ganging up on me like my girls do." He eyed them with something like affectionate pride in his gaze.

Maizie said, "Did you mean it when you told that guy we're family?"

That made her move, shifting so she could look Maizie in the eye. Kenna wanted to say a number of things, but for a girl raised in anything but safety, sometimes Maizie needed Kenna to say things plainly. "You're stuck with me now." She let that sink in for a second, then turned back to Stairns. "What else is going on?"

"Navarro wants to see you. He specifically mentioned dinner." Stairns glanced at Maizie.

"I said if you were going, then we're all going."

Stairns shook his head. "To which I replied that if anyone is meeting him, then it should happen here in town. Not out at his ranch in the middle of nowhere."

"I do want to see if Ramon is okay," Kenna said. "Did you two come down here together to find me?"

Maizie nodded.

"I did wonder if you had put a tracker in my shoe, or something." Kenna gave the girl a soft smile.

Maizie's jaw flexed. "I've got something I need to give you. So you never get lost again."

Kenna wouldn't argue, even if it invaded her privacy.

Stairns said, "Someone we know and appreciate insisted that she needed to be in the area so she could adequately locate you personally."

Kenna held out her fist. Maizie tapped it with her own.

Maizie had faced her fears and come down here because it meant helping Kenna get rescued.

"I'm glad you're both here," Kenna said. "It's good to see you."

Stairns just nodded and said nothing.

Kenna glanced around at the room she hadn't looked at much, mostly so she could take a minute and blink away the hot tears that gathered. Even when she'd been alone, she hadn't really been completely abandoned. But still, having them with her now made all the world of difference. Especially with Jax in the hospital.

"Who is this Ramon guy?" Maizie went to her laptop. She

cleared her throat as she moved away from them both, her back to them. "I can look him up."

"Ramon Santiago was at Quantico the same time as me."

"Santiago?" Stairns frowned. "Why do I know that name?"

"Give Maizie about thirty seconds and she can probably tell you, but he was undercover. A few years after we graduated the report came through that he had missed more than one check-in, and the last contact the handler had with him he'd shown signs of erratic behavior. In the end he was written off as working for the cartel he'd been undercover with."

"So he's a turncoat?" Stairns' expression gave away exactly what he felt about that.

Kenna would have agreed with him except for what Ramon had told her. "He said he was the one who called the FBI to come and rescue Jax."

Stairns shook his head. "That call was anonymous as far as I know, but if this Santiago guy did help them out, they might want a follow-up conversation."

Kenna stretched her arms above her head and rolled her shoulders.

Sleep was good, but she still had the urge to get moving so things loosened up a little. Which only made her think about Jax and all the exercise he'd made her do every day after she was shot.

"Ramon was hung out to dry." Kenna paused. "He said he didn't leave the FBI of his own volition." She wasn't sure what she even believed, or if her memories of being held by Kart and his men would skew what she remembered about all of this. "I don't know."

Stairns gave a nod. "I'll make some calls and find out." Before she could speak, he lifted both hands. "I won't say that

I found their AWOL agent. I'll just look into what he was investigating and who the handler was."

Kenna nodded, more than relieved that he understood her concerns without her having to be firing on all cylinders.

"You want to go back to the hospital or see the local doctor?"

"I have no idea if I trust either, but whoever is working on Jax had better be legit."

"Don't worry about that," Stairns said. "The FBI flew in a Red Cross doctor from the other side of Mexico specifically to take care of him."

"Good." Kenna blew out a breath. "What do you know about the man that captured us, Kart? Or his boys? There's only one left as far as I know."

Maizie flinched. "I have him listed as Ian Kartom."

Was he dead, or had he survived somehow? "That's him. He said Sheriff Elliot Preston is his cousin."

"I found that connection as well," Maizie said.

Stairns nodded. "And ever since, she's been throwing a wrench in every travel plan he's made to get down here. Delaying him at every turn."

Kenna laughed.

Maizie frowned at her.

"What, Maze? It's brilliant."

Maizie swallowed. "Thanks."

"What is...?" Kenna put together the girl's hesitation. "Elliot Preston?"

"I recognized him."

"One of..." They didn't need to say it out loud if they didn't have to. It made Kenna sick enough as it was knowing what had happened to Maizie since she was tiny. She'd been held captive of a dangerous man in Las Vegas who believed he lived above the law. Until Kenna killed him.

Now he had no hold over Maizie because he was dead.

"I saw him around." Maizie's expression blanked, the tone of her voice hollow. "The sheriff."

Stairns said, "You should've told me, kiddo."

Kenna had heard him use the same tone of voice talking to his grandbaby. Or helping Ryson's toddler daughter get more fish crackers.

He folded his arms. "Well, I *was* thinking we need the evidence to prove he's the one behind Jax and Kenna being kidnapped. But now I'm thinking I won't waste everybody's time. I'll just put a bullet between his eyes."

"Find a grassy noll, I'll be your spotter." Kenna might sound like she was joking, but a huge part of her was deadly serious. Her brand of justice felt very much in line with that adage, *God's children are not for sale.*

"You're both talking about murder." Maizie sat completely still, not backing down. "Not self-defense, just straight murder. That makes you no better than any of them."

Stairns said, "'There is none good. No not one.' That's what the Bible says."

"So you want to be just as bad as them."

Kenna knew what the girl was saying, but she also knew what Ryson had told her. And what she'd heard on the radio listening to sermons. "Humans are inherently sinful. I realized that when all I wanted to do was get Jax and get out of that compound, no matter what happened to any of the other innocent people in there. In the moment I didn't care if they lived or died—or who might have cried over losing them. All I cared about was me."

Maizie stared at her.

"Just like we all have the capacity for good, we all have the capacity for great evil. No one is exempt. I don't care how good someone thinks they are, we all live just a series of choices away from total destruction."

Stairns nodded. "We like to think we're better than the bad guys. And there are so many things they do that make me sick to my stomach. But you're right that I shouldn't take their actions as the right path and use their tactics to eliminate the problem. That might even the score, but it doesn't make the world a better place."

"Sometimes all you're capable of is evening the score," Kenna said. "But I do want to make the world a better place. It's just hard to see that a righteous path could make a difference against all the evil in the world when you're in the middle of the evil. But you know that, Maze."

The teen nodded. "It doesn't scare me that you could take a life. Either of you." She glanced between them. "It actually makes me feel safer."

Good. "I don't like the person I am when all I'm after is vengeance. So let's get the evidence and prove to the world exactly who Elliot Preston is." Just so long as he didn't come anywhere near Kenna or Maizie, she absolutely wanted to take the guy down. "So what about those military guys that ran the compound?"

Maizie clicked the mouse on her laptop. "The one you called Kart was a squad leader in the army. He had more than one report made against him, complaints of all kinds. Harassment. Theft. None of it was ever proven, but people transferred out of his squad on a regular basis." Eight pictures appeared. "These are the guys who stuck for longer than a few months without filing a request to be transferred to a different team."

Kenna pushed off the bed and went over to the teen girl. She squeezed Maizie's shoulder, then crouched beside her and studied the faces on the screen. She pointed to the ones she recognized. "Ramon Santiago killed this guy, Benjamin. That's Anthony. Navarro cut off his hands and had me take them back to Kart. I don't see the fourth guy that was there at the compound." She straightened. "He left a few days ago with three young women, drug mules he was taking to Seattle. I want to say his name was...Walken? Something like that."

"Maybe they met him in the army, but he wasn't in their squad," Maizie said. "I'll run his name and see if it pops in association with the three of them."

"Thanks, Maze." Kenna turned to Stairns and mouthed, *I don't want her coming to dinner.*

He mouthed back, *Who is going to protect her?*

"I know you guys are talking about me," Maizie said. "I'm just being polite enough to not get mad about it."

Kenna strode across the room and filled a cup of water in the bathroom. She downed the whole thing, refilled it, then moved to stand with her shoulder against the open bathroom door.

"I don't want to stay here alone either. So I guess I'm coming with both of you to the Navarro ranch."

Kenna could understand that. "Did anyone at the compound find Kart's body? I want to know for sure that he's dead."

Stairns frowned. "I can contact the local police and see if they've been through the place since it was attacked."

She had met the local chief in Kart's office. "Don't trust anything the chief says any farther than I would be able to throw him." Which was basically not at all.

His brows rose. "Is that right?"

"Maybe he polices the community and keeps people safe. But he also takes money from the Navarro cartel and Kart's operation. So he's sketchy at best."

Stairns glanced at Maizie, who had the man's picture up on her computer.

The teen said, "I don't recognize him, if that's what you want to know."

"Fair enough."

Maizie turned back to her computer. "I'll get copies of the reports they log in their computer system and see if that gives us the information we need to know."

"Short of going back to the compound and checking it out for ourselves?" Stairns glanced at her. "Don't worry. I'll be doing that alone."

Kenna didn't realize she had reacted. She took a sip of the water and tried to steady her shaky hand.

"I went out there last night," Stairns said. "The whole place was crawling with Navarro's men, so I stayed out of the way."

If they'd found Kart alive, they would probably have killed him. Which meant he was dead—or he had escaped.

"Anything else I should know before we get ready to go to dinner at the Navarro ranch?" She still needed to take a real shower, plus drink about six cups of coffee and take one of the pills in the medicine bottle Stairns had given her.

Maizie glanced over her shoulder. "I hacked the medical office computer system because Valentina had so many appointments."

Kenna froze.

There was something wrong with Ryson's wife? "Is that why he didn't come down here himself?"

Maizie nodded. "But it's not what you think. It's twins."

Kenna gaped. "They're having another baby?"

Maizie grinned. "Maybe if it's two girls, he'll name them Kenna and Maizie, but I can't suggest that to Valentina yet because no one is supposed to know. She's not very far along,

like nine weeks maybe. I've been reading up on multiple pregnancy online. It's pretty gross."

The first time in a very long time Kenna found herself in a
conversation about pregnancy not overwhelmed with grief.

But laughing.

Chapter Seventeen

The front door to Navarro's house opened before they even walked up the front steps. Kenna lifted her chin to the man holding the door open, aware of Maizie right behind her. The teen had given her a cross necklace, the metal pendant chunky enough to hide a tracker.

They stepped inside, and she positioned herself to see whoever came toward them and keep Maizie in sight at the same time.

The teen had opted for jeans that completely disguised the shape of her legs, whether that was by design or because it was a fashion statement Kenna didn't know. But personally she wasn't going to give up skinny jeans. Ever.

Maizie also had a sweater on, despite the temperature, and her hood pulled up so only the wavy front strands of blond could be seen. For now all she wanted to do was hide in whatever way she could, which was fine by Kenna. They had good reason to believe she was safer if she did. Later she could choose what she wanted to do with her life.

Kenna was thinking of talking to her about online college. Not that the girl couldn't test out of basically anything, since she was so smart. But if she wanted to make a life for herself, she needed qualifications rather than a shadowy past, no medical history, and a whole lot of trauma.

Stairns stepped in last and took the lead when Navarro appeared.

The cartel leader strode down the hall toward them. "Drinks?"

Stairns lifted his chin. "If that's what you called us here for."

"Dinner is almost ready." He led the three of them to a terraced dining area.

Maizie hung back, leaning against the adobe exterior with one foot on the wall like she didn't have a care in the world. Unless, of course, a person already knew that she did everything out of an epic sense of self-preservation that bordered on justifiable defensiveness. If she was honest, Kenna had lived a lot of the last few years doing exactly the same thing.

Not drawing attention to herself.

Hanging back.

"Sit. Please." Navarro waved a hand at the table. Eight chairs—three on each side and one at either end.

Kenna pulled out the end of a three-side, farthest from Navarro as she could get. She glanced over at Maizie. "Sit down, kid."

The girl pushed off the wall and slumped into the chair, immediately pulling out her phone. She looked for all the world like a recalcitrant teenager—and Navarro wasn't impressed. He would dismiss her. *Good.*

Kenna lifted one foot, bent her knee, and set her shoe on the chair so her shin pressed against the table. That way she could recline like someone with no care over facing Navarro.

"No thank-you for me?" His brows rose, and he sat back

while an older woman in black pants and button-down shirt poured him a drink, then one for Stairns. "I did rescue you."

Kenna folded her arms. "I figure you'll get whatever you were promised." She just had no idea what it was.

Stairns sipped from his glass.

Kenna raised her hand at the offered whiskey and told the server lady, "Water. Please. For both of us." She motioned to Maizie and back.

The server returned with their drinks, then trays of appetizers.

Maizie only took one after Kenna had eaten. Yet another thing that Kenna wanted to note so she could address each one in turn. Figure out why the girl did what she did and if it was a habit or learned behavior that she needed to break if she wanted to be free. Maybe Maizie was simply checking to see if it was poisoned first—rather than respect for Kenna's position in her life, or in consideration of not appearing rude.

Stairns set his elbow on the table, his chair turned to face Navarro. "Several months ago, during the summer, Kenna here met Camila in Colorado."

Navarro's body language exuded tension, as though waiting for a bomb to drop.

Kenna wasn't going to toss it to him. Would Stairns really give her up?

"She was one of a group of migrant workers being held by Brian Preston, the brother of Sheriff Elliot Preston, who I happen to know is on his way here. He thinks Kart is holding Kenna for him." Stairns paused. "Elliot and Kart are cousins."

Navarro frowned.

Maizie didn't look up from her phone. *"Primos."*

"Ah. And this"— Navarro waved a manicured hand toward Kenna—"is supposed to be compensation for my retrieving your friend here? That my bride was in Colorado months ago?"

"Perhaps you could ask Preston what happened to her." Stairns sipped his drink.

Navarro wasn't going to let this go without them giving him more.

Kenna said, "I'll tell you what you want to know."

They all turned to her.

Maizie's hand hovered over a tiny taco. She pulled it back.

Kenna shrugged. "I can't help you find her, but I can tell you I set her free from that place. We had to go inside in the middle of the night—"

"We?"

"I got help from one of the other migrants. He wanted to make sure the rest of them got free, and that someone in authority found out what was happening to them." Hadn't done much good, though. "They killed Elliot's brother, and they all escaped. Sorry to say, I don't know where Camila is. Not since I saw her last."

In Vegas...when she and Jax had witnessed Luca and Camila getting married.

"You're a private investigator, aren't you?" Navarro wiped his hands on a cloth napkin. "I'll pay you to find her."

"I don't have time for any new cases right now."

Even if she did, she wasn't going to disturb a young woman's freedom for the sake of a cartel leader with an obsessive need to reclaim a person he believed to be his property.

No, this wasn't a case she would be taking.

Luca and Camila deserved to have a life with *their* baby.

"Perhaps I...misspoke." Navarro cleared his throat. "Out of an abundance of gratitude for what I did, rescuing you from those Americans, you will find her for me and return her to this ranch."

"So you can...what? Kill her for leaving you?" Kenna shook her head. "You don't think it was Kart that's to blame, since she ended up in his cousin's operation? Trafficked in the hope of a better life, then put to work against her will."

Maizie stiffened very slightly.

Kenna said, "She's free now," having decided honesty would serve her better right now than anything else. "Camila gets to decide her life, not you. She's free to make her own choices. And if that means coming back, then it's up to her."

She wondered if telling him about Luca, and how the kid seemed to care about her, would make a difference. Navarro might be willing to let her go if he understood she had made her choice. Then again, he was just as likely to hunt them both down and end their lives for choosing to be free.

No telling what the cartel leader would decide to do. This whole thing was a gamble, and Stairns might have chosen a path that destroyed a young couple—and the happy life Camila's baby might be able to have as a free person.

Nothing was worth taking that from an innocent baby.

Navarro said, "I'll be sure to have a word with Elliot Preston on his arrival."

If they destroyed each other, Kenna would have two less things to worry about. And she might also be giving Navarro's young nephew the chance for a new or better life.

The glass door opened, and Ramon stepped out with his arm in a sling. His face was slightly pale but looking a whole lot healthier than when she saw him last. "Kenna." He rounded the back of her chair slowly and sat opposite Maizie, a chair down from Stairns.

She said, "You look better."

"I'm alive." Ramon lifted a brow. "I can say that, at least."

Whatever deal he had going with Navarro, he'd been rescued along with her—and maybe that was part of why the cartel leader had done it. He'd hammered against Kart and his operation in multiple ways and come out the victor.

But what deal had the ex-fed made with Navarro that meant the cartel leader protected him, and invited Ramon to his table? She didn't want to know what Ramon had done to prove his loyalty.

Or what he still had to do.

"Benjamin won't be a problem anymore." Kenna glanced around. "What about the rest of them?"

"Anthony didn't make it here. As our *guest*." Navarro sipped his drink.

He'd either been killed or lost his life as a result of Navarro's treatment—both of which amounted to the same thing.

"No one found Kart after," Ramon said. "Not his body, and not him."

Kenna flinched. "He isn't dead?" Or here as a captive. "He's out there?"

Maizie stiffened. She paused from tapping her phone screen as though she was chatting to someone. Kenna figured she'd already gained access to whatever security system Navarro had set up in his home.

From there, Kenna hoped Maizie could connect to the rest of Navarro's operation and find out where he did his business. That way they could take down the entire thing from the inside. Send all the documentary evidence to the Mexican authorities—and the Drug Enforcement Agency. Whoever would listen.

Ramon's jaw flexed. "We will find him. Don't worry about that."

If his expression was to be believed, Ramon would personally ensure Kart's death. She had to respect a man determined to dish out payback for keeping him captive. What she didn't know was if this was Navarro's directive, or if Ramon had permission to take care of his own business here.

Kenna didn't want to stick around long enough to find out.

She would rather get out of Mexico back to the US, find somewhere to rest, and be safe for a while—maybe with Maizie. Take a vacation. So long as she wasn't going to be asked again to come back to DC and testify. As far as she was concerned, any meeting between her and the FBI would happen on an isolated tarmac in some out of the way state. They would have a single conversation before Kenna disappeared again.

If it wasn't for the sake of Jax still being here, she'd have split as soon as she woke up.

Kenna bounced her other knee, trying to beat back the restlessness.

Navarro said something to Stairns. They both got up, taking their drinks to walk away along the pool through the garden.

"Surprised to see you." Ramon shoved an appetizer in his mouth.

Kenna shrugged. "Figured we'd pay our respects, since Navarro is the one who cut me loose from the compound."

"I'm not that surprised he didn't only do it to rescue me."

Kenna set her foot down and leaned onto the table. "He did it for information about Camila."

Ramon didn't seem to be too surprised about that, either. They'd talked about it.

Kenna said, "If you want out, I can help you."

He stared at her and didn't once even glance at Maizie.

"I won't be here, but if Kart comes or the fourth guy shows back up and finds it all decimated"—the one who'd taken those mules to Seattle would return at some point—"you could be in for retaliation."

"You're not going to volunteer to stick around and protect me?" His lips twitched.

"Because you need it?" Kenna said.

That would mean either Navarro hung him out to dry, or Ramon didn't have the strength to protect himself against attack because of his injuries.

He sighed. "I'm good here. I'll be all right."

"You ever need anything…" She figured she didn't need to finish.

Ramon's phone chimed in his pocket. He started to dig it out.

"That was me." Maizie didn't look up from her phone. "Now you have Kenna's number."

"And yours?" Ramon's brows rose.

"Nope." Maizie's expression remained blank.

Kenna scratched at her jaw, covering her smile.

"She's with you?" Ramon glanced at Kenna.

Kenna shrugged one shoulder. "We're family."

Ramon would know what that meant—and the implication was far more than colleagues or hired help. He would never have the connection she had with Maizie with Navarro, and he knew it. But maybe he could make a choice like Camila and reach for something better.

Take a chance on hope.

Wasn't that what they were all doing? Chancing that the future might be better than the present. One step of faith at a time. Not because any of them deserved it, though if anyone was to then it would be Maizie.

Navarro and Stairns came back over.

"Mr. Navarro and I have settled our business." Stairns put his empty glass on the table.

"Now we eat." Navarro waved both hands, and servers exited four different doors, bringing over dishes and bowls.

Maizie stiffened until they retreated, and Kenna squeezed her arm. *You're all right.*

"It is time to celebrate the defeat of our enemies." Navarro spread his hands. "Dig in."

Kenna said, "Must've been quite the windfall, raiding the compound." She figured he'd made off with everything Kart had been holding. Drugs. Money. They'd set free the workers, but likely kept everything else.

Navarro reached for the meat. "Consolidation of assets is good for business."

Kenna stuck to rice and beans, not sure how her stomach would appreciate a rich flavorful meal so soon after days of next to nothing.

Ramon's phone buzzed again.

Maizie said, "Not me."

He tugged it out looked at the screen, then glanced at Navarro. "He landed."

Navarro nodded.

Ramon turned to Kenna. "We have a man looking for Kart's associate in the US. Tying up all the loose ends. So you don't have to worry about retaliation."

Because their plan was to retaliate first before that could happen?

"And if the Americans were the cause of our business disruptions, as you say," Navarro said, "then surely it will stop after that."

Kenna nodded. "I hope I was right."

That didn't mean she wouldn't ensure their downfall eventually. While also keeping Maizie protected. That part was nonnegotiable.

Kenna *wasn't* letting a dangerous criminal go free.

Navarro stared at her from the other end of the table.

Just then, the door whipped open so fast it hit the stone surface of the bar and the glass door shattered across the patio.

Maizie let out a short scream. Kenna set a hand on her arm and stared at the woman who ran in. She raced to Navarro, who was crying and pleading in Spanish too fast for Kenna to even pick out the few words she did know.

She glanced at Ramon. "What's going on?"

Ramon pushed his chair back and stood. "The child. The new nanny was stabbed. There's blood all over the floor, and the boy is missing." He started to sway.

Kenna stood. The last thing she wanted was for the three of them to be dragged into something else—or implicated. She'd been a distraction before. Would Navarro think the same thing might've happened again? She didn't want to offer to find the child.

She didn't want to be dragged in.

Chapter Eighteen

"Come on." Ramon waved for Kenna to go with him.

She didn't like it, but she went.

As the former fed led Kenna into the house and down the halls, someone followed behind her.

She glanced back and saw Maizie right there. Kenna nodded, not wanting the girl to be far from her. At least not any more than it seemed Maizie wanted the same thing.

Yelling erupted from the opposite end of the house.

They raced through the house to a different wing she hadn't visited before. It took on a more casual feel than the areas where Navarro would entertain guests.

Ramon passed a couple of the cartel guys, headed the opposite direction. No one looked happy. The boss was on a rampage. Hopefully, the alert had gone out quick enough that they could track down whoever had taken the boy before they left the property.

The nanny lay on a blue rug in the center of the room, blood soaking into the fabric beneath her. Kenna knelt on one side while Ramon did the same on the other. Between the nanny's lips, air bubbles tinged with blood gathered.

"She's alive," Kenna said.

Ramon nodded.

She glanced at Maizie, who stood beside the door. Out of sight of anyone entering. Her back to the wall. "See if you can find me towels."

The girl pushed off the wall and headed through to what looked like a bathroom.

Ramon lifted his two fingers from the nanny's neck. "Her pulse is pretty sluggish. She might have lost too much blood already."

"We still need to try and save her."

Maizie handed Kenna a stack of white towels.

Kenna covered the wound on the nanny's chest and leaned her upper body on it. "I did this for you, and you lived." Ramon could say whatever he wanted. She was still going to do what she was going to do. What she believed God asked of her and the life He'd given her. "It's always worth trying."

"You think I'm going to argue with you?" Ramon shot back. Still, there was some hesitation in his expression. "I know you don't care if she was a nice person or not."

"Because every single life in this world is precious. If you write people off because they've done bad things, or you believe they'll never change, and then you let them die? That's a chance they could've changed, and you stole it from them."

Even if she was sometimes no better than any of the terrible people she'd been surrounded with. Even if instead she wanted desperately to believe she was so much more worthwhile than they were. All because they chose to victimize others.

No one could be so far gone that they weren't able to be saved.

A child who could grow up to be a deadly cartel leader was still innocent—no matter what he might do in the future.

There was only a tipping point between her becoming the things she hunted in the dark and dragged into the light. Between being swallowed up by the need for vengeance and being the person she wanted to be.

And it was hope that kept her moving toward what God might have for her. The future she wanted. A life in the light, full of the kind of peace she'd never felt before outside of tiny glimpses.

"Call the doctor," Kenna ordered. "Get him here so he can try and save this woman."

Ramon started to argue.

"Just do it." She wasn't in the mood to listen to someone debate while a woman's life drained into the carpet.

"Maybe you should have just taken some medical training." Ramon pulled out his phone, dialed a number, and spoke in rapid-fire Spanish. When he ended the call, he said, "Or I should have. If we knew how to stop the bleeding and fix her up, we could get her to tell us what happened."

"Now you're getting it."

Navarro strode in at full speed and pulled up short. "What is this?" He kicked the nanny's foot.

Maizie let out a whimper.

"The doctor is on his way," Ramon said.

"Take her outside and finish what this"—he used a Spanish word she didn't know, a descriptor for the man who had stolen the boy—"started when he took my nephew." Navarro squeezed his hands into fists, making the tendons in his forearms flex. Added to the red face and the bulging vein in his forehead, she guessed the guy was about to blow. "Then the two of you will go find my nephew."

"We need her alive so she can tell us who did this." Kenna

used a softer tone, but she wasn't about to back down. And she wouldn't let anyone take the life of this woman simply because she had chosen the wrong employment opportunity. "Unless you have that information this woman needs to live."

"Graciela should have fought until her last breath to save my nephew."

Kenna wasn't going to point out that it looked like that's exactly what happened. "The doctor is coming, and we're going to try and get information from her. She could tell us why your nephew was abducted from this house and who did it."

Behind Navarro, Maizie shifted, drawing Kenna's attention.

Kenna said, "What is it?"

Navarro spun around to the teen, who tapped furiously on her phone.

Kenna didn't ease up on the pressure she had on the nanny's wounds, but she would turn it over to Ramon if she had to. For now she watched carefully to ensure the cartel leader wasn't going to approach the girl under Kenna's protection. "What do you have?"

Maizie turned the screen so she could see it. "Who is this?"

A shadowed figure carried a child over his shoulder, the footage from a paused video on the phone. Maizie had accessed whatever security system Navarro had in place.

The cartel leader stiffened.

Ramon said, "How did you—"

Kenna cut him off, not needing them to get into the fact Maizie had hacked them. Not when it could mean the difference between a child being recovered rather than found dead. "That's Kart."

"This man came into my home and stole from me?"

Navarro flinched, every inch of him a brutal cartel leader. He spun back to Kenna. "Find him. *Now*." Then he whirled around and stormed out.

Ramon let out a tight hiss between his teeth. "He's not going to let that go. It's not his priority right now to do anything but find his nephew before Kart gets off the property, but you can be sure he will come after you about getting into his computer network."

Maizie's face had paled.

Kenna didn't like the look of fear in the teen's eyes. She turned back to the nanny, Graciela, and refocused on Ramon. "He can try. But if he wants to come after us, then he's going to realize eventually that there is no way for him to find us. We can hide."

Regardless of that, there were other ways to end this than to simply run forever. They could make a deal with Navarro—finding his nephew in exchange for him dropping the issue of the hacking.

But she would have to see how this played out.

The doctor strode into the room. "I came as fast as I could." He pulled up short. "You."

"Yeah, me," Kenna said. "Blah-blah. Whatever. Help this woman."

"She doesn't have long. She would need a surgical suite, and a full team of medical staff to save her life." The doctor tapped his index finger in different spots on Graciela's chest. "Her lungs are filling with blood. It would be my guess that her heart got nicked."

"So there's no way to wake her up and find out what she knows?"

The doctor shook his head. "All we can do is make her comfortable."

"You aren't even going to try and get her to a hospital?"

"Unless you have a helicopter around here somewhere there is little chance of her making it that far."

Kenna hissed out a breath of her own. Ramon shot her a look. She shifted her weight back and stood. "I don't want to hear it."

Ramon stood as well, something like compassion on his face. "Trying to save someone's life is never a bad thing."

Kenna strode past him into the bathroom, got some soap, and scrubbed at her hands and arms. She tried not to look much at the tinted water swirling the drain like the chance Graciela had of living. It just washed away, gone forever.

She splashed water on her face and patted it dry with a towel. Tiny motions that helped to center her. The way she always did when her emotions rioted from adrenaline.

Kenna headed through the bathroom to the hall. Maizie moved with her the last couple of feet as they stepped out. Ramon did the same, and the three of them ended up in a huddle in the hallway.

The doctor pulled the sheet from the bed and used it to cover the nanny.

Maizie leaned over to speak low to Kenna. "He gave her something."

When the doctor stepped out the room into the hallway, Kenna said, "Did you put her out of her misery?"

There were so many things wrong with everything that'd happened to her since she woke up the first day in Mexico. Terror after terror. At this point she would hardly be surprised if he took things into his own hands.

The doctor held no compassion in his expression. "What do you think Navarro pays me for?"

"I wouldn't think he would waste money on paying you if he could just dump people in the desert and let them die on their own."

"But then the police would find them, and that means paperwork and more payoffs."

Kenna folded her arms. "So you avoid having to make more deals or owing anyone a favor. I guess that makes your life easier, doesn't it?"

She didn't like the sound of that when it meant the doctor used his job and his position to cover up what amounted to murder.

She let out a long breath.

Maizie's phone buzzed. "Stairns wants us to meet him in the foyer."

In the entryway Stairns lifted his chin. "Maizie, do you know what car he was driving?"

The girl nodded. "It looks like a white pickup truck." She showed Stairns her phone. "I tracked him through the house to the garage, where he stuffed the kid in the passenger seat and left with him."

Kenna glanced at Ramon. "Would he have been stopped on his way out of the ranch?"

"Depends which way he went." Ramon looked at Maizie.

"All I know is that he didn't go out the front."

Ramon nodded. "He took the back exit, probably because he knows we don't have cameras on that side."

"So he's gone, and he has Navarro's nephew."

"And you are going to get him back for me." The man himself strode into the room. "Kenna Banbury, the private investigator who finds missing people. You want revenge on Kart for what he did to you. This is how you get it."

She didn't move. "That's for me to decide."

"I'll give you one million US dollars if you return him to me alive." Again, he tried a tactic that bore no weight with her. He really thought that revenge or money could sway her into finding the boy for him?

But rather than convince him that it was more of a moral imperative when a child was in danger, she said, "Tell me everything you know. And give me full access to this place, no questions asked."

"So you can turn it all over to your DEA?"

"You either want him back or not. I have no loyalty to you." She paused. "The longer I stay in this town, the more likely it is that Kart or his cousin Elliot will find me. Your rescuing me from that compound will be for nothing." She was the one who would shoulder the weight of the risk. And no one else. "If I'm going to find the boy for you, then I have to do it my way. Which means you don't get to tell me what I need and what I don't."

He glanced at Ramon, then at her. "Since you two are such good friends from the FBI, Santiago goes with you and doesn't leave your side until you bring me back my nephew."

"Fine." Maybe she shouldn't have agreed so quickly, but she needed to start walking so she could shake off the prickling tension.

"After all, you failed to bring back my bride. I trust you won't fail to bring back my heir." He turned around and strode away.

Kenna glanced at Stairns, who shook his head. "Not here."

They headed for the car, where Kenna sat in the back with Maizie.

Ramon settled in the passenger seat and turned to look at her. "If we don't find the kid, then it won't be worth me coming back here. If I do, he'll just kill me for failing."

"I asked if you wanted help to get out of this." She was still prepared to help him if that was what he wanted. If she was going to provide him with safe passage to a new life, then there was a whole lot that he would need to debrief her on.

That was the only way she'd be satisfied she could let him go free. Because if she allowed someone who would only hurt others, or worse, to be loose in the world, then it was her responsibility if they did exactly that.

"If I do that, then none of the others get help."

Kenna frowned. "What does that mean?"

"Camila? The boy she was with?"

"You arranged for them to be sent to America?" Her brows rose.

Ramon said nothing for a few seconds. Then he said, "We all have our part to play."

"She didn't go free. She was a captive."

"At least she was free of Navarro."

Kenna wasn't sure she agreed with that assessment.

Stairns pulled through the gate onto the dirt road that led to the highway into town. But he immediately took a right turn and drove around the ranch land. Acres and acres that stretched as far as she could see, with the canopy of stars overhead.

She would be able to appreciate the beauty of this country if she hadn't been living in terror for days. Kenna might have a glimmer of safety right now, but for a little boy that peace was gone.

Maizie tapped the screen of her phone before swiping and tapping again. "They're headed northwest at the far end of the ranch."

"We will break an axle going that way," Ramon said. "And how on earth do you know that? There are no cameras out here. There's no nothing."

Kenna leaned over to look at the screen of Maizie's phone. "I don't think you want to know." Looked like a UAV satellite feed to her. What had she retasked, and who was currently trying to take back control of their tech?

Maizie said, "Northwest. That's the way he went."

"What I want to know," Stairns said, "is why Kart took the boy. And what he plans on doing with a child."

"He's probably been planning it since the compound was raided. A way to hit back at Navarro where it hurts the most." If Kenna were going to get vengeance on her enemy, she would also go after their most vulnerable spot.

Kart only recently discovered the existence of a child in the cartel leader's life. But he hadn't wasted time coming after Navarro.

An eye for an eye.

"But it doesn't matter," Kenna said. "Because we're not going to let that happen."

Chapter Nineteen

Maizie stiffened in the seat beside Kenna, then shifted, still looking at her phone but far more tense than she had been a second ago.

Kenna leaned over to the girl, her elbow on the back window shelf. "What is it?"

"We have no idea where he is, or what he plans to do with that boy." Maizie didn't look up from the phone. "We don't even know what the kid's name is."

Ramon said, "His name is Javier, and he's three years old."

Maizie sucked in a breath through her nose.

Kenna rested her fingers on Maizie's shoulder. "Which is why we aren't going to rest until we find him."

Stairns pressed down on the gas. "Where does this road go?"

Ramon glanced around at all of them. "It leads to the American's compound. But none of you are supposed to know that, and you didn't hear it from me."

"So he just went back home? What is there at the compound for him?" Kenna asked, even though none of them would have the answer. "The guy should be taking the kid and fleeing as far as possible so that Navarro never finds him. Or is he regrouping and making contact so he can demand a ransom?"

Maizie shuddered.

Kenna flexed her fingers, then moved them off the girl's shoulder. After a lifetime of unwanted touch, Maizie didn't need anything that would remind her of the life she used to have.

"Is he going to kill Javier?" Maizie asked.

The fact the girl could feel empathy for another child in her situation was a good thing. It meant that everything she was inside hadn't been seared to the point of being unable to feel. There just wasn't enough time to unpack that with Maizie right now—though Kenna planned to do it later, when they were home.

"We don't know what his plan is," Kenna replied. "But it doesn't matter, though, because we're going to get Javier back before the worst happens."

Whether or not Navarro had other men in front of them. If they were already racing toward where Kart had gone with Javier. Chasing him after he stole the boy and the vehicle from the ranch. It didn't matter. Kenna just hoped they weren't going to get in the way. Or cause more problems when she showed up to get the kid back.

"He could be doing anything to the kid." Maizie paused, her breaths coming faster. "And we have no way to stop it."

Stairns hit the brakes and pulled onto the dirt beside the road. It was slightly less compacted than the surface of the street, but not by much. There didn't look to be anything around them. Just a whole bunch of nothing, plus the lights of the ranch behind them and the lights of town over to the east, across the desert hills.

"Ramon, get out." Stairns pushed his door open.

He and Ramon climbed out and closed their doors. Then stood chatting in front of the hood in the glow of the headlights.

Gauging by their body language, Kenna realized Stairns was giving her the space to talk to Maizie. She shifted in the seat to face Maizie, but also give the girl some space. "I need you to listen to me."

Maizie closed her eyes.

"Not everyone who is taken suffers the things that you did."

"He's scared."

Kenna nodded. "Yes, he probably is."

"He doesn't know what's going to happen to him."

"He wants to get home to his uncle. But the place where he felt safe is the place where he saw the nanny who cared for him get killed. So he doesn't understand how to find where he wants to be. He doesn't know how to get that peace back, because it's up to his parents and caregivers to provide it for him."

Maizie blinked and opened her eyes. "What is he going to do?"

"He's going to retreat into a place in his mind that will keep him protected. It's what little kids do to keep themselves safe. They build walls in their minds that protect them from trauma."

"It won't work."

For her, it likely hadn't. Maizie had still been captive when she was old enough to understand that it wasn't just short periods of trauma or a one-time event that her mind needed to protect her from. It had been every day of her entire life up until just a few months ago. She didn't need to be anywhere near anything like that again.

"Go with Stairns back to Colorado," Kenna said. "Go home to the trailer and help me from there."

Maizie glanced at her, the sheen of tears in her eyes. "Is that what you want? To get rid of me?"

Kenna shook her head. "I want you to be safe, and I want you to find peace."

"Elizabeth said I'm not going to have peace unless I find it for myself. You can't give it to me."

Kenna said, "I want to."

"I know." Maizie sniffed. "That's why I chose you."

"I'm really glad you did."

"You know, Stairns would cut off his arm if he thought it meant I could let go of some of this."

Kenna nodded. "I know."

She hadn't made the choice to leave Maizie with him lightly. Not considering the history that she had with Stairns. But if she was going to move on from forgiving him for the way he'd ended her FBI career, then she had to keep trusting him. As it turned out, one of the best places where Maizie could've ended up was with Stairns and his wife, Elizabeth.

Kenna lifted two fingers and waved to Stairns. He and Ramon got back in the car, but neither asked if she and Maizie were good. They simply carried on like it was business as usual.

Stairns said, "So should we go check out that compound?"

"Sounds good to me." Kenna needed to get out of the car and do something. Move. Sitting in here was beginning to heat up her body too much. Enough that she felt flushed and adjusted the vent to give her more air. She almost felt like she had a fever, but it was probably just all the stress, coupled with the aftereffects of the drug Kart had given her.

She glanced at Maizie and the teen looked over.

They shared her small smile, a tiny moment of solidarity.

There was so much she wanted to do with and for the girl. Safe times Maizie could rest and focus on healing, and vacation adventures to create new memories. All of which meant Kenna would have to take a break from solving cases at some point. In order to not let too much time pass and risk never being able to share some peaceful moments of her own with the girl.

Stairns pulled into the compound, the car bumped over the fallen gate, and he sped down the road toward the main building. Half the buildings were rubble, parts of them still smoldering. The other half weren't going to be habitable anytime soon. She doubted Kart had come here to hole up. More than likely he just needed to retrieve something from the location, and then he was gone.

It wasn't lost on her that it would be some kind of payback to leave Navarro's nephew dead in the middle of all this destruction. Doing that would send a clear message to the cartel leader as to how Kart felt about what happened here. The question was, after Kart delivered that blow whether he would come after Stairns for being the one to make the deal with Navarro in order to get Kenna back.

Stairns parked. "I'll hang back with Maizie if the two of you want to go and look around. You know more about what is where in this place than we do."

Kenna could have kissed him for that suggestion. There was nothing she wanted less than to give Maizie an up-close-and-personal view of the hidden parts of the compound. But she and Ramon would have to look through everything.

"Copy that," Kenna said.

She and Ramon traipsed to a doorway still intact, though the door itself lay on the floor inside.

"What are we looking for—apart from Kart and Javier?"

"If he's not here, it's because he took something and left."

Ramon paused. "Or he used this location as a way to access somewhere else."

Kenna turned to him in the dim light of the hall. She should have brought a flashlight. That one bare flickering bulb at the end of the hallway didn't give her much of a view of his face, and the dark expression in his eyes. There had to be a generator still working somewhere.

Her stomach flipped. "What somewhere else? Where would he go?"

Ramon said nothing.

"What do you know about accessing other places from here?" Kenna asked. She had tangled with people who used underground tunnels, caves, and hallways carved out of the earth just a few months ago and had no desire to revisit anything like it.

"Only the rumors I've heard. It's how I think some of the people have been going missing." Ramon waved her on. "I'll show you, but I only got a quick glimpse of the room once before I was discovered where I shouldn't be."

Her phone chimed. Kenna played the voice recording message from Stairns.

"We took a look around the back of the building. The white pickup truck he stole from Navarro is here."

Kenna recorded a response back. "Do you see him anywhere? Or any lights on?" She sent the message.

A second later her phone chimed, playing immediately since she had the app open already. "Nothing. Keep your eyes open."

She followed Ramon to the end of the hallway. Down a set of stairs with a couple of sections that had collapsed on one side. Thankfully, most of it was intact enough for them to descend. "You really think we should be going down here first, instead of walking through all the surface level parts? We could actually do a room-by-room search in a way that's effective."

Ramon shook his head. "That would be a waste of time."

"Because you know something I don't know?" Kenna stood waiting while he pulled open the door. "How do I know you're not just taking me down here so you can put a bullet in my head?"

Ramon slid a gun from its holster on his hip, turned the pistol, and handed it to her. "You keep hold of this. Maybe one day when we're eighty, you'll actually trust me."

"I doubt it. More likely we'll be playing Ping-Pong at a retirement home in Florida, and you'll cheat so you can win, and I'll put poison in your pudding in retaliation."

He barked a laugh. "That's how you relieve tension? I have to say, it works pretty well."

"It's a gift." Kenna followed him through the door. "So what are we doing down here?"

They walked by a row of small rooms. Kenna didn't hang around long enough to contemplate what happened in each one of those. It was a different building than the one she and Jax had been held in, but not so far from the captivity they had experienced.

"There's supposed to be a tunnel from one of the back rooms, that some of the guys knew about—but not all of them. Like a couple of the military guys had a way in and out that the others weren't aware of." He led her down the hall to the end. "Maybe it was in the original plans, and Kart knows about it. But I don't think Benjamin and Anthony at least knew it was here."

Whether they did or not, both of them were dead now.

Navarro's men hadn't managed to kill Kart. The fact they let him live was the reason Navarro might lose his nephew.

She knew Navarro expected them to execute the American when they found Javier.

Another way Kenna had begun to creep closer and closer to who these people were, as though their corrupted morality had begun to infect her.

"Here we go." He opened the door wide to reveal a small musty-smelling office with wood wainscoting, maps taped up on the walls, and a few filing cabinets. A huge safe stood in the corner, the door hanging open. At least one shelf had been emptied.

"He must have come in here to get something from this." She made her way over, rummaging through the envelopes and files on the two top shelves, beneath which were a row of guns. Several were missing given the indents in the foam that indicated something heavy had rested there.

Kart had stocked up, and now he was heavily armed. Or Navarro's men had discovered this room and taken the American's weapons.

Kenna wanted to gather the rest of the contents of the safe just in case it could be useful later. It could give them information about the entire operation Kart had been running down here, the names of his associates all over the place, and exactly how extensive they needed to be in order to dismantle the entire thing. Maybe Stairns could come and grab it before they left.

She texted him so Ramon wouldn't hear her telling her colleague they were going to be sure to destroy the entire operation.

After which they would send the feds on some international cooperative task force after Navarro.

"There's more than one reason to be in here." Ramon crouched in the corner by the wall. She saw a flash of pain on his face, but it was gone in a second. He pushed against the lower half of the wall with both hands, and the door clicked, then opened.

From waist height down was a tunnel made of cement like an old sewer pipe. And that's exactly what it smelled of.

Kenna wrinkled her nose. "You hear anybody in there?" She would rather have regrouped and figured out what all this information in here meant for where Kart might have gone.

Ramon stayed silent for a second, then shook his head. "I don't hear anyone."

"Then we have less reason to believe that he would've gone that way than that he might be somewhere in the rubble of the compound above us, and if we don't make a move and go find him? We could end up losing Javier."

And that was the last thing she wanted to happen—being responsible for the death of a child. Not even the nephew of a man who should for all intents and purposes be her sworn enemy. Or at least someone she never made deals with. Whether or not Stairns had.

Right now she was going to do everything she could to find his child. "We can't take the risk that we don't find him."

"If we don't, then Navarro will kill us all."

Chapter Twenty

"Can you still hear me?" The phone line crackled. Ramon's voice sounded far away. In that tunnel, underground.

Nope. Not me. No, thank you.

From the back seat of the car, Maizie said, "I have him close."

Kenna stared out the car window. They were crawling along with Stairns keeping the speed low so they wouldn't get too far ahead of Ramon.

For the first time in her life, she found herself torn between what she wanted to do, and what she'd always done. Everything in her strove to save the life of a child. This time was no exception.

But with everything she'd experienced—more like *suffered* —the past few days, part of her wanted to leave more than anything. Even with Jax in the hospital. Maybe she should go see him again, but until he woke up, he wouldn't even know she was there.

The residual fear and need to escape was still inside her. Making her antsy, and there had been no way at all she would've gone in that tunnel. She'd have had a full-blown panic attack. Right now she was battling some serious anxiety —the need to flee.

"Just think," Ramon said over the open phone line. "You could have been down here with me, crawling through this concrete tunnel all the way to the end."

At least she'd managed to keep him from seeing the panic. "I have zero desire to reenact a movie-style prison break."

He chuckled, but the sound had an edge to it. Whatever was in him that caused him to go the way the FBI thought he had, and make deals with bad guys rather than double down on proving his own innocence, bled through everything he was like a kind of darkness—in his manner, his tone of voice, and what he believed about himself and the world.

Kenna had lived with the need to not fall into a bitterness against the FBI that could characterize her if she let it. But then she wouldn't have Stairns in her life, here to watch out for Maizie. If she hadn't opted to forgive him for the wrong he had done to her, then she'd have missed out on the friendships she now had.

She glanced over at Stairns in the driver's seat. "Any updates from our friends with badges about Jax and his condition?"

"I have a buddy in the loop who is supposed to text me if anything changes."

From the back seat, Maizie said, "And as soon as I get back to my laptop at the hotel, I'll be able to see what the latest is. Assuming they do things electronically and they update their computer records regularly."

Ramon said, "I have a friend who is on staff at the hospital. I can make a call if you want."

"Thanks, guys." Kenna rubbed her hands to her knees. "I appreciate it."

Still, she couldn't quite get rid of the snag her thoughts had encountered before she and Ramon agreed he would be the one to crawl through the tunnel. Because she'd had zero intention of doing so. She understood he was focused on not disappointing Navarro. But his statement about failure leading to their deaths? She couldn't let it go. If Navarro wanted to go scorched earth, that was fine.

Would he hunt her all the way back to Stairns' house, putting Maizie and everyone else at risk?

She didn't want that.

Kenna had to focus on the fact there was a scared child out there.

A lot like Maizie, and the well of deep empathy the girl had for anyone who might be in her situation, but without it being overwhelming fear for little Javier. If Maizie could channel that empathy into positive action, she would be a strong advocate for victims trying to heal and regain their sense of self and freedom. One day, anyway.

Ramon was the one who had let Luca and Camila go, all so they could have a chance at a better life. She could hardly believe he was the one who sent them on their way. Something that could almost be construed as being out of the goodness of his heart. If that were even believable. As it was, this was a dangerous game that Ramon played. And he was worried about Navarro killing him? The guy was working both sides, and intermittently rescuing people as he felt like it.

How did he choose who deserved freedom and the shot at a good life, and who didn't?

She lifted the phone. "Are you going to let Javier go to a new life somewhere safe when you find him?"

If the boy was "never found" as far as Navarro was concerned, Ramon thought he and Kenna would pay the price. Maybe that kept him from rescuing the child until now.

"I have a friend in Mexico City who will take the boy to a home in Manzanillo where he'll be safe. America is too much of a risk right now." Ramon grunted, and she pictured him in her mind dragging himself along that concrete pipe. "We've been talking about doing it for a while, but now that Kart took Javi, I might not be able to risk trying to rescue him."

Kenna shook her head. "What am I supposed to think other than that *you've* been behind the random disappearances this whole time?" The guy's entire life was a gray area.

Ramon grunted again. "I might be a lot of things, but I'm not a killer."

"But you do rescue some of them?"

"When I can. When it's worth it for the person, and I can be inconspicuous."

Kenna looked at the ground beside the car, imagining him down there. "So who do you think is out there killing people?"

"I don't think you want to know."

She frowned. "What does that mean?"

The phone line crackled. Maybe Ramon, exhaling against the microphone.

"My handler told me to leave the case alone. I was supposed to be focusing on a couple of Texans doing deals with their neighbors to traffic drugs across the border. We were trying to shut down their operation. So when it cropped up that someone was murdering people and carving a W into their backs, I took it to my handler."

"So this has actually been going on for the better part of ten years?" And he hadn't bothered to do the work to get it shut down. Kenna couldn't believe it. After she'd seen Lola on the dirt, dead, she'd wanted to find out who did it.

Ramon seemed to pick and choose what he put his energy toward. What was the point in saving a few people if a killer was left unchecked?

She fisted her hand on her knee. "You need to give me everything you have on this guy."

Ramon snorted. "You think I have the case file?"

"I think you're going to at least write down everything you can think of and give it to me so I can take a look."

As if she would walk away when the killer was out there? She might not have time to look into it right now, but she could at least go over everything. Maybe turn it over to Jax or some of his colleagues so they could present it to the FBI.

The Bureau could open a new case and assign agents from the local office closest to the majority of the killings. Then they would have a shot at shutting this person down.

"I'm at the end of the tunnel."

"We overshot the exit," Maizie said. "It's almost a quarter mile behind us and to the east a ways."

Stairns turned the car around and pointed the headlights in that direction.

Ramon emerged from the ground and waved two fingers. "I'm coming over."

When he was beside her open window, Kenna leaned her elbow out.

He pointed. "I see tire tracks. Maybe he came out this way, but there is no way to tell how long the tracks have been there."

She climbed out of the car so she could get in the back with Maizie. "What now?"

He reached up and squeezed the back of his neck. "You and I should go see the priest."

She studied his expression but couldn't read the intent there. "Okay."

·   ·   ·

An hour later, they had dropped off Maizie and Stairns at the hotel and walked the couple of miles to the church.

"Any particular reason why we need to sneak over on foot to see the priest?" Kenna asked.

Ramon shrugged.

"Does it have to do with Kart and Javier?"

"Maybe."

Kenna rolled her eyes. "Well, does it have to do with you rescuing people sometimes?"

He said nothing.

"Then tell me what you know about whoever has been killing people for the last ten years."

"Could be longer than that, considering he was well into his methodology when I realized it was happening." Ramon tucked his hands in his jeans pockets as they walked. "He was getting clever, and I have almost believed each one was random. Except for the letter on their backs."

"And you were certain it wasn't some kind of cartel hitman?"

Ramon shook his head. "No one would've bothered to kill these people. They didn't mean anything to any of the cartels, so far as a discernible pattern. And it happens up and down this side of the country, probably into the US as well."

So they hadn't been targeted hits. But that didn't mean the person killed had never mattered to someone. People were dead—and that meant the person responsible should be stopped.

Ramon continued, "I had a couple of the case files opened and sent to my office before my career was ruined. But whoever got them wanted me to focus on the cartel and my assignment. I was written up as a turn coat, and they probably just passed them to someone who put them in a drawer. Otherwise, it wouldn't still be happening. I'll give you dates and names as much as I can remember so you can dig them all up."

Literally, or figuratively, she wasn't sure. But the sentiment was the same. "I'll do that."

Ramon sighed. "You'll have all the time in the world to work on it once we find Javi and you go back to your life in America."

"I guess I will." But she'd heard something in his tone. "Are you regretting your choice to stay here instead of going back and fighting for your career?"

"Hardly." Ramon climbed the steps to what looked like a back door to the church. He clicked down the latch and pushed the door open.

"I'm surprised they don't keep that door locked."

Ramon led her down a dark and quiet hallway, to the door at the end. He knocked softly.

"Come in."

It was after midnight, but the priest, a fit-looking man in his seventies, looked as awake as he had in the afternoon when she saw him last.

"What can I do for the two of you?"

Ramon settled onto a couch that didn't look sturdy enough to hold anyone's body weight.

Kenna opted to wander the room, looking at the bookshelves and the hand carved statues.

"Have you seen Kart in the last six hours?" Ramon asked.

The priest frowned. "What's going on?"

"He took Javi from Navarro's ranch."

The priest muttered something under his breath, maybe a prayer. "I will say mass for the boy's safe return."

Kenna turned to them. "So Kart hasn't been by, looking for something?"

The priest shook his head.

Ramon sat forward on the couch and set his elbows on his knees. "He hasn't asked you for safe passage across the border?" He clasped his hands together. "We think he might be making a run for it."

"I haven't seen him." The priest frowned. "And I doubt he would come here looking for a sympathetic ear. He doesn't strike me as the type, and that's not usually what he comes here for."

"What about the doctor?"

Kenna glanced between the two men. She'd have asked what Kart usually came to the priest for, but Ramon either knew or didn't care.

"Perhaps you should ask him," the priest said. "I do not wish to be involved in this business."

"You don't need to worry about Navarro retaliating." Ramon shrugged one shoulder. "He won't even know you were involved."

"Navarro isn't the one I am concerned about." The priest glanced at Kenna.

She blinked. "What threat do I pose to you?"

"Only the general risk to life and limb being around you." He stared at her.

"You'll have to fill me in because I think I'm missing something." For some reason the priest believed she presented a serious threat to him. And why would he think that?

"I believe some time ago you met a dear friend of mine in Albuquerque. A key player in our effort to ensure the freedom and safety of victims we come across." The priest paused. "Both here and across the border in the town of Hatchet, and even farther north as well."

A friend of his. Hatchet.

That could only be one person.

Kenna said, "You have this Underground Railroad-type of

thing going on, and it was going up to Hatchet?" That couldn't have been super secure, given the entire town turned out to be connected to all kinds of shady business.

"Since you uncovered the issues with that town we have sought alternative routes," Ramon said. "And our success rate has increased dramatically."

She had met the priest in Albuquerque. The priest who was killed by Peter Conklin, a man who turned out to be a serial killer. Sadly not the person who had been murdering people down here over the last decade or more, or that would have stopped.

"The priest was your friend?" Kenna said.

"I considered him my brother," he said. "And you failed to keep him alive."

She ducked her head, a lump rising in her throat. "He was a good man." It hadn't taken long knowing him to understand that he'd been a force for good in the world. He'd even encouraged her to seek the light in the darkness. To be that light to the dark places around her.

"'None are good, no not one.'" The priest stared at her. "But I understand what you mean. I considered him dear to me."

She sniffed. "I'm sorry for your loss."

Stairns had lived, but the priest had been killed. Both good men. One was a servant of God and the other was a man who strove to make amends for his mistakes. Even Kenna had barely survived that encounter with a serial killer's lair in a hotel in Albuquerque.

Would this situation turn out to be a trap like that?

Things would make a whole lot more sense if evil was eliminated and good got to continue and thrive. But life seemed determined not to work like that.

Ramon squeezed his fingers together. "Now that we all understand where we're coming from, you haven't seen Kart?"

The priest shook his head.

"If you hear anything about Javi, or where Kart might have taken him, will you call me? I'd like to make sure the boy is safe."

"So would I," Kenna said.

The priest glanced between her and Ramon. Finally, he nodded. "I will pass on anything I learn."

"Thank you." She didn't reach out to shake the man's hand, unsure if he would want to accept it. "For everything you do."

He only stared at her, then his gaze flicked down to the cross necklace. She didn't tell him it was a GPS tracker.

"Right." Ramon stood. "Let's go."

He wrote something on a notepad he left on the priest's desk. As they headed to the door and out the same hallway they'd come down, Ramon said, "We keep it low-key, but I know what they do."

"The priest...and who?"

"The doctor."

Of course. "So they pinpoint people they can save, and they rescue the individual. And that's the way you got Camila and Luca out?"

"We alternate through methods. We don't always work together, but we have an understanding. They have channels I don't know about. Missionary charities where they can get the paperwork to get people across the border under fake names using missionary work visas. They can transport them all over, and then the people disappear."

"I just hope they end up somewhere safe when they get where they're going," she said. "Not like Camila and Luca."

"I did everything I could to get them safe." He ran a hand

through his hair. "There had to have been a breakdown somewhere."

Kenna paused, her fingers grasping the handle for the exit door. "So it's their fault they couldn't get free?"

"I thought they did." He tipped his head to one side. "And no, it wasn't their *fault*."

"Pretty risky if you ask me." She pushed open the door and stepped out into the night. "Too much chance it will go wrong—which it did."

"Life is risky."

She couldn't argue with that. "Some people only know safety their whole lives. It's why I do what I do, so the ones who might've been targeted by a dangerous person never have their quiet lives disturbed by an individual who means them harm."

"But you never meet them. You never even know who they are."

"Why would I have occasion to do so?" She shrugged. "I know I'm saving lives."

Ramon only stared at her.

Kenna blew out a breath. "All this business you've got going on rescuing people and setting them free—or so you hope—is great and all, but how does it get us any closer to finding Javier?"

She was with Maizie on that. Worried sick over what the boy might be going through right now. Though, she refused to let anyone know how much it was tearing her up inside.

Ramon said, "We need to know where he'd take the kid to lay low."

"Or if he simply grabbed him and started driving," Kenna said. "Which means he could be hundreds of miles away by now."

Ramon shook his head. "Easier to just kill him and be done with it. Less hassle."

"Do you even hear yourself?" Listening to it made her sick to her stomach. "We need to *find him*, Ramon. Before the worst happens. Not because it's in our own best interests."

Chapter Twenty-One

Kenna braced her hands against the tile and closed her eyes while water from the showerhead pounded on her back and shoulders. Her body flushed under the heat of it, but probably just from the temperature she'd turned it to—close to the temperature on the surface of the sun.

She prayed for Javier, all too aware of how many hours he'd been gone so far.

Every place they'd looked and hadn't found him narrowed the list of where he might be. But when the answer was "anywhere in the world," that didn't help her narrow down how far Kart could have gone. No matter how she tried to spin it in her own mind, there were still far too many places to look.

"I know You can keep him safe."

She didn't much care that Navarro might retaliate if they didn't find him. Or if he didn't like what they found. She'd rather push on and find the kid.

Ramon had opted to kick down some doors in town and ask local sources he had for information. They wouldn't talk as readily if she was there, so she'd come back to the room to see what Maizie had. The teen was on research, and Stairns had gone to morning mass at church. He'd wanted to ask the priest afterward if there had been any news from someone in town about the boy.

What she wanted was to go by the hospital again and sit with Jax, even if he never opened his eyes. She wanted to see the monitors and listen to the beep of his heartbeat.

"I don't want to lose him."

She knew she would survive if she did lose him. She'd lived through the death of a man she cared about before. That one hadn't killed her, but it had been close. What was between her and Jax might be new, but it wasn't any less real than what she'd felt for Bradley. She had figured out that much the past few weeks—months—or just the last handful of days since they'd landed her.

The truth was, Jax pushed her in all the right ways to be a better version of herself.

Maybe it was better that he was unconscious right now. He didn't have to see the turmoil she was in right now. Her head was a mess. Case in point? She didn't like thinking about the fact she couldn't help wondering if he would be disappointed in the person she was right now. Talk about mixed up.

If Jax died, would she be like Ramon? Maybe she'd be somewhere making deals with the worst kind of bad guy for survival. Or would Stairns and Maizie keep her from slipping over the edge?

Kenna didn't want to find out.

But she couldn't make a bargain with God to save his life just because it would in turn serve to keep her alive and on the right path. She had to be on the right path on her own, without Jax's influence—but she liked the gift he was to her life.

Kenna nearly snorted, shaking her head under the cascading water.

Now wasn't the time to get nostalgic.

She shut the shower off and grabbed a towel. The hotel bathroom wasn't big enough to turn around in without hitting something, but she managed to dry off and dress in the shorts and T-shirt that Maizie got for her.

But thoughts about Jax lingered. Something about the past week or so had made her sentimental...and homicidal. Sure, her feelings for him did separate her from the dangerous men she'd met since she got here—and at other times in her life—proving she was a better person. They thought she was weak for doing the right thing rather than being strong because she did whatever she wanted and called it freedom.

Everyone had the capacity for good in them just like they had the capacity for evil. Each person in the world had to decide which they were going to be. They all had to choose.

There is none good, no not one. That's what the priest had said.

She knew the difference between who she wanted to be and who she would be if she allowed herself to slip into the darkness. The slide started with shutting off care and concern for those who needed her protection. That was the difference between her and people like Navarro, or Ramon. They seemed to have given up and called it who they "had" to be like there was no choice to be made.

Kenna woke up and made the choice for herself. Who she was going to be. The kind of person she would strive to be that day.

Every day.

It was part of her survival to continually move forward. To press on and look for how she could grow. Like reading more about Christianity. Listening to her friends. Researching.

That had been on hold since they were ambushed in DC

and brought here, but her need to pray had grown. More out of desperation than anything else. And yet, for a long time, God had been the one who listened to her thoughts. The yearnings of her heart. When there was no one else, He had been there.

Rather than seeing it as invasive, she sought comfort in never being truly alone.

Kenna strode out of the bathroom to find Maizie at the tiny desk on the hard wood chair typing furiously at the computer. "What's new, Maze?"

The girl started, then glanced over. "Huh?"

"You were pretty focused there. Sorry I disturbed you."

"Oh." Maizie's expression changed. "I shouldn't do that."

The teen thought she should be more conscious of her surroundings? "You're safe here, so it's fine to lose your awareness in what you're doing."

Even if there hadn't been anyone else in the room while Kenna had been in the shower, that didn't mean the girl was at risk—at least, not any more than she would normally be.

Kenna sat on the end of the bed and started to put her boots on. "Anything new with Kart, known associates, other properties he might own...or Jax?" She'd rather hear about Jax not Kart, but Javier had to be the priority until he was found.

Maizie pushed out a breath between tight lips. "I want to find him so badly." The teen rubbed her hands on her thighs. She wore wide leg jeans and that same zippered sweater with the hood—thin material in concession to the heat.

Meanwhile Kenna had on shorts and a short-sleeved T-shirt. Anyone who looked at her would see the scars on her forearms, but she'd rather have opted for Maizie's tactic and kept them hidden. Usually she wore a sweat-wicking base layer that cooled her under whatever shirt she had on. She also tended to avoid hot climates, especially in summer. That way she didn't have to do the bare-arms thing.

But right now that wasn't an option.

And it had her on edge.

Don't think about it. Who cared if people saw her scars? It wasn't a secret what'd happened to her. If they couldn't see them, people asked about them. Practically everyone she met knew her history—or so it seemed.

Maizie tapped her mouse pad. "Stairns is across town. He looked at a house that was under Benjamin's legal name. There are two more, one owned by Anthony. Crash pads by the sound of it. But it'll take him all day to drive between them."

"Nothing at Ben's?"

Maizie shook her head. "Stairns said it looked like a place Ben had just so he could go do all the things the Bible says will keep you out of heaven."

Kenna frowned, figuring out what that meant. She could guess. "That's one way of putting it."

Maizie said, "He's on his way to the one Anthony kept now. Apparently, it's on the side of a lake. The maps app has a satellite image that makes it look like it's a fishing spot. Unless he had a cabin or something there's nothing else there."

"Everyone needs a getaway. Even bad guys," Kenna said. "Maybe he takes a tent and camps."

Maize glanced over her shoulder. "I wonder who owns it now they're dead."

Kenna smirked. "I say we put them on the market as the owners, sell them, and give the proceeds to a children's home. Or some kind of trafficking victim's assistance place."

Maizie shot her a grin, shadowed though it was. "I found a few of those. We could make a big anonymous donation. I've been reading testimonials from the people who live in one."

"Yeah?"

Maizie nodded. "Elizabeth wanted me to see what they do. Not really so I can go stay there or whatever." Her tone took on an edge. "I don't want…"

"No one is going to make you go anywhere you don't want to go," Kenna said. "Or do anything you don't want to do."

"What if I don't want to make my bed?"

Kenna glanced at the perfectly made bed, wondering if Maizie had actually slept since she and Stairns arrived here.

Maizie said, "I mean my bed in the trailer."

"Ah." Kenna wanted Maizie to make her father's trailer her home, still she winced like not making the bed was the worst. "You're going to be a slob?" She even added a mock gasp at the end.

"I know." Maizie sighed. "I'm a terrible person."

Kenna chuckled.

"Maybe I am, since I haven't found Javier yet."

Kenna squeezed her shoulder. "This isn't a country where you can run an ID and get a surveillance hit." Far as she could tell there weren't any cameras on the street in town, and she hadn't seen many camera doorbells.

"Nothing on social media either." Maizie sighed. "This Kart guy is too smart for that. He knows how to stay below the radar." Maybe that was why he'd moved to this part of the world in the first place.

"Let's think this through." Kenna went back to finish lacing her second boot and set her foot on the carpet. "If he kills Javier, he would want Navarro to know. If he wants money, or some other kind of payback, then why didn't he contact Navarro for that as well? What's he waiting for?" She couldn't help thinking there was something she was missing here.

Unless Kart had contacted Navarro and no one told her.

"Does it have to do with Sheriff Preston coming?" Maizie said. "Maybe he's holed up waiting for his cousin to get here until he does what he is going to do."

Kenna had been under the impression Elliot called the shots. She thought over that...waiting for instructions from the boss? "Bonus, Navarro is going to be out of his mind with worry until Kart delivers the message. Maybe cousin Elliot really is the one who calls the shots." She worked her mouth side to side. "But with all of Navarro's men out looking for the boy—"

"And us."

Kenna nodded. "There's a whole lot of attention on the town, and people out looking for Kart." She bounced her knee. "What is his endgame?"

"I think he wants to believe he's the big man, but he actually has to wait for Elliot for orders."

Or Kart would turn the boy over to Elliot, maybe.

Perhaps that was the ultimate payback for Navarro—to know the boy was a captive. Kenna pushed off the implications, not wanting to swim in thoughts of the worst things a man could do to a child. She prayed it wasn't that.

And prayed Maizie wouldn't have to live with the knowledge another child grew up the way she had.

"Give me a lead." Kenna sighed. "Something." She didn't mean for her tone to be so short, but frustration ran hot. She had to do something or she would drown in the worry. The fear.

"I'm working on it."

"I know you are, Maze." Kenna shifted over on the bed and grabbed the phone Maizie had given her right after she was rescued. It looked like one of her dad's old flip phones. She hadn't thought they even made those anymore. "Huh."

"What is it?"

"I have messages. It's Ramon. Just says, *Call me.*" She shook her head and dialed the number, putting the phone to her ear.

"Finally."

"What's up?" She had her boots on, and she was ready to go. She just didn't want to leave Maizie here alone—and unprotected.

"Word in the hospital is your boy woke up."

Jax was awake.

"Friend of mine is a nurse, and I had her switch to that floor so she could keep me apprised."

"Thank you." Kenna sank back onto the end of the bed, more relieved than she could find words for. But there were more things than just Jax to discuss right now. "What about Javier? Anything on finding him?"

"Nothing. No one matching his or Kart's descriptions have been admitted to the hospital. No one's seen either of them on the street. I called the doctor, but I'm waiting for a call back."

"You really think Kart might actually have reached out to him?"

"I think it's worth asking everyone," Ramon said. "He ain't invisible, and three-year-olds make noise. Someone will see them eventually."

Kenna winced. "Thanks for updating me about Jax. I appreciate it."

"See if he knows where Kart might be."

That was a long shot. "Right." Kenna hung up and stood. "I need to—"

"I know." Maizie sat back in the chair. "I'll deadbolt. This room can't be accessed through the window, and there's no adjoining door. I'll wedge the door with a chair and keep my gun close."

Kenna blinked.

"Stairns taught me how to shoot. And a bunch of self-defense moves, but they're more like 'how to do serious damage' than actually escape someone. He showed me some of those, too." Maizie motioned to a backpack on the floor. "I also have a knife and pepper spray."

Kenna stared at her.

"I'll be scared, but I'll also be okay."

She wanted to hug the girl.

Maizie's expression softened. "Go. I'll survive."

That made her want to repeat what she'd said before to the girl. That the goal here, for both of them, wasn't simply to survive. The goal was to live and thrive.

Kenna gripped the door handle.

"Go."

"Get the weapons out. And get that chair." She didn't want anyone coming in uninvited.

Maizie came over to the door.

Kenna waited in the hall until the deadbolt clicked into place. The sound of Maizie wedging a chair under the handle. Since Stairns had the rental car she walked to the hospital, formulating a plan to get past the agents at the door.

Thankfully it was early still, so the heat of the day hadn't built to full force. But it meant a night Javier had been scared.

She wanted to be out finding him, but seeing Jax might give her mind a break from trying to push for an idea. Then her mind might come up with something while she thought about other things. Not exactly a hardship, even if it sometimes made her feel guilty. She should have one-hundred-percent focus on the search regardless of if it was unrealistic to avoid sleeping or eating. Or the fact they had no leads.

She snuck in a side door and took the stairs to the second

floor. Two FBI agents outside the room sat in chairs—no, they were slumped over. She didn't see any wounds, or blood.

Kenna stepped out into the hall and let the stairwell door click shut behind her.

It was too quiet.

She drew the weapon Stairns had left for her and crept down the hall. The two agents were about to fall to the floor, chin to chest. She checked the pulse on the closest one and found a faint thrum. Surely the hospital had security. Or staff to sound the alarm. But there was no one around.

What is going on?

Kenna found a cell phone in the inside suit jacket pocket and used the agent's thumb to unlock it. She found what looked like conversations with the handler in his texts. She dialed the number.

"ASAC Barnes' office."

"Your guy in Cielo Ardiente on the detail for Special Agent Oliver Jaxton, and his partner, have both been compromised. They need backup immediately."

"And your name—"

Kenna tucked the phone back where she'd found it without hanging up.

Then she prayed, grasped the handle, and stepped into the room. Her heart squeezed in her chest at what she saw. "Get away from him."

Chapter Twenty-Two

"Back. Up." Kenna lifted the gun.

Jax strained, his body leaned over toward her. Reaching for...the call button. He spotted her and gasped.

Kart turned from his spot over by the window, a gun of his own in his hand. "I've been waiting for you to show."

She held hers raised. "Put it down. Backup is on the way, so you get *one* shot to leave here alive."

His mouth curled up at the corners. "Straight to the point. I like that about you."

Jax managed to right himself. They'd taken the tube out of his throat, but he didn't look like he could push over a piece of paper right now. Kart moved the gun to point at Jax, who tensed. "I know you."

He was still out of it, then? But memories were coming back. Maybe he remembered Kart along with the torture. If not for the fact Javier wasn't here, she'd have shot him right now where he stood.

"Remember what I said?" Kenna kept her focus on Kart. "He dies, you die."

Kart chuckled.

"There's nothing funny about any of this," she said. "Where's Javier?"

Jax glanced between them. "Kenna?" His voice sounded raspy, and he was definitely confused as to what this was.

The guy probably wanted to know where his detail might be. Then again, if this was the first time he'd woken up since the compound, then he needed to be caught up on a lot of things.

She couldn't get into it all right now, though. Not with Kart here...but no child.

What was the plan?

"Why are you even here?" Kenna asked. She wanted to shoot his leg, or some other fleshy part of him and get him to start talking. But the risk he might shoot Jax was far too high. "What do you want?"

"I wanted to see you. Obviously."

Kenna wanted to scream at him and demand answers.

He thought he had the power here, but he didn't. As soon as he told her where to find Javier, he would realize it was true.

"I go where I want. I do what I want."

"Is that right?" She lifted her chin. "Like drugging FBI agents so you can sneak in here?"

"I had some help, but I have to say that was pretty creative." Kart swung the gun over to her and smirked. "How about I kill you instead of him?"

"I'll kill you at the same time, most likely. Then it will be over for both of us." She stayed where she was, standing her ground.

Jax shifted in the hospital bed. "Kenna." He said her name like a warning.

Kart said, "You kill me, you'll never find Javier."

Kenna shrugged one shoulder. "Assuming the child is

even still alive. Which is unlikely." Let him believe she wasn't convinced the boy had survived the past few hours with him. And at the same time she'd told Jax there was a child's life at stake right now.

Where were the medical staff? Or security? Even the FBI.

Stairns had surely called the closest office by now to send down agents to look through the compound Kart had occupied. But that would've been in the wee hours of the morning. Now it was barely eight, and a coastal hurricane was all any news report wanted to talk about.

The hospital should be teeming with patients and staff. Not two agents who'd been drugged, or tased, or otherwise knocked out.

Why not just shoot them?

She got the feeling yet again that he had orders from someone else. Kart wasn't in control of the situation he'd found himself in. Like at the compound when it had been clear he'd like nothing better than to kill her, or even hurt her a little bit for his own amusement. But he hadn't.

Because they'd been waiting for his cousin, Elliot Preston.

And Maizie had told her the sheriff was still on his way down here, though encountering travel setbacks.

It could be that Kart was currently under the same orders as before. Not to kill her.

Had he really dumped the child somewhere and set up this elaborate scheme...for what? To get her to show up when she heard Jax was alive. Information that had come through Ramon.

Which made her question Ramon's honesty as well as cast doubt on whether the former fed had been working against her all this time. Or undermining her ability to find the child. Did Ramon know where Javier was? If he did and it had all been subterfuge, he was a seriously good actor.

"The boy is alive," Kart said. "For now."

"So what happens next?" As much as she tried to fight it, she had to shift her weight. Soon her arm wouldn't be able to hold the weight of the gun, raised like she had it. Did he know that she lacked the strength? Was that why he seemed to be stalling. "What's the plan here, Ian?" She used his first name to throw him off balance, and by appearances it worked.

He hesitated.

"You probably want to hurry it up before we're swarmed with people." She tried to sound nonchalant.

"Why do you think I came here, but to kill the FBI agent so he can't tell anyone what happened at the compound?" He almost smirked.

"He doesn't know anything. He doesn't remember anything." Kenna stared him down. "Problem solved." He didn't need to kill Jax. "So let's get going. We can settle this elsewhere."

"You know, you almost had me fooled that it might've just been basic human consideration—"

"Which you know nothing about," she pointed out.

"But you really do care about him." Kart studied her. "Maybe you even love him." Kart was only trying to bait the two of them. He wanted her off her game as much as she wanted the same from him.

Out the corner of her eye, Kenna saw Jax look at her. "So you kill him, and I kill you." She paused, her gun still trained on Kartom. "What does that get you?"

"I'll die knowing you have nothing, and I won."

Kenna chuckled. She might lose, but she wouldn't have nothing. "That's not the definition of winning. You'll be dead, and I'll still be here. The one who carries on my legacy? That would be me when I go hunt down everyone under your protection. Everyone who is connected to your life, personal and professional. Everyone you've ever cared about. I'll bank-rupt their businesses. Ruin them financially. Spread their secrets all over the internet. I'll destroy their lives."

Surely he'd heard the term *scorched earth*.

"A little bloodthirsty there, Kenna." His brows rose. "I like it."

She pressed her lips into a thin line. As if he might've corrupted her into acting like this? She could be that vindictive all by herself.

Maybe he just didn't understand how loyalty worked, or the way she was with family. How people who looked out for each other in her small circle were all in, the way they couldn't be if the circle was larger. When it came to the people she cared about—even if it was only Maizie, Stairns and his wife, Ryson and his family, and Jax—-all that protective instinct distilled in a way that meant she went to bat with everything she had in her.

Thank You.

She had the God-given will and the skills to do this—and she thanked Him that Kart was here, not where Maizie was.

Kenna lifted her free hand. She switched her gun to her other hand, making it look like it was purely so she could pull out her phone. He didn't need to know she wouldn't be able to hold up the gun much longer.

She hit the middle button and held the phone to her ear, listening to it ring.

Kart stared at her like he couldn't believe what she was doing. Jax might be smirking, but she couldn't let that smile distract her right now.

Maizie picked up. "Hello?"

"Everything good?" Kenna kept her expression passive, so Kart wouldn't see the fear that had frozen her solid.

"Yes." The teen sounded confused.

She could've collapsed on the floor from sheer relief. "Just checking." Kenna cleared her throat. "I'll call you back."

They needed to develop some code words.

She snapped the phone shut and stowed it back in her pocket. This wasn't a ruse, or distraction, so someone could hit back at her by attacking Maizie. If it was, then maybe Stairns had been the target instead of the teen. He could take care of himself, and she would call him as soon as she could.

Did Kart have others working for him, or with him?

Kenna said, "Let's go, Kart. Leave the fed, and let's go."

He chuckled. "Leave your gun. Then we go. Together."

Kenna was done stalling for help that was apparently not even coming. Trying to figure out what this was, and whether it had even worked to convince Kart that killing Jax wasn't worth the risk. He wanted her, but he could table tying up the loose end of a conscious Jax. For now, anyway.

She side-stepped slowly. "I'll be leaving my gun with Jax."

Kenna handed off her gun to the man in the hospital bed. Then she gave him her phone, since that was better than it ending up in Kart's hands. The last thing she wanted to do was hand the guy all her personal contacts. But Maizie could still track her with the necklace.

Jax held on to her hand a little longer than he needed to. "Do you know what you're doing?"

"Always."

She shivered, and it had nothing to do with the chill air pumping out of the vent in the ceiling. The air-conditioning at max in order to beat the heat outside just rose goosebumps on her arms and legs. The shiver was more about leaving him. She wanted nothing more than to sit with Jax and talk. Find out why no one had responded to the quiet on this floor of the hospital. Find out where the closest able-bodied fed was right now.

To Kart she said, "Let's go."

She wanted to give Jax some parting words. A "take care" last word or a joke that was just between them. Her mind stayed traitorously blank. She couldn't think of anything that would lighten the mood or ease his worry or pass on some kind of message.

Neither could she tell him how to contact Stairns and Maizie—hopefully he would just call the last number she dialed. There definitely wasn't the chance to tell him that he should be cautious of Ramon Santiago. Or that the man was even here.

All she could do was glance over her shoulder and try to put everything into her expression instead. So that he understood she knew what she was doing.

At least, she hoped so.

Jax must have caught something of her intention—or her frustration. He nodded.

The trust in his gaze was something she always wanted to see. The respect of a good man. She would never be anything like Kart if she had the choice. She needed to button up the part of her that would go scorched earth if anything happened to her friends and be the person that still small voice wanted her to be.

The part of her that couldn't be an FBI agent anymore because she didn't fit the bill. She would never make the cut. Didn't need to end up like Ramon Santiago, walking the dark side.

She wasn't good like Jax. He didn't need to know she would never measure up. Maybe he knew and didn't care. But she could have integrity anyway.

Kart shoved her shoulders. She nearly stumbled, jogged from her dissonant thoughts by his jerky move. Her thoughts probably made no sense, anyway. Maybe the only person she was kidding was herself, and her ability to be in denial was back in full force.

She'd been doing pretty well with accepting reality lately.

This whole Mexico trip had been upsetting. In so many ways.

Kenna blew out a long breath. "Elevator?"

He shoved her again. "Stairs."

Kenna winced. In the echoey concrete stairwell, she chanced a glance back at him as they rounded the landing between floors, headed down to one. "Where's Javier?"

"Somewhere you don't need to worry about him."

"Unlikely. Unless you've returned him to his uncle or dropped him off at the best children's home in the world." Either way the kid wouldn't emerge from this unscathed.

"He's alive. I've got someone watching him."

Kenna focused on holding the rail in case he tried to send her down the stairs at high speed. After all, his intention could have been to kill her in here, out of sight of anyone. Or injure her badly enough she would be incapacitated.

"Door."

She pushed out into a parking lot behind the hospital. She thought she spotted movement at the edges of her awareness. A spark of disquiet that things weren't quite right out here.

But were they friend, or foe?

Surely the FBI only wanted to ensure their people—including Jax—were all right. They'd proven already they didn't care about her. Yet another person who believed she didn't measure up, but she tried not to care about the opinions of people she'd never met. It didn't matter if they assumed she would never rise to Jax's level when she'd only fallen from grace so far that she now occupied the same dark places the bad guys did.

It could be Ramon's voice in her head, his doubts whispered in her ear.

Or it could be the stone-cold truth.

She'd never felt this way with Bradley. But then, maybe with her being the daughter of a famous investigator and him being the son of a politician she simply hadn't felt off balance. He'd been the one who had to prove to the rest of the agents they worked with that he wasn't a political hire, good for FBI public relations. She'd been the blue-collar, grass-roots investigator with a nomadic childhood. He'd grown up with a silver spoon and roots.

Jax was a little more down-to-earth than Bradley, even if he'd been raised upper middle class. Certainly he'd never had his birthday at an Applebee's.

Still, she felt more off balance with Jax now she wasn't an FBI agent. She had more to prove these days, if she wanted to convince people they should be together. And yet, why did she even care what people thought?

Everyone they knew was all on board with the thing growing between her and Jax.

Her front collided with the trunk of a car. Not the pickup Kart had stolen from the ranch. She'd been too distracted with thoughts of Jax and their relationship—if she even wanted to think of it like that—to realize where he was walking her.

Now reality hit her all over again.

Kart clicked a button on a set of keys, and the trunk lid lifted. "Get in."

She whirled around to him, already stating her objection. His gun hand slammed down onto her forehead and Kenna crumpled.

She felt herself being lifted, and then he dug in her pockets. She pretended she couldn't fight back so he thought she was helpless. That meant swallowing back bile that threatened to make a mess everywhere—which she would have to lay here in.

The trunk lid closed.

She hissed out a breath into the darkness. Kidnapped again, but thanks to Maizie she could be tracked.

Kenna grinned, feeling a tiny chuckle bubble up in her throat. She tugged the pepper spray he hadn't found from her pocket. He was going to regret this. She would get Javier back, and get free, and Kart wouldn't be able to stop her.

The car swerved all the way across town. She guessed it took about twenty minutes, and then he hit the brakes and she rolled against the carpeted side wall.

Kenna rolled her eyes. He had to have done all that on purpose just to throw her off balance.

She heard him slam the driver's door and waited for the trunk to open, ready to pounce at him and hit him with the pepper spray.

Nothing.

Kenna kept waiting.

What was he doing? What could he possibly be...

The trunk lid flipped open.

She launched up, her finger already on the button, and realized that Kart held Javier in front of him. Anything she sprayed at him, the child would get full in the face. Tears running from his eyes, nose leaking.

"Nice try." Kart took the pepper spray from her and stepped back, still holding the boy. "Better luck next time."

Chapter Twenty-Three

Kenna blinked awake, sucked in a breath, and started to sit up. Little hands grasped at her arm, and she heard a whimper, though it might have been her.

The back of her head pounded. Kart had knocked her out almost as soon as he'd forced her to walk inside the house at gunpoint. After that it had been nothing but black.

She'd gotten a look at the woman in the house in the seconds before he slammed his gun on the back of her head and Kenna had crumpled to the floor. Thin, jeans cut low so she could see both the woman's hip bones. Stringy blond hair that hung to her waist and dark circles under her eyes.

Kenna blinked some more, and the room came into focus. A grungy bathroom. She was in the tub, presumably because he'd dumped her in here. She lay with her body at an awkward angle, and her head pressed against broken tiles behind her.

She hissed out a breath. Her jaw hurt, along with everything else.

Javier stood beside the bathtub, dried tears on his face.

His hair stuck out in every direction. Kenna reached out and rubbed her thumb over his cheek. "Hey, kid."

She didn't even know if he spoke English.

The child whimpered. His bottom lip pouted out, but he said nothing to her.

She didn't like the overwhelming fear in his eyes. Who knew what he'd been through? The best she could think of was that he'd been ignored and neglected and was simply hungry and in need of a bath so he could sleep and heal. The worst wasn't something she wanted to think about.

Muted shouting came from the other side of the closed bathroom door. The whole room was barely larger than the bathroom at the hotel she shared with Maizie.

Time to plan.

The last thing she wanted to do was lie here and wallow in her current situation. She would rather let Kart believe he had won, that he'd captured both her and Navarro's nephew successfully. That Kenna had been subdued enough she wouldn't be able to fight back even if she wanted to.

But why did he need both of them?

And why go to such lengths at the hospital to do it? She could only think his intention really had been to kill Jax. Maybe he hadn't been expecting her and she disrupted the plan, so he'd taken her instead. So he'd have her when Elliot showed up.

Playing both ends of his game so he could produce a result either way.

She couldn't get her thoughts together well enough to figure it out.

Kenna looked around and spotted a washcloth on the edge of the cracked sink. A grimy rag. Close enough to her that she could reach over the toilet and grab it. She wiped the kid's face, trying to give him some semblance of care even in the middle of this.

The boy clambered over the edge, sliding into the bathtub, and landed on her. Kenna grunted.

He cuddled up to her, his face in her neck. She pretty much melted.

Kids weren't usually people she had around after she saved them, and she wasn't always sure what to do or say with them. Not beyond, *Do you want to get out of here?* and *Let's go.* This one let her know what he needed, which was good because she didn't know enough Spanish to reassure him.

She could do *this.*

Kenna switched up her plan to get out of the empty tub in favor of staying where she was, rubbing her hand up and down the little boy's back. He shuddered and sighed against her.

"Okay." She kept her voice gentle, hoping he understood the sentiment. "We're gonna be okay."

The muffled yelling escalated. She could make out broken English in a higher tone, from the woman she'd seen when she came in the house. Kenna didn't like making snap judgments but the impression she'd gathered in just a couple of seconds was that the woman was likely a customer of Kart's.

Someone hooked on whatever he sold locally.

She hadn't been Hispanic, but Caucasian. So maybe someone who'd come down to Mexico for some of the same reasons Kart had—to escape the laws and regulations north of the US–Mexico border. Down here there were likely the same laws and regulations in effect. It just depended on the local police and what they chose to enforce. And how they did it.

So effectively, just like anywhere else.

The woman seemed like someone he thought he could

bend to his way of thinking. Or who he could coerce for a favor in exchange for...whatever she wanted from Kart. Drugs. Something else? Kenna had no idea. But she couldn't imagine the woman was all that reliable.

The kid started to drift off to sleep, letting out a long shuddering breath.

She did the same, trying to relax so Javier rested rather than absorbed the tension she felt. Getting up wasn't going to be so fun, considering how hard her head pounded right now. She would have to eventually though, in order to escape.

"You can't do this!" The woman's muffled yell hit her.

"I do what I want, Shey," Kart's voice boomed across the house. "I'm leaving."

The woman said something without yelling, but the tone sounded desperate. Kart said something else.

A couple of minutes later the front door slammed, shaking the whole house.

Kenna wasn't going to think about whether she could handle a woman alone. If Kart really had left, then it was a better time to take a shot at leaving than when he was here. Even with a child relying on her.

Now or never.

She prayed, whispering the words as she sat up. Sat on the edge of the bath. Got her feet under her. They'd taken her shoes but left her with socks. She had dirt smudges and scratches all over, so she didn't look in the mirror.

Her arms rang with pain, up to her hands and down to her elbows, but she ignored it and held Javier on her hip to take some of the weight off her arms.

She listened at the door.

Then stared down at the chrome handle, wondering. It had to be locked from the outside if they'd been shut in here specifically. She tapped her knuckle on the door. It sounded hollow. She grasped the handle and turned it. Then the handle stopped at a point and didn't give any more.

Kenna listened some more.

Wherever the woman had gone, she was quiet. Maybe on the back porch, smoking.

Please, Lord.

Now or never.

Kenna backed up and kicked the door.

It splintered open, away from the handle. Her foot caught on the shards of wood and flared with pain. She ignored it and kicked again, then slammed her hip and shoulder against the door. It cracked open. A chair wedged on the other side of the door handle stayed in place. Kenna kicked it away.

Teeth gritted.

Head pounding.

She stepped into the hall and looked both ways, letting out a long breath as she scanned and listened. No one came running.

She patted Javier's back as she walked, as a nanny or someone might do to sooth a crying child. The hall opened to a filthy kitchen on the right. Trash and dishes piled up. Empty containers and pizza boxes. Flies buzzing around.

Farther down she saw blond hair, where Shey sat on the couch, head lolled to the side.

Kenna raced past her to the front door and flung it open. Her socks slid across the floor, and she stumbled against the wall. The woman screamed behind her.

She didn't even look. This could be the end, or she could survive and rescue a child.

A bullet exploded behind her.

Run.

The round embedded in the wall beside her, and the woman continued firing wildly.

Kenna raced outside, across the grassy weeds and the gravel of the front yard. Her foot jabbed on something, but she kept going in her socks, pushing everything from her mind.

The gunshots continued from inside the house, but Kenna held tight to the boy and ran. He jostled in her arms and came awake, crying again.

"It's gonna be okay, Javi." Kenna jogged down a side street, along what counted for a sidewalk. Ignoring the pain in her foot.

A car roared around the corner at the end of the street.

Kenna crouched beside a parked car while it whizzed past and took a few measured breaths. Then she lifted up and continued. She'd saved the boy, and now she just had to get out of here. Back to town. To a phone, or some other way to get help.

"Okay, here we go." She waited and looked around the corner. A couple of boarded-up storefronts. Two men across the street spotted her.

Then Kenna walked, heading straight and making a beeline for...she didn't know. But she would get there in one piece with the child in her arms. Assuming her forearms didn't give out and she dropped him on the ground.

"Hey, woman!"

Realizing one of the men had been calling out to her, she turned her head to the side, just slightly. "No, thank *you*."

"Woman, you stop!"

The other one yelled something in Spanish.

She walked faster.

Another car engine revved. Actually multiple cars, which rounded the corner up ahead and sped toward them. Two Mercedes pulled over by her. Kenna backed up to the building. Her back hit the bricks and she held on to Javier. What else could she do?

The first car's doors opened. Ramon climbed out and said something to the two men, barking an order full of authority. They backed up and walked away.

Kenna let out the breath she'd been holding. "How did you find me?"

Ramon looked her up and down and winced. "Come on. Get in." He held the back door open, and the guy who'd been in the back seat went to the second car.

She slid in and shifted Javier to the seat beside her.

Ramon got in the front passenger seat and turned to the boy. He spoke softly in Spanish and used the word *Papa*, which caused Javier to nod. Then he gave the order to the driver, who pulled out.

"How did you find me?" she asked. They turned the corner at the end of the street, and the second car went the opposite direction. She frowned. "What are they doing?"

Ramon sighed. "What question do you want me to answer first?"

"Just start talking." Kenna felt little fingers on her arm and shifted to hold Javier's hand.

Ramon looked from the boy to her. "We know what house it was, so they're going to pay her a visit."

"They should take her to the police so she can be prosecuted as an accessory to kidnapping."

Ramon said something to the driver.

The guy let out a burst of laughter.

"It's the right thing to do." Kenna might have it in her to be vicious and vindictive like them, but that didn't mean she had to act on it.

"This is cartel justice. You think we need the police getting involved?" Ramon snorted. "People will find out Navarro is vulnerable and crawl out of the woodwork to challenge his authority."

"Street justice isn't a reason to take lives."

"So you'll never understand this life." Ramon shrugged one shoulder. "Doesn't mean it's wrong."

"Great." She patted the shoulder of the seat. "Hey, drop me in town by that café."

"You don't want to see Navarro? He will want to thank you for helping find Javier."

"I didn't help. You set me up, and I got kidnapped." She glanced out the window. He was the one who had called to say that Jax was awake, because someone he knew at the hospital passed on that information. But way more had gone on there than just Jax being awake.

He shifted in his seat. "What are you talking about?"

"The hospital. You said Jax was awake—"

"And was he?"

Kenna blinked. "Well, yeah."

"So what's the problem?"

"Something went down there. Kart got in and took out two FBI agents. He was waiting for me. But why would he do that if he had Javier already?" She needed to think this through, but she also couldn't believe Ramon hadn't known there was something more going on.

Ramon shook his head. "You think I know?"

"Well, how did you know where to find me?"

"That guy with you. Stairns. He passed on a message that you'd been taken from the hospital and called with your location. Turns out you rescued yourself."

"Right." Did that even make sense? "Great. You found me."

He got out his phone and made a call, speaking in Spanish so fast she switched off listening and instead focused on Javier and the road outside the window.

When they were nearing town, she said, "Drop me off in town, remember?"

He held up two fingers and didn't stop talking. His voice rose, and the tone shifted. He barked a couple of things, then hung up. "There was an incident at the hospital. Someone put the call out on their phone system that the second floor had a quarantine situation."

"So he cleared out the floor." She hadn't seen any staff or security when she went to see Jax and found Kart with him—or on the way out. "And made sure no one disturbed him."

"It's resolved now, and there are feds crawling all over the place now, apparently. So my guy, he works security, can't get to his station."

Kenna's stomach tightened. Feds crawling all over didn't sound good. "Are they moving Jax?"

"Don't know."'

She'd given Jax her phone. "Let me borrow your cell."

Ramon flinched. "We'll drop you off and take Javier home. You can find your people yourself." He spoke to the driver, who nodded.

"Fine." She would walk into the hotel lobby looking like she'd been dragged through a berry bush with only socks on her feet. No wallet, no phone, and no weapons. *Great.* "This whole situation has been just great. I'm never gonna want to come back here after this."

Not that she'd been planning on a Mexico vacation, but still. The dangerous men who lived in Cielo Ardiente had soured her on the whole country.

She just wanted to get her friends and get out before Elliot appeared. Maybe she should get Maizie to use Kenna's credit card to get them a full security detail, so they had a safe way to leave. Enough with the distractions and the danger. Maizie needed to be back at the trailer in Colorado.

"This town is my life," Ramon said. "Some of us don't get a choice whether we like it here or not."

"Didn't mean to hit a sore spot. I'm just tired and frustrated."

He might not have picked this life, but he could have stopped before he made one of the choices that got him in the employ of a cartel leader. He could've made his way back to America and done the work to clear his name. Or lived under a fake name and had a quiet life where he didn't break the law.

His phone rang, and he held it to his ear and listened. "Okay. *Gracias.*" He hung up. "Navarro wants you at the ranch."

"Ramon. Let me out in town." She gripped the seat and leaned forward. "I'm not going to the ranch. Let. Me. Out."

He shook his head. "Boss's orders."

"I don't care!" She twisted and flipped the lock on the door. It would hurt when she hit the asphalt and rolled. She'd have to shift the boy's head from her lap where he'd fallen asleep.

Ramon grabbed her arm. "Don't."

She turned back to glare at him and stared down the barrel of a pistol. "Seriously?"

"Boss's orders."

Chapter Twenty-Four

Ramon opened the car door for Kenna. As she climbed out, wind from the storm front moving in from the coast whipped at her hair. She glared at him and nearly got knocked over by a housekeeper-type lady who gathered Javier from the back seat and raced with him toward the house.

Kenna leaned against the back quarter panel as Navarro stepped onto the front stoop, every inch the lord of the manor at this ranch. Did he really think she would simply bow to his will? She'd had enough of this place and these people who did whatever they wanted.

The housekeeper stopped so Navarro could speak to his nephew, which only made the boy start to cry. She had no idea why he'd settled down with her. Kenna didn't have "a way with kids" like some people seemed to. She was just who she was, no pretense. She figured kids respected a genuine person. They might actually be better at discerning that stuff. One day she might have children of her own, but Kenna couldn't imagine bringing them into the life she had now.

"Come in." Navarro waved her over.

Kenna folded her arms. "No."

Ramon stiffened beside her. The few other men around seemed interested in how this was going to play out.

"I'm going back to my hotel so I can take a shower and get out of here." She shrugged. "I'm not staying." She wanted to say, *And you can't make me*, but figured that might sound a little childish.

Too bad she was irritated and at the end of her rope enough to consider it. Kenna was about ready to throw a full-blown tantrum that would make Javier proud. She was glad Jax wouldn't be here to see it.

"You don't get to order me around," she added. "I don't work for you." She had nearly no power here if he wanted to push it—no weapons and zero way to pressure them.

Navarro stepped aside.

Stairns came out, followed by Maizie. Neither looked like they were here of their own accord. Tight expressions. Maizie hugged herself, a defensive mechanism to protect her space.

Kenna strode over to them and pulled the teen to her. It would look like a hug but was more like Kenna standing between Maizie and whatever might come at her. She whispered, "What happened?" low in Maizie's ear.

The girl wrapped her arms around Kenna's waist. "They kicked the door in. I screamed a lot, but no one helped me." She shuddered. "Stairns was already in the van."

Kenna glanced at her former boss. Stairns had a knot on his forehead, his eyes glassy—and mean. She'd never seen him this unhappy, and she didn't blame him.

The wind blew hair across her face. After tucking Maizie behind her, she turned toward Navarro. "Your men were abducting my friends, rather than saving your nephew? Interesting."

"It's called strategy."

"What do you want from us that was more important than Javier?"

His brows rose. "I have plenty of men, and I know how to..." His expression pinched. "What's the word? Right, I know how to multitask." He lifted his chin. "Inside."

Kenna stared at him. The last thing she wanted to do was to follow orders, with no argument. The last thing she wanted to do was go inside. Least of all right when he asked. Defiance was her only option right now.

Maizie's hand slipped against Kenna's.

She clasped her fingers, so the girl knew she had both Kenna and Stairns to watch her back.

Stairns went inside first. Then Navarro. Kenna followed them, Maizie beside her.

The TV in the living room played a news report, scrolling text along the bottom with a vacation town she recognized. An anchor struggled against wind and rain, the sound muted but subtitles showing up one word after the other.

"What's going on with the weather?" She glanced at Maizie.

"The hurricane changed direction. It's headed inland."

Okay, not super high on her priority list, but it could present a problem. "They always lose power the farther inland they come. It won't hit hard here, just over on the coast."

Maizie didn't need to look so worried. Although, probably her expression wasn't completely about the hurricane.

Navarro said, "I'd invite you to sit..."

She twisted around, still holding Maizie's hand, and glared at the cartel leader. Then she realized Navarro had probably killed people just for looking at him wrong.

Half a dozen men stood around the room, all armed. Not the first time she'd faced down something like this, and it probably wouldn't be the last. Ramon had conveniently disappeared again.

Traitor.

Kenna gave herself a second, so she didn't say something she shouldn't and get them all killed. "Maybe you could get me a drink, considering I just saved your nephew's life."

"You did lead my men to find Javier. For that I suppose I should be grateful." Navarro stared at her. "And yet Kart remains at large?"

"So how about letting us go? We can find him for you. Eliminate the problem." Both Maizie and Stairns stiffened at her words, but Kenna would be happy to turn Ian Kartom over to the feds—or even the police in Cielo Ardiente.

Navarro settled onto the couch. "I'm afraid I can't do that." He sat with his elbow on the back, his knees splayed out. Studying them with the eye of a hungry man at a meat market.

"If any of you touches her"—she nodded in Maizie's direction—"I will kill that person."

"The three of you are my guests here. My men know how to keep their business elsewhere, and not in my home." It almost sounded like a threat.

"*Guests* can leave whenever they're ready to go." Not that she knew a whole lot about social norms. "In that case, we'll be going now."

Navarro nearly grinned. "Stay. Listen to my proposition."

"I'm not for hire, and you have nothing that I want except a door for me to leave through."

He sighed. "Sit. Please. You are my guests until I say you can leave, and what happens to you is at my discretion."

She didn't move.

"For the time being, the three of you will remain here." Navarro's expression took on an edge. "I have a shipment coming in tonight at midnight. I got word Ian Kartom plans to intercept that shipment with the help of hired assistance from America. You'll be there with my men to ensure that doesn't happen. Another layer of...protection, shall we say."

Kenna's clenched down on her jaw so hard that it ached. "No, thanks." She didn't want to go up against a group of armed men. Especially not to protect drug money, or illegal substances—or whatever this "shipment" was.

"The health of your friends here depends on your cooperation."

"I've had enough of being a victim and being kidnapped." It was literally all that'd happened to her since she got here, and she was *done*.

"Be that as it may, you have the skills to ensure my delivery gets here on time and your loyalty will not be in question."

"You think someone in your circle is working with Kart? So sad. Why not just go ensure the shipment gets here all by yourself."

Navarro glared. "I'm not leaving my nephew."

"So you'll put this shipment in the hands of someone you definitely shouldn't trust?" Made perfect sense to coerce her. After all, she'd be completely neutral and have no intention of calling the FBI to intercept. "Why would Kart grab Javier and then me if he has his eye on this shipment?"

"Merely a distraction from his true purpose."

"Right. He just wanted to irritate you before he stole from you." So Elliot still wanted her, and it was up to Kart to deliver her.

"His designs are to throw me off my game," Navarro said. "Ensure my focus is diverted from the shipment, and threaten those I care about." Mostly she figured he cared about blood and money. And he probably saw power as equally valuable.

"What is it? Drugs?" She wanted to know what the shipment contained. "Because I'm not sure I care if you get that safely delivered back here."

"Inside the truck is six million dollars."

Kenna flinched. She had no filter right now—especially not on her expression—so why wouldn't he be able to see her surprise. "You just keep that kind of cash lying around?"

"As if I have to explain my business model to you?"

Kenna shrugged. Maybe he should. She could tell the FBI, via Jax, and he could get the credit. They should do that. If Kenna ever got intel they'd need, she should have him turn it over. Be his confidential informant who gave great tips.

"The money will get where it's going. Or your friends will be killed. This is your only priority for the next twelve hours." Navarro waved, and two men stepped forward with guns. "Your friends will be escorted to my guest suite. You may join them shortly to...clean up before the job tonight."

Kenna tried to get between the guy and Maizie. Stairns aided with covering her, but when one of the men pointed his gun at Stairns' forehead, Maizie slipped between them.

"Lead the way." Maizie lifted her chin and glanced back at Kenna with an expression very much like, *I can do this*.

Which was exactly what Kenna didn't want. After everything she'd been through, Maizie shouldn't *have* to.

She stared at them as they left the room. "If there's even one single scratch on them..."

"Yes, yes. Scorched earth. Biblical plagues." Navarro strode to the wet bar and poured himself a drink. "Whiskey?"

She shook her head. "How about a knife?"

He tipped his head back and chuckled. "So you can stab me? Hardly."

Kenna's legs were about to give out. She slumped onto the couch as far from where he'd sat as possible and put her feet on the coffee table. The bottom of her foot smarted, but she didn't bother looking.

Navarro strode over with his glass. He frowned at her foot. "Did you bleed on my carpet?"

She leaned over the end of the couch at the spot where she'd stood. "Looks like it."

She'd been through so much stress the last few days, her body wanted to shut down. She was about to lose consciousness. That kind of nap left her dead to the world—which wasn't good for needing to be aware of her surroundings. She wanted to go to the hospital where Jax was recovering, curl up in a chair beside him, and sleep as long as she could. If it wasn't for the fact Maizie and Stairns were here.

A niggle of worry in the back of her mind said she might not get a warm reception from him. After all, they hadn't talked much since they arrived here. He hadn't been mad—he'd been injured. In pain. That didn't mean he blamed her for what happened, but since the FBI were subdued and Kart had invaded his hospital room, he might now, though.

Kenna folded her arms and tried to figure out how she would stay awake now that she'd sat down. Her energy seemed to drain into the floor.

"You should rest before tonight." Navarro took a sip.

She let out a sigh. "I don't care about your money."

"But you care about your friends. That's why you're going to do exactly what I ask."

"You're a scumbag, you know that?" She'd been close to being able to leave. Now he was going to make her stay because he threatened people she cared about. She would have to commit crimes to satisfy him.

Navarro chuckled over his glass.

"How am I supposed to even trust that you'll keep your word and they'll be unharmed?" She might've appealed to his empathy over what Maizie had been through, but she doubted that would work. With a man like this, who had no heart? He was pure evil.

Kenna was sick of being scared.

Kidnapped.

Threatened.

Terrorized.

She continued, "You really think I'll be able to do anything to help with the state I'm in?"

"You'll make it work."

"Why don't you just hire better people, ones you can trust?" She turned only her head to look at him. "Then you wouldn't have to worry about being stolen from." Or do the job himself.

"Since you failed to kill Ian Kartom, we're all going to have to deal with his actions. I protect what's mine."

And she didn't? "None of this has anything to do with me. I didn't ask to be here, and everyone seems to think I can solve their problems."

"It's what you do, isn't it?"

"For criminals? No." She needed to be clear. "I help people who have no one else to turn to."

"That's it." He pointed at her with his glass. "I have no one else."

"With six million coming in? Hire someone. Pay for loyalty."

She needed to pay for a ride out of here—like an armed escort. Soon as she could get a phone, Kenna was going to have Maizie recite her credit card number and get some private security people over here to pick them up.

With helicopters.

And maybe a tank.

Surely he understood how loyalty worked, and she didn't

need to explain it to him. He'd even understand paying money for quality work. "There are literally a dozen other ways to do this that are more effective than kidnapping and coercion."

"You seem to only want to argue. As far as I can see the deal is already done." Navarro's phone chimed. He leaned forward to look at the screen, the cell lying on the tabletop. "Sleep. I'll tell you when it's time to go."

She didn't want to.

Like she'd said to him, there were a dozen other ways to do this. And a dozen other places she'd rather be right now. Navarro thought he could order people to do whatever he wanted. Which left Kenna bruised, filthy, and exhausted. The last time she'd slept had been in a bathtub holding onto his nephew.

She hadn't had quality rest in days.

Kenna sucked in a breath and pushed up off the couch. "Which room is she in?"

Navarro said, "I'll walk you."

"Whatever." As soon as he'd closed the door behind them, Kenna crossed to Maizie. She lifted the necklace over her head.

Maizie blanched. "You can't take off your tracker."

Stairns stood by the wall, saying nothing.

"I know where I am. What I want to be sure of is where *you* are." Kenna dropped the necklace over the teen's head.

Maizie pressed her lips together.

"Tuck it out of sight," Kenna said. "But I want you to keep it on, just in case."

"And if you get taken again? That's been happening a lot lately, and I don't have any of my stuff here." Maizie gasped.

"I know." She touched Maizie's shoulders and turned the girl to face her. Kenna didn't want to be alone and captive.

Not again—ever. But she knew what she could handle, even if she was battling with the end of her strength right now. "Keep it. Please." She squeezed Maizie's shoulders, then let go. "And when we're done with all this, we're both getting one each. Matching ones."

Maizie didn't smile, but that was okay. She unzipped the top couple of inches of her sweater and got the necklace situated inside and under her collar.

Kenna glanced between them. "I'll be back soon."

Chapter Twenty-Five

Kenna stared out the windshield at the jetties, boats lined up. A tourist spot an hour from Cielo Ardiente—maybe more. This wasn't the kind of place she'd think a delivery would come in. Which was probably exactly why Navarro chose it. "Where is the money coming in from?"

Ramon had parked out of the way, where they could watch a row of boats. Nothing headed this way out in the dark still water. At least, not with lights on. "Does it matter?"

"Matters where it came from in the sense that will indicate how it was obtained." Though, Kenna could easily guess it was dirty money—blood money—no matter what his answer would be.

"Because you want to secure your spot on that pedestal?"

Kenna fisted her hands on her knees and tried to be calm. Maizie and Stairns were captive because of her.

Like Jax had been. And now he was injured as a result.

With Jax she'd been thinking that she'd put him in this position—being here in Mexico. A good man, brought low because of her actions and choices. The great divide between him as a federal agent and a devout man who did the right thing.

And then there was Kenna with her tendency to hunker down when things got heavy. To retreat to her solitude. Focus on the job, and the things she could do *alone* to make the world a better place.

Helping the FBI hadn't done her any favors.

Trying to speak the truth only landed them here.

Right before she'd left, Kenna had checked on Stairns and Maizie one last time. Stairns had told her not to worry.

I've got this, Kenna. Do what you have to and don't worry about us.

Both of them knew it wasn't like she could switch off worry any more than he could. But knowing he was there to stand between Maizie and anyone who came at her made the world of difference to Kenna's peace of mind right now.

Ramon shifted in his seat, the way cops did after hours of surveillance. "There it is."

A boat piloted into the harbor, one man at the helm and another two armed with rifles on the bow. They pulled into an empty slip, and one man jumped out. Once they had the boat secured, they started to carry big duffel bags to a waiting semi-truck in the parking lot, close to the end where the slips were. Ramon had parked them on the opposite side.

"There a reason we're so far away?" she asked, not taking her attention from the men loading up the truck. One watching for anyone in case they approached. They knew what they were doing enough this was going fast. No one wanted to hang around where they were vulnerable, focused on loading up rather than protecting all the money.

Navarro's ill-gotten gains.

All the while, the wind and rain hammered around them. It was like they didn't notice.

"Are you going to ask questions the whole time?" Ramon muttered under his breath. "It is what it is. Just cool your jets."

She pressed her lips together and watched. Navarro had told them to escort the money and make sure it got back to him—that was all. But she'd figured they would be closer to what was happening than this.

The fire in her middle she'd been nursing since she first woke up in Mexico hadn't gone anywhere. But why wouldn't she be spitting mad? She was perfectly within her rights to be downright angry at all of this. And why should she keep quiet about any of it when she just kept getting dragged back into things?

Her friends' lives in danger.

Her life in danger.

Coerced into breaking the law in ways that could land her in serious trouble if she didn't keep things tight. The last thing she wanted was to be implicated in other crimes. To have to testify for even more things, or even face a legal battle.

Kenna was going to have to find a lawyer soon enough, but where did she find one she actually trusted? She'd seen so much corruption lately she needed someone either she knew, or her friends trusted.

The man on lookout tensed, said something to his friends, and readied his weapon. The muzzle flashed several times, the gunshots muted through the car so that she only heard the dampened sound of it. Still, she flinched.

From the other end of the parking lot, a group all in tactical gear raced across the lot.

"Feds?" Kenna said. They kind of looked like it, but she wasn't sure the way they moved correlated. The FBI taught tactics for raids. This seemed more like a swarm.

Ramon huffed. "Figures. Did you call them?"

"With what phone?"

As Kenna watched from the passenger seat of the car, they circled the truck. One of the men went down. Gunfire sounded like a conversation in the night. She knew they'd be yelling to the others to get down. Drop the weapons and take arrest positions. *Hands up, don't move!*

They sat there and watched it all go down. Maybe these were feds after all.

"You knew they'd be coming?" Kenna frowned. "You knew the feds would be here to intercept, and you didn't do what it would take to get the money out before then. You just cost my friends their lives. I'll lose all three of them." In horrible ways. "And their blood will be on your hands."

"Calm down."

Kenna sucked in a breath.

"That's not our delivery."

She glared. "Start talking, Ramon. Before I kill you where you sit and go fix this myself."

"Take a look over there." He pointed to the right.

She followed the line of sight and gasped at what she saw. *Elliot.* She'd seen an image on Maizie's computer of Sheriff Elliot Preston. If he was here, did that mean Kart wasn't far?

"Kart must have told his cousin that the delivery would arrive tonight." Her mind assimilated ideas faster than she could process which was wrong and which was right. "But did he really tip off the feds? Why would he do that?"

"To get a deal for Kart. Or secure Elliot's position as a law-abiding sheriff."

"After Kart distracted Navarro by kidnapping his boy and took me to the same house?" Did Kart really consider his biggest threats right now to be Kenna and the cartel leader? If he was trading information to the feds that was one thing, but why do it this way?

Finding him in Jax's hospital room might've been because

he'd been there making a deal. But why take out the guards only to kidnap her? Or had someone else called in the contagion on that floor? Maybe he had to make it look like he was still doing what Elliot ordered him to.

She wanted to wring the guy's neck. Then ask a hundred questions, figure out what was going on here. There was no mystery here she wanted to solve. But neither did she want to further Navarro's criminal empire.

If it wasn't for her friends, she would make Ramon let her out. Then find Kart before he got away with all of it in exchange for talking—and securing a win for the FBI.

No matter which way she sliced it, he was betraying his cousin and covering his own fate with safeguards, so he had a shot at getting out. If she was to take a page out of his book, she might get further than she had so far with this.

But would she like the person she became?

"And you knew it was going to happen." She shook her head. "What are we going to do about the delivery now? It's being seized."

"Yeah, but watch."

She was about to burst out of the car, just to try and release some of the tension. "This is unbelievable. You could've told me."

"You weren't gonna risk messing up your job. And now we know there is someone in Navarro's operation sympathetic to Ian Kartom, or working with him and Elliot Preston, who handed him the information about tonight's shipment. Just a case of figuring out who it was."

"Maybe there's no one. Or it's you." She shrugged, trying not to give off how she felt about Elliot being here. "You don't know how he found out about the information."

"We knew he was going to intercept." Ramon glanced at

her. "How else did he get the info than someone who knew about the delivery told him?"

"Maybe *you're* the leak. Or someone else got sloppy."

Ramon chuckled. "Now you're getting it."

"Navarro knows about this?"

"I'll be reporting in. Keeping him posted about the status of the delivery."

"By the looks of things, the status is that some of his money is going into the pockets of those feds. If that's who they are." Kenna shook her head. "I'd have thought they'd be recuperating after Navarro hit the hospital to get Jax out."

Ramon shrugged. "Maybe they don't care about justice... and it's your job now."

"If it's up to me to keep him safe, then give me that gun you brought for me so I can go get the delivery back and we can get Navarro his money." If he didn't let her and her friends go free, they were going to have serious words.

Ramon turned on the car engine. He backed out of the space they were in with no headlights, then turned and drove half a mile. He pulled in behind a warehouse with its own jetty. No boat.

"What is this?"

Ramon sighed. "See for yourself." He hit a button on his phone, and a garage door on the side of the warehouse rolled up. He pulled in and parked alongside a pickup with a camper shell that looked to be packed tight with...

"The money." In bags or bundles, wrapped up. Kenna climbed out, went over, and peered in the window. "The delivery was already here? The whole thing was a ruse."

"Now we know."

She turned to him. "You could've told me."

Ramon shrugged. "Too many people know, and it pollutes the results. That's why I'll never clear my name. I can't sort out who knows what, and who has too much to hide. Those feds out there? They're worse than you and I because they *pretend* to fight for justice. In the end they're as dirty as Navarro, but at least he's honest."

"The rest of the FBI isn't like a few agents here...ones who might not even have been agents."

"Pretty good ruse if they're not. Maybe the feds that grabbed your friend from the compound weren't feds either." Ramon made a *huh* sound in his throat. "I hadn't considered that, but now that I think it certainly could be. Maybe the ones at the hospital were just hired guys posing as agents."

"It's not a conspiracy." She'd had enough of those. And it wasn't that easy to pretend to be an agent with any accuracy—especially not when they'd encountered Stairns. Both Kenna and her former boss would've seen through it.

"Everything is a conspiracy. You wanna see with clarity? Buy a pair of binoculars." Ramon chuckled at his own joke. "Because you won't get the truth from people—especially if they have power."

"So you're lying, too."

"Guess you have to figure out about what." He sighed. "Just get in."

Kenna settled in the passenger seat of the truck. The whole unloading of that boat had been a ruse to draw out a mole, but it hadn't worked. Whichever one of Navarro's men had betrayed him was evidently working with Kart, and perhaps a whole group of dirty FBI agents. Or they'd passed on information in exchange for a kickback.

She doubted any of them had any loyalty to anyone else in this.

Just the money they'd get paid.

All she wanted was to get her friends and get out of this situation. They needed safety and a way home. Or at least away from the people here and their ill intentions, sucking the life out of Kenna every second because she couldn't see a way through. Or out.

Ramon pulled the truck onto the street and headed away from whoever those men had been, quickly making his way to the highway that led inland back to Cielo Ardiente.

"So how are you going to figure out which of Navarro's men betrayed him?"

"You let me worry about that." He glanced aside at her.

"No." Kenna flinched. "No way is Navarro going to drag me into a witch hunt. I'm not doing anything else for him."

"How do you know your friends didn't escape already?" Ramon chuckled. "Maybe they left you behind again."

"I hope they did. For their sakes." Kenna clenched down on her back teeth, wanting to scream. She'd need a phone or computer to track the necklace and find Maizie. Exactly why she'd given it to the girl.

Everything will be all right.

But neither her heart nor her mind wanted to believe it. She sat with her fists clenched, sitting completely straight trying to get a handle on this. Trying to pray didn't work. There was no peace. No answers. Nothing but frustration that had gotten worse and worse since she got here.

All her trying.

All her working.

None of it did any good when everyone around her dragged her into their schemes. Forced her to do their will as though she had no say. Everyone here had an angle, and she couldn't get herself out of it to even start untangling the mess without seeing how she wasn't that far removed from these people.

There are none good, no not one.

That was what the priest had said.

I give up.

There was nothing she could do to fix this. What was the point striving so hard? Or twisting herself in knots to get a win? It wasn't doing her any good. She'd been rescued. She'd been kidnapped again. She'd done what she could to keep Jax alive—and now her friends were caught up in this.

No matter what, things just got worse.

What is the point? I can't do anything on my own to help them.

She wanted to scream.

Control isn't the same as peace.

Ryson's voice rang in her head as though he'd spoken aloud here with her. But it was only Kenna and Ramon in the truck and he hadn't said anything. Her friend's words stuck in her mind.

Control isn't the same as peace.

Right now she had neither.

No control of any of this. And no peace.

She'd hit rock bottom, punched through, and found something deeper. Every nightmare she'd ever had. Every fear. Every inch of control torn out of her fingers.

And for what?

Come to Me, all you who are weary and burdened, and I will give you rest.

Tears rolled down Kenna's cheeks. Did she really have faith in the only one on her side right now? The only one able to help.

A God who saw her mess and wanted to give her rest?

"What's wrong with you?" Ramon asked.

She gasped, crying. Her whole body shaking.

I give up.

The past had repeated itself, and she hadn't been able to

save the man she loved. Again. Not enough strength. Not enough on her own. Brought to the end of herself.

To a place she found God, ready to extend His hand to her.

Kenna closed her eyes, whispering prayers of thanks in her mind. It didn't change where she was or where her friends were. But the peace that settled on her knowing God had them all in His hands gave her a warmth she hadn't felt... maybe ever in her life.

Thank You.

No matter what happened, she wouldn't be alone.

Headlights from an oncoming car flashed across the windshield. The vehicle parked on the side of the road up ahead.

Ramon flashed his headlights and pulled over behind the vehicle.

"What's going on?" Kenna asked, her throat hoarse. "Why are we stopping?" She swiped at her face and cleared her throat.

Ramon gripped the door handle. "Stay here. And try not to have another mental breakdown."

Chapter Twenty-Six

Kenna looked around at the dark of night, and a boarded-up gas station that looked like it had gone out of business years ago. Not super surprising considering they were in the middle of nowhere between the coast and Cielo Ardiente, a hurricane behind them.

She swiped at her cheeks and felt the smile on her lips. Almost giddy at the well of peace and joy surging up in her. The situation hadn't changed. Her friends were still in danger, and she was being forced to be the accomplice of a dangerous criminal. Nothing about this was different. But from the core of her being, Kenna was a new person.

She wanted to sit here and bask in it. Absorb this feeling, so different from who she'd been for years. Then again, she didn't know what she should do next. How did this work, anyway? She needed some direction.

She needed Jax.

Outside she saw Ramon walk to a dusty Toyota. The driver's door opened and the priest climbed out, then both back doors opened. The two nuns were stocky, their visible features no-nonsense in the light of the headlights. They looked like they could take care of themselves *and* keep a bunch of rowdy kids in line.

Ramon spoke with the priest while the nuns stood like bodyguards.

She looked at the dash clock, no idea how long it would take to get back to the ranch since she didn't have her phone to map it. Still, they needed to get going if they were to make their deadline to deliver the money and save her friends.

She grabbed the handle and shoved open the door, not sure what to say to the priest and nuns about her...what was it, a conversion? She didn't know how to tell them about her change of heart. Change of life status. Did they even want to know?

Whether they did or not, she needed to find out how long this was going to take.

The wind pushed the door back against her, so hard she had to fight to get it open and get out. Sand blew in gusts.

Kenna shielded her eyes from the flying dirt. "Ramon!"

He strode over to her. "I'll just be a sec." He slid open the back window on the camper shell, her side. Right behind her seat. He pulled out a duffel, stuffed full. Not part of the wrapped stacks of what she presumed were cash.

Peeking in, she saw two pallets, bundles stacked to the ceiling. Shoved in tight and wrapped up. No one would guess it was all money.

And he had an extra package?

"What's going on?"

No one answered her.

Ramon handed the duffel to the priest, talking in Spanish fast and quiet. They shook hands, then he strode back over. "Get it. We need to go." He glanced behind the truck, up the highway where they'd just come.

Kenna looked as well. "You see something?"

"Get in, Kenna."

He was mad at her? As if any of this was on her. She'd played along and he could tell Navarro that, thank you very much.

"What was that?" She buckled her seatbelt even though he didn't. "What did you give the priest? And is there someone following us?"

"There's always someone following us." He peeled out. "And I'm not just talking about that hurricane."

She didn't like the sound of that. "So why'd we stop?"

"Doing my civic duty. Or my devout duty to the church. Probably both, considering how much money was in that duffel."

Her brows rose. "You just gave money to the church?"

"It was a donation."

She checked the side mirror. Maybe there were headlights behind them, but it could be anyone out here on the highway headed inland. "And you made a planned stop to do that? In a way Navarro won't know you skimmed some off the top."

"How do you know it wasn't my money?"

She glanced over. "Was it?"

He chuckled. "The church doesn't care if it's dirty money. Maybe it's better that they have it. Then it'll get used for something good, right?"

"So you jeopardize my friends' lives for a church donation. Couldn't you have done it another time?"

"Chill, yeah?" Ramon huffed. "We've got time. And Navarro can't know, so you're not going to tell him we stopped."

"You think I'm going to lie for you?" She wasn't sure she was supposed to do that. More now than before she'd surrendered to what God wanted to do with her life. She'd given up, given Him control. Turned things over. If she was going to let

Him lead her, then it wouldn't be to tell a lie—even to a bad guy. She wasn't sure if it was okay to lie to save a life.

She needed a pen and paper so she could write down all these questions.

"When he asks if we stopped?"

Kenna sighed. "I'll tell him you needed to pee. Maybe you had to go, even if you didn't." It was still iffy, but maybe better than the outright lie. "You're the one who put me in this position. Are you going to threaten my friends to get me to cooperate? Because I'm getting a little sick of that happening."

"Poor you."

"Don't." She shook her head. "There is nothing similar about our situations."

"No? You saw those feds back there. You think they're going to report that they murdered the guys Navarro hired to make it look like a shipment came in? Or that they were hoping to score a payout from it?"

He didn't know what those men had planned, though. So how could he surmise anything?

He continued, "They've got Kart in their pocket, and they didn't run that like a legit operation."

"We don't even know who they were." She'd gotten the feeling they weren't feds, even if they were pretending to be.

"I know they're coming up on us." Ramon glanced at the side mirrors. "So you'd better prepare." He motioned with one hand. "There's a rifle behind the seat. You can roll the window down if they start shooting. Hit them back, try to slow them down so we have a chance a making town."

"That's it? You donate to the church, then you're back to murder?"

"It's not murder if they're trying to kill you."

Kenna pressed her lips together, not wanting to get into an argument. Wind rocked the truck. She reached for the rifle so she'd have control of it rather than Ramon. Who knew what he'd use it for. She was done being threatened.

God, help me.

She needed His help to do and say the right thing here. Lives were at stake, and rather than it being the victim in whatever case she was working, instead it was her friends. People she considered family.

She glanced at Ramon. He really thought he could play both sides? "You're working your way up onto a high horse of your own, I think."

He barked a laugh.

"It wasn't supposed to be funny."

"So we're not that different, you and I?"

"Never said we were different. A lot of your story and mine have correlations." She watched the side mirror, the rifle across her knees now. An older weapon she hoped was the kind someone had taken care of. "But you could have proven your innocence. You could have made it so your story was heard." She never would've given up the fight. "Instead you chose this?"

"I get to do good here. Do what I can, and maybe one day I'll prove what Cecilia Warren did to me."

Kenna flinched. Her roommate from Quantico. That's who had done this to Ramon? That was unbelievable. They might not have kept in touch, but she would never have imagined Cecilia doing something like that.

Before she could say as much aloud, Ramon said, "I'm here, and I get to earn redemption on my terms."

She frowned. "Does that work? Proving yourself. Proving you're worthy. I didn't think redemption was something that could be earned." She'd listened to enough sermons to know grace was a free gift. Which had nothing to do with trying to persuade God she was worthy of anything.

"How do I know I have it if it's not based on my actions?" Ramon shook his head. "That's messed up. Anyone could just ask for forgiveness, and whatever they've done means nothing." He thumped a hand on his chest. "*I* make the world a better place."

She had been doing the same thing. Believing the same thing since she left the FBI—because she'd been essentially forced out. Like losing everything was her fault somehow. But who could carry on under the weight of that much guilt? Or the weight of who they were. She knew she didn't measure up and that there were parts of her that never would deserve redemption no matter what good she did. So maybe it was easier to swallow that she had to be given grace.

"We all want to make the world a better place," she said. "Or I trust that most people do. But it doesn't get you anything in return. No one even knows you made that donation back there except the priest. And he's not going to let slip that you're the one funding whatever they use the money for."

"Relocating victims. They set up a house. Once in a while, when I can, I 'sell' him a group, so his cover is listed as a client. He gets them to a safe place where they can heal."

She blinked. "Not one at a time?"

"I have no idea who takes the ones who disappear," Ramon said. "I always thought it was Kart." He braced. "Here they come."

She leaned forward and looked at the side mirror. Headlights lit up the road behind them. A car passed on the other side, coming at them. The driver laid on the horn as they passed, but she didn't know what they were trying to communicate—a warning, or an order not to involve them.

Whichever it was, they passed.

Then the first gunshot pinged off the back of the truck.

Kenna flinched.

"I've got this," Ramon said. "You take care of them."

Great. She turned the gun so it pointed at the carpet between her feet, not ready to roll the window down and start firing. "How far to cover?"

They'd been out in the open up to this point. Ahead she could see the yellow glow of civilization where the mountains dipped into a flat area. Rain started to pepper the windshield, fat drops that accompanied the wind.

"There's a river up ahead. The bridge will bottleneck us, but once we're past that we can head into town and try and lose them." Ramon's voice was tight. "We just have to hang on."

She expected frustration to come to the forefront, but it didn't. There was a stillness inside that seemed to settle her where normally there would only be more turmoil. Another gift on top of the salvation she believed she had received.

Help us get to the ranch if that's what is meant to happen.

She didn't know what God might have planned and didn't want to mess up His will. So how did she decide if she was meant to suggest to Ramon that they take another route, or try another plan?

Another gunshot cracked the driver's side mirror.

Ramon gripped the wheel.

She looked out the one on her side. "They're right on us. If they shoot out a tire or send us off the road—into the river— we won't be able to get the money to Navarro in time." Or at all.

"And all you care about is your friends, not us."

"I don't want any casualties," she said. "No matter who it is."

"Then roll down your window and shoot back."

That was his answer, just shoot back? Kenna gritted her teeth. "Get us to that bridge."

Town was closer now. She watched the dash clock and the speedometer, though she didn't have a good view from this angle. No one obstructed the road in front. The hurricane and the bad guys were behind them.

Kart, his cousin, and the men who dressed as feds? Maybe they'd all realized what happened—that they'd been duped—and jumped onto a pursuit. Determined to steal the money, no matter what.

Stopping had allowed them time to catch up.

She shuddered, not wanting to think what Elliot might have planned.

The donation had been a good thing in the midst of a bad situation. And it turned out, there were dangerous consequences. She didn't like these circumstances no matter which way it turned out for any of them, all she wanted was to get past this.

Then they would *run*.

The car or truck behind—she could only see blinding headlights now—eclipsed everything. A heavy thump impacted the back of their truck. The whole thing shook. Ramon fought to keep hold on the steering wheel.

He hissed. "They'll try and run us into the river."

Kenna didn't want to get in a crash. "Put your seatbelt on so it doesn't kill you if we do end up in there."

He did as she ordered. "Are you going to use that gun?"

"Don't rush me." She was waiting for just the right time, hoping the wisdom she had came from God. Her skills—ones He'd made sure she had for exactly this night and what they would have to do. "Hold it steady."

He bumped up onto the bridge.

Kenna pressed the button while the window rolled down. Wind whipped at her hair and her shirt, and rain sprayed into the cab of the truck. She ignored the weather that wanted to push her back to her seat and got the gun and both arms out the window. Kenna rested her elbows on the open window ledge. Fast as she could, Kenna sighted the vehicle behind and squeezed off a shot.

She pulled again and sent a few more rounds into the passenger side window, splintering the windshield glass.

An armed man leaned out. She squeezed and put a round in him.

He slumped down out the open window.

She shot a couple more times toward the hood and managed to hit the target. Hopefully, that would disable the vehicle enough they'd have to break off pursuit. She couldn't see more than the one trailing vehicle.

"One down." She settled back in her seat. "Now you need to lose them."

Ramon bumped over the bridge going faster than she would have.

Kenna gripped the door handle and held on. Then spotted a dark house built on the far side of the river, someone's dream property with a view.

The truck recoiled against the ground, and Ramon jerked the wheel in a two-handed grip to the left, causing the back end to spin out.

She gritted her teeth and prayed.

A bullet shattered the driver's side window, and Ramon grunted. Probably the shock of it caused him to let go of the wheel with his left hand. Still, he drove toward the street behind the house, where the front door would be located in the backyard, which adjoined the bank of the river.

She pushed out "not the time" thoughts about what kind of place she might like. As if she needed to get sentimental when everything was upside down.

Whatever You want.

Ramon bumped the corner and took out the low fence around a planter. He kept going, ignoring everything around them. "We need to switch places."

She twisted to him. "Did you get shot?"

Ramon grunted. "You need to drive or we're not going to make it."

Chapter Twenty-Seven

Kenna unbuckled herself, slid to the middle, and grabbed the wheel. "Keep pushing down on the gas pedal." She held the wheel with both hands and got them on a straight road, driving down the center line. "Which way gets us to the ranch?"

Far as she could tell, it was still at least thirty minutes to the ranch, and they had little more time than that if they wanted to make Navarro's deadline. Free her friends.

Ramon gasped.

She held the wheel straight and glanced over at his left shoulder. He had his right hand braced on the wheel, sweat coming down from his temples. His far side was covered in blood. The bullet could still be in there and it would do serious damage, considering it lodged in a major joint.

She told him, "Hang on."

His left arm lay limp in his lap. He swayed forward and leaned against her left shoulder for a second before pushing off the dash with his right hand and slumping back against the seat. He pressed down on the gas pedal.

"Ease off the speed." She winced. "We don't need to go so fast we're out of control."

Kenna spotted a car on a side street. She flashed the headlights as a warning, praying they didn't pull out in front of her. She didn't want to crash.

They passed under streetlights that swayed with the gathering wind. She knocked the lever for the windshield wipers up to fight harder against the pounding rain.

The vehicle behind them sped up and bumped the back of the car.

Kenna hissed out a breath.

Ramon sucked in a painful gasp.

"I got you." She wasn't going to let go or allow those men to run them off the road. But she needed help. "Give me your phone."

He only grunted.

Kenna held on to the wheel, all her attention on the road ahead of them. "We're not gonna make this unless we get help."

He groaned but reached with his right hand and dug out a phone from under his leg. He thumbed the home button and gave it to her unlocked. "Redial."

The number wasn't saved. She prayed it was Navarro, even if he was the last person she wanted to ask help from.

Then Kenna's mind clicked a piece into place. She'd left her phone with Jax.

She didn't want to speak to Navarro.

She wanted to talk to Jax.

"Lord Jesus." Kenna prayed he still had her phone—and he was conscious and able to answer. She picked the number out digit by digit, praying she remembered right while switching her attention from the road to the phone with each number. "Let this be you." She bit her lip and wedged the phone between her ear and shoulder, pulling her neck at an odd angle. *Please.*

"This better be Kenna."

"Jax?" She managed to gasp out his name. He sounded good. A whole lot better than the last time she'd seen him. But would he be able to help? She didn't want to only be calling him because...

"You need help."

"You could say that." She winced. "But you're in the hospital." She bit her lip. "Can one of the agents there—"

"I'm up. And they're not the ones who will be helping you."

Her throat clogged.

"You called me. Not them." She heard him moving around. "What do you need?"

"You probably shouldn't be up." A tear rolled down her face. She was only being selfish, asking an injured man for help. But she didn't want anyone else.

"Kenna, where are you?"

"We're in town in a truck with a camper shell." And the bed of the truck was full of money. "The weather is bad. I don't know if you'll want to—"

"Don't tell me what I want."

She pressed her lips together. "We're being pursued by Kart and a group of men, including Elliot Preston. I don't think they're feds, but they dressed like them. I have no idea."

"I see." He paused. "You're on speaker now. Tell me again where you are."

"In the middle of town, heading west. And if I don't get this truck to Navarro, Maizie and Stairns are dead."

"Okay." His voice took on a grim tone. "We're mobile."

"Are you well enough for that?" She didn't want him to overexert himself and end up more injured than he was.

"My head is pounding, but I'm not alone and you won't be either."

Ramon was with her, but she figured that wasn't what he meant. Warmth spread through her middle because he knew what she cared about. He cared about the same thing. "Jax..." She barely knew what to say.

"I know." Car doors slammed on his end of the line, and he grunted.

He wasn't okay. He was going to push through so he could be here to help her.

She wasn't going to argue with the wisdom of it, since she would do exactly the same thing if it were her. They both knew it.

She spotted a sign and gave him cross streets.

Ramon shifted. "The old furniture store."

"What?" She didn't know what he meant by that.

Ramon gave a street name, then said, "Tell them to go there."

Jax said, "Got it," before she could even relay the information. He must've heard. "We're getting directions to it." He grunted again. "Five minutes."

The wind struck the vehicle, and Kenna fought with the wheel. The cell phone slid from where she was holding it between her chin and her neck down to her lap, then hit the seat and fell on the floor.

She ignored it and gripped the wheel. "Which way?"

Wind buffeted the camper shell, and she fought to keep the truck straight. She actually thought it might be loose on one corner.

"Keep going." Ramon pushed down on the gas pedal, and the needle passed forty.

"What are you doing? You're going to crash us if you don't ease off." It was too dangerous.

"That's the idea."

"We can't—" Kenna started.

He grabbed the wheel between her hands at the top of the wheel and jerked it to the right. They barreled through a chain-link fence, splitting the gate open. The truck bumped over uneven gravel and sprayed it behind them.

The trailing vehicle headlights flashed in the side mirror.

Kenna stared at the looming rundown building in front of them. "Slow down, Ramon."

He pressed down on the gas even more.

"Ramon. Slow down. Hit the brake." They headed right at a roll-up loading bay door. "Ramon!"

They crashed into the door, and it splintered.

Ramon shifted his foot to the brake.

Kenna held on to the wheel for dear life.

He jerked it to the left, and they slammed into debris as they went. The camper shell tore off the back of the truck and went flying. Clouds of dust filled the room, smearing across the windshield and making a white mess that obscured her view of the dark interior. Headlights lit up machines, but he steered them down the middle.

"You can't possibly have a plan besides killing us."

Ramon said, "Hang on," then hit the brakes before she could ask what that was about.

Kenna split the difference between locking her arms straight and absorbing the sudden stop. Still, her head slammed forward onto the back of her hand. She blinked. Coughed, then sucked in air. "You could've warned me."

Ramon grunted. "Sorry."

Kenna twisted around to look at the doorway they'd made by punching through the loading bay door. Vehicle headlights filled the open space. "They'll be here in a second."

"Hopefully, the feds will be, too." His face was far too

pale, but there was no time to look at the wound and nothing to put on it. "Until then, I guess it's on you to protect the traitor."

Kenna shoved the door open. She climbed out with the rifle, brushed hair back from her face, and used some of the rainwater from the side of the truck to slick it down so it didn't get in her eyes and cost her life. She headed for the back corner of the truck and stayed back for cover, but held the gun ready.

Two men appeared at the opening, lights on the front of their rifles switched on.

She squeezed off a shot and hit the first one, then aimed for the second. He dove back for cover. She put a couple of rounds in the wall beside where he'd been standing a second ago.

"Kenna Banbury!" That was Kart. "Come out with your hands up, and we won't shoot you."

A man who'd opted to testify and make a deal with the feds, suddenly in charge of the operation? She didn't think so. No way these guys were legit. If he really was giving up the cartel or his own operation in exchange for lighter sentences, there was no way they'd let him run the show.

She gritted her teeth. All he wanted was the money. She needed to save her friends' lives, and if that meant she delivered the money to Navarro, then so be it. She would make the deal. She would do nearly anything and didn't want to be pushed to the breaking point on exactly how far she'd go to save Maizie and Stairns.

Hurry up, Jax.

"Kenna Banbury," Kart repeated.

"I hear you!" She tried not to sound as irritated as she was, but the anger and frustration still bled into her tone.

"Come out with your—"

"We can't do that!" she screamed, cutting him off. "Ramon is hurt. Your friends shot him, and now he's bleeding out. He needs medical help!" Her throat burned. If she yelled back and forth much more, she'd wind up losing her voice.

"Surrender yourself. We'll take care of Ramon."

More than likely they'd shoot both of them. "I know you only want the money!"

"These are federal agents. They're here to help."

And she was supposed to believe that?

"Come out. We'll rectify this situation."

Kenna drew in a few long breaths, trying to calm her racing heart and ease her breathing so she didn't react in a panic. The last thing she needed to do was get trigger-happy and end up shooting Jax—or one of the real feds. In fact… "I want to see some ID! If those are real feds, then they need to prove it!"

"Come out, and you can verify who they are."

A low metal creak drew her attention—and a whole lot of confusion. Almost like Ramon was out of the truck.

"That's not going to happen!" Kenna sucked in a breath and yelled again. "We're taking this money to Navarro!"

"It's federal property now. They're gonna seize it!" Kart yelled back. "But no one wants more bloodshed, so stand down."

Kenna felt movement behind her and stiffened.

"Just me." Ramon didn't sound good.

At least it hadn't been Elliot. Where had the sheriff slithered off to?

She backed up, making space between her and the truck so she'd still have line of sight on the opening and be able to get a look at him. His left shoulder made her want to be sick. He held the arm across his body with his other. "You need a hospital."

"My life doesn't work like that." He spoke through gritted teeth. "Give me the gun. Take the truck and keep going straight. There's an opening at the end. You can get the money to Navarro and get your friends back."

She flinched. "I'm not doing it alone. I'm waiting for Jax."

"So take him when he gets here." Ramon pushed out a breath. "Get the money. Get your friends."

"I'm not leaving you here to die." She had already lost enough people. "You're coming, too."

Ramon shifted. "Here goes." He lifted his chin.

She spotted the open door, making sure they weren't about to be ambushed. Then glanced where Ramon had indicated and saw FBI agents—the real feds here—breach the room.

One of Kart's friends breached the opening.

Kenna took a shot and heard a scream and a thud.

"Nice shooting."

Before she could respond to whoever that was, Ramon said, "Take the truck and get out of here."

"Sure." That was Jax. "Who are you?"

Of course. He had been in the hospital, and before that unconscious. He hadn't even met Ramon. Before she could explain, Ramon cut her off.

"You don't wanna know." He paused. "Just get Kenna out of here."

One of the agents took her spot, covering the opening from the back corner of the truck. "How much money is in that back of that?"

Kenna heard the tone of his voice and knew it was only curiosity, not the intention to betray his oath. "It's enough we could split it and be rich, but then my friends would be dead."

"Shame." The agent shook his head.

"Yes, it is." She patted his shoulder and turned back to Jax and Ramon, a smile tugging at her lips. Then she got a look at Jax and choked back a gasp. "Get in the truck. You shouldn't be on your feet."

He groaned, not looking any better than Ramon did. "You first. Slide over so you can drive."

She handed the gun to Ramon. "You sure about this? You can come with us."

"They'll take care of Kart and his friends." Jax motioned to the others.

Only three agents. That was all?

She didn't like the look of this.

"Get going, ma'am." The agent who spoke had a vest over his white shirt. "Before you're in any more danger. We'll take care of this."

Jax leaned on the door. "Kenna?"

She didn't like this. Normally she would be the one who had everything handled, and instead she found she needed to give up apprehending Kart for the sake of saving her friends—and getting Jax off his feet.

"Go, Kenna."

She glanced at Ramon, not wanting to leave him. But maybe it was best for him to go with the feds. Have the chance to say his piece and maybe even clear his name. The fact it was her roommate from Quantico that had betrayed him and painted him as a traitor didn't sit right, but somehow the truth had to come out.

Kenna's hands shook. She gave Ramon the rifle and moved to Jax. She passed him, lifting her hand to squeeze where his neck met his shoulder, then paused long enough his lips brushed across her forehead.

Neither of them said anything.

"Straight. He said go straight." She put the truck in gear and stopped the windshield wipers.

"Buckle up."

Kenna did the same as Jax, and then they both shut their doors. "Here we go."

"Fast as you can. Give them the element of surprise." Jax looked out the window. "Okay. *Now.*"

She hit the gas and peeled out, through the warehouse to the far end. A lobby. The doors were busted, and the whole mouth of the building was like a gaping wound. The result of an explosion, or something like that—maybe another crash.

Ramon had known it would be here.

He'd punched a hole in the loading bay on the way in, knowing they could get out this way. Pretty hefty gamble considering they could've totaled the truck on the way in.

Gunfire behind them made her squeeze the wheel so hard her forearms hurt. She bumped down the entrance curb onto the street.

A series of shots hit the back of the truck. She turned them toward the street and drove as fast as she could, praying Ramon and the other feds were protected and were successful here.

Jax said, "You know how to get to Navarro?"

She headed for the ranch. "You know about the cartel?"

"They filled me in when I woke up. After they woke up." He waved a hand. "It's a whole thing."

"I'd love to hear the story, but right now we need to get this money to a dangerous cartel leader and use it to buy back my friends."

Jax grunted. "So basically it's date night."

Chapter Twenty-Eight

Kenna wanted to laugh at that so badly. Instead, she ended up crying, even though that was the last thing she wanted to do right now. She had Jax beside her in the truck. God had met her in that prayer. But even with those good things, there was still so much more that seemed out of control.

Then again, all of it had been outside *her* control.

The balance of good things and bad things—that scared her to her core—created a wash of emotion she couldn't hold back.

Jax said nothing. He just let her get it all out, until she was gasping long breaths and still trying to drive. She slowed to yield before she pulled onto the highway and grabbed the phone off the floor. She put it in the cup holder, then took a second to wipe her dirty face and get ahold of herself. "Sorry."

"Nothing to be sorry for."

"I wasn't crying about the prospect of dating you, by the way." Her throat felt hoarse, and her entire body ached like she needed two days of sleep—after a scorching hot bath.

Then after all that, she could get dressed up and *only then* they could talk about a date.

Where would he take her if they ever got the chance?

She wanted to know if he was a ballpark-and-hotdogs kind of guy, or sushi for dinner and her in heels. She could go either way when the occasion called for it. And not just if it was an undercover operation.

"I appreciate the clarification," he said.

She glanced over for a second, long enough to see he had his eyes open, but they were lined with pain. "Are you up to talking? We need to put our heads together."

"Yeah." He sighed. "I woke up in the hospital. That guy was there."

"Kart." She said his name like a curse word.

"Then you, strolling in like a white knight there to save me."

She wanted to point out that in getting taken she'd saved Javier, Navarro's nephew. But that would take far too much explaining when she wanted to hear his story right now.

"You got him to take you and leave me." His tone indicated his opinion of that. "The agents on the door rushed in a few minutes later, and one of them fell. They'd been drugged by Kart and his men."

"I never saw anyone else with him...until tonight." She stopped herself, not liking the accusation in her voice. The feds Jax trusted weren't necessarily dirty. "Sorry, carry on."

"It's all right." He squeezed her knee. "They told me they'd been given coffee by a nurse, and right before they passed out. They realized once they woke up that the agent from San Diego wasn't legit. They double-checked his credentials, and the guy was pretending to be an agent so he could get intel on what they were doing."

Kenna blew out a breath.

"And it turns out they've all been tracking Ian Kartom, his friends, and his business for months. Trying to piece together exactly what he does so they can build a solid case against him and get everything—not just part of it."

"Seems like he does a little bit of everything." She paused. "Do they know about the sheriff, Elliot Preston?"

Jax shook his head. "They didn't say anything about him. Maizie told me, though."

"You talked to her?" That must've been before she and Stairns had been captured.

"Thanks for leaving me your phone. I know how hard that must've been."

"You could use it, and I could use it to call you. I didn't want Kart finding Maizie."

Though, she hadn't managed to keep the girl safe, had she? Maizie was currently being held. And if any of Navarro's men had touched one hair on her head they were going to learn from Kenna personally why that was a bad idea—if Stairns hadn't given the lesson already.

"We'll get them back."

Kenna nodded. She drove faster than she felt was safe, but not so fast they'd be out of control. Given everything the truck had been through, she wasn't surprised the temperature was rising.

They were probably leaking something, but with the rain it was almost impossible to tell. The money was going to be a soggy mess by the time they got to the ranch. Assuming it didn't come apart and fly off in the wind.

She pushed out a breath. "So you spoke to Maizie, and you got the lowdown from the feds about their investigation you landed in the middle of." But they hadn't connected it to Elliot Preston, or the US, and they didn't know the cartel.

"They called for reinforcements after they were drugged but only got two more agents from the San Diego office. Just actually legit ones this time." He sighed. "One went to the compound to assess the situation there. The others came with me when you called. Which I'm very glad you did."

"Me, too." She swallowed against the lump in her throat. "We're almost there."

"And this entire situation connects to a sheriff the feds know nothing about?"

Kenna nodded. "Elliot Preston." How did she explain this? "Remember Luca and Camila? We went to their wedding in Vegas."

"Sure."

"Ramon sent them north, hoping they would be able to break free. Or he had it set up but it fell apart." She shook her head. "But they were caught up in Kart's operation—which connects to the Preston brothers in Colorado. Elliot seems to be the leader on both ends, and he's supposedly on his way here." She hadn't seen him yet, so who knew? "I think Camila might be pregnant with Navarro's baby. I'm so glad they're nowhere near any of this. Thank You, God, that they are long gone and safe."

He shifted in his seat. "Yeah?"

She heard the hope in his voice and looked over. "I prayed." Kenna stared at the lines on the highway ahead. "When I had nothing else and I couldn't see a way out, I prayed."

"And God met you there?"

She nodded.

Jax held out his hand. When she laid hers in it, he kissed her palm and held her hand against his chest.

"Are you really all right?" Kenna bit her lip. "Or do I have to worry that you'll suddenly have a brain aneurism, or some kind of stroke?"

"Isn't there always a risk of that?" He exhaled, and she felt it against the back of her hand. "Any of us could die at any moment."

"That doesn't answer my question," she said. "What was the prognosis?"

"I'm fine." He chuckled a little against the back of her hand and then groaned.

"You're as bad as Ramon."

"That's another thing you need to explain to me." But she didn't hear anything but the question in his voice. "I have internal injuries, but they did surgery. I need to not rip anything, and I shouldn't be heavy lifting anytime soon. So give me a gun and point me in the right direction."

She tugged her hand free. "How 'bout you just stay behind me?"

"As long as we go in together."

"Sounds like a plan." She pulled off the highway at Navarro's ranch and headed down the lane.

"Before we get there, who is that Ramon guy?"

"I could barely believe it when I saw him." Kenna shook her head. "We went to Quantico together. He was undercover, and the report is he went off the reservation, didn't check in. Dropped off the map and supposedly went dark side. Now I'm not so sure. I think he might've been implicated so someone could save face."

She didn't mention the agent she'd been roomed with. There would be time later—after this was all over—to look into it. Maybe even to clear his name.

She continued, "Did the feds who've been looking into Kart's operation say anything about a killer? Someone who carves a W into their victim's lower back?"

Jax made a *huh* sound. "Not that I can recall. They're more interested in the drug money, the mules, and migrant trafficking. Illegal weapons sales goes to the ATF, but they don't want to share, so they're keeping that under wraps until the very end."

"Politics." She pulled up in front of Navarro's house.

The wind was barely moving the trees here. Had the hurricane turned again, or lost strength when it came this far inland? She could see the weather system in the distance, in the sky to the east.

She put the truck in park, and the phone in the cupholder illuminated. A call in progress. She touched Jax's arm and pointed to it, motioning for him to keep quiet.

He barely whispered, "Who?"

The front door to the ranch opened, and Navarro stepped onto the front step, a phone to his ear. Listening to their conversation through an open phone line? If that was true...

We just told him everything.

She hung up the call because there was no point in pretending she didn't know he'd just overheard everything. Including what happened to Camila and his baby. "I guess he knows it all now."

She and Jax both climbed out. No matter what, she wasn't going to back down.

"We brought your money." Kenna lifted her chin. "So it's time to let my friends and I go."

"When you bring my enemies on your heels?" He tucked the phone into his pocket.

She turned and looked at the gate. "I don't see anyone."

"Ramon filled me in. Says he's working with the feds to take down Kart. They got his men captured. The mercenaries Kart is friends with are all secured or dead. But Kart escaped."

Kenna stiffened. "Our deal was that I bring your money,

and you let my friends go. Or are you going to go back on our agreement?"

He almost looked amused before he turned to Jax. "My name is Héctor Álvarez Navarro. They call me El Falcón."

"FBI Special Agent Oliver Jaxton."

"I know. I did attempt at one point to ah...purchase you as it were. From Ian Kartom and his band of disgusting hooligans."

Kenna frowned.

"Sorry that didn't work out," Jax said, his face deadpan. "You might have been more hospitable than they were."

"Unlikely." Navarro motioned to the door. "Let's go inside."

"I'll just grab my friends and get out of your hair." She stepped into the foyer behind him, the whole place running like usual and not like a major disruption was underway. "If you've got a car we can borrow. Or I'll need a ride from someone."

Navarro chuckled. Outside, the driver of the truck revved the engine and pulled away. "You did make good on our agreement. I suppose it's on me to hold up my end."

"So why are you stalling?" she asked.

Jax touched her hip.

Kenna wasn't going to back down. "I want to know they're unharmed. That was also part of the bargain."

"It certainly was."

She heard a *but* in there and didn't like it at all. "There's been enough bloodshed since I arrived here, don't you think?"

Navarro chuckled again.

"How is Javier since he was kidnapped? Is he doing all right?"

Navarro's brows rose. "I sent the child to live with my aunt. He is safe and will be cared for."

But not here. Either he had no interest in family ties unless it was Camila's child, or he had simply had the boy killed. Was this man vicious enough he'd murdered his own nephew for the sake of eliminating the vulnerability?

"I'm sorry," Kenna said. "I'm sure you'll miss him."

"No more than I missed his mother." Navarro shrugged. "That's the way life goes, I suppose. Like discovering someone I'd made an agreement with has withheld information from me."

"Because you heard that whole conversation." Kenna shrugged. "We already told you that Camila was lost in Preston's organization."

"And yet you neglected to tell me of a *wedding*."

"If she didn't want to stay with you, then why make her? She would never be happy."

"I will have my child."

Kenna's stomach clenched.

"And until then, I will take yours." He lifted his chin. "I received a visitor a short time ago, a sheriff from Colorado. While you were transporting my money here, he told me all about you and your friends. And the girl." His eyes gleamed.

"He was here."

"Correction," Navarro said. "He *is* here."

Ice settled into her core. "Where?"

Jax shifted to stand beside her. "Elliot Preston is here?"

Navarro said, "You assume I wish for you to eliminate this problem? And yet you're the federal agent."

"He's a sheriff," Jax said.

But Kenna had a better grasp of the depth of the man's depravity—and that was without even meeting the guy. "He's dirty."

"We discussed a partnership." Navarro, of course, was unbothered by Elliot's sordid dealings.

A gunshot cracked off across the house.

Kenna flinched. Jax raced past Navarro, a pistol between his hands.

She looked at Navarro as she went after him. "If anything happens to that girl, you're the one who will answer for it." Then she raced after Jax.

He didn't move like he normally did, considerably slower and almost stiff.

A door crashed open, and Stairns stumbled out, clutching his stomach. Blood in his hands. "She…"

Jax reached to catch him.

Kenna yelled, "Don't!" She shifted Jax aside and caught Stairns. They both slumped to the floor, him partially on her knee. "I've got you."

"Looks like it." Stairns gasped.

"What happened?"

Jax disappeared into the room Stairns had come out of.

"We'll get help. Get you to a doctor." She wanted him—and all of them—as far from Navarro as possible. A man who would keep a person in trade until he had what he wanted. *No. No way.* "Where is she?"

"Sheriff—" Stairns began.

"Elliot Preston," Kenna said.

"—took her." Stairns gasped. "Saw you were here. Laughed and—" He coughed.

She twisted around to Navarro. "Call the doctor!"

"He won't come out in this weather. Not even for you."

She had no idea what that meant.

Jax came back out of the room and shook his head. "Window's open, and she's gone." He dropped a stack of towels into her lap.

She pressed one against Stairns' gut. *Not good.* "We need

a car, Navarro. Preston just *took* her, and we need to know what vehicle he's in and where he took her."

A red haze had settled over her vision. She was rambling. Navarro didn't care about her, or her friends, or what she wanted.

They needed to get Stairns to the hospital, or he wouldn't make it through this. Then she had to get to a device she could use to track the necklace.

Thank You, God.

She could find Maizie no matter what.

Jax walked toward him, gun raised pointed at the cartel leader. "Order your men to get us a vehicle. We're getting our friend to the hospital before he bleeds to death."

Navarro made a call and spoke in Spanish.

"Now ask what vehicle Elliot Preston is in and which direction he went."

Navarro's jaw flexed. He spoke into his phone.

Not happy. As if any of them cared.

Stairns moaned. "I'm sorry, Kenna. I tried to stop him."

She shook her head. "You did what you could." And he might've given his life for the teen Kenna had taken under her wing.

God, help her.

They had to get her back.

Stairns shifted. "N—" He coughed, his whole body spasming.

"Don't worry about him."

Jax shifted. "Navarro, I will kill you unless you say what I told you to say, not some junk about open gates."

Navarro stiffened. Spoke again. Then to Jax he said, "The sheriff killed two men on his way out. He's gone. But Kart just arrived."

"I want a description of the car Elliot Preston is driving."

Headlights flashed across the open door, reflecting off the tile floor. Kenna stiffened, expecting Kart to walk in.

A shadow darkened the doorway.

Kenna braced.

Chapter Twenty-Nine

I an Kartom stepped into the doorway, a desperate and dark look on his face.

Where did Elliot take Maizie? Kenna wondered. From what Navarro had said, they weren't even on the ranch property anymore. Stairns was about to bleed out.

Ian took a step.

Gunshots cracked off behind him, from somewhere outside. Kart's body jerked. Blood bloomed in the center of his chest, and he fell to the ground.

An FBI agent appeared at the door. "Sorry we're late." He rushed in. "Jaxton?"

"I'm good." Jax faced off with Navarro. "We need to get Stairns to the hospital."

The second FBI agent stepped over Kart's body, then searched him for weapons and ID.

The first one crouched in front of Kenna. "Stairns?" He didn't wait for an answer. "Let's get you to a doctor, yeah?" He lifted her friend, who grabbed for Kenna's hand.

"Don't worry. Just go with them." She shook her head. "I'll get her back."

The guy carried Stairns in his arms to the door, and the other agent got what he'd collected from Kart. He checked outside, then watched out for Jax as Kenna stood. She barely had the strength to push herself up the wall but rallied and went to stand in front of Navarro.

Jax went to the door, then turned back. Gun raised and a lethal expression in his eyes. "Kenna?"

"We can't just leave him here with his money." Six million—or however much it was after Ramon took some out. "He should be arrested."

"Come with me so we can get Stairns to the hospital."

This man was responsible for her friend's fate. He'd let the sheriff in here. If Maizie was lost and Stairns didn't make it, then Navarro would be the reason they were lost.

His eyes glinted. She saw a flash of Navarro's teeth, and his shoulders turned. The intent telegraphed in his expression and the twist of his body.

She flung up her left hand.

Navarro's knife sliced across the blade of her forearm. Kenna cried out.

Jax pulled the trigger on his weapon, and Navarro hit the tile.

She gasped and held her arm to her front, backing up.

Jax ran over. He pulled Navarro's phone from his pocket, straightened, and slid his arm around her. "Come on, Kenna."

They stumbled together to the door.

His voice rumbled in his chest, under her cheek. She heard him say, "What were you thinking?" Then her awareness swam, and she heard his words as though below the surface of water and he remained above it. Free while she drowned.

But she couldn't.

Stairns...

Maizie...

Hot wind whipped her hair around her face. She barely felt the sting of the cut on her arm. Jax walked her to the car, and she tumbled in beside Stairns. Her former boss sat against the rear passenger side door. He'd lost so much blood he looked dead.

Kenna scrambled across the seat and pressed two fingers to his throat.

She felt his pulse—barely.

Kenna didn't like the noise that burst from her throat. Jax tugged her back against him, half in his lap. Lying awkwardly against his side. She tried to twist around. "I'm hurting you."

"Shhh." He wrapped his arms around her and held on, the hold not unlike a straight jacket. Both his arms covering her arms, keeping her from moving. Flailing.

Losing it.

"We need to put pressure on."

"We'll be there in five minutes," one of the other agents said.

She gasped. "We need to—"

"Kenna."

She swallowed what she'd been about to say and sat there in his hold, shuddering. Blood. Pain. *Maizie.* "Jesus, help us."

Jax's lips touched the side of her forehead, beside her hair. "Amen."

She squeezed her eyes shut. Elizabeth. She would have to call Stairns' wife and tell her what happened.

Please don't let him die. It's more than just Maizie and me who need him.

She sucked in a breath that caught.

"Here we are." The car swung into the parking lot and bumped up the curb. Whichever agent was driving pulled right up to the emergency bay doors. The two of them shoved open their doors. She didn't even know their names, but they might have saved her family.

The agent caught Stairns before he fell out and hauled him up and inside through the sliding doors. She spotted a couple of doctors, or a doctor and a nurse. A gurney.

"He gave his life for her."

Jax didn't let go.

"If he doesn't make it..."

"Kenna, don't—"

"If we don't find her..." She squeezed her eyes shut and fought back the panic building. "I can do it when it's me. I can handle it." She'd found the end of herself. Instead of an iron core of strength her dad had instilled in her, Kenna had found...God. At the end of it all, she'd found Him.

Maizie didn't have that.

"She's trapped in her nightmare, and I said she would never have to face it again." Kenna gasped. "I need a phone." She had to find Maizie.

"That girl is a different person now. Not the kid who suffered all those horrible things." Jax paused. "She's strong."

"It's only been a few months." She felt the burn of tears, but her eyes remained dry. "She can't go back there. She won't survive."

"You did. You faced your nightmare, and you're still here."

He really thought she'd done that?

Kenna sighed. "Whether I'm whole or not remains to be seen."

How did she know she hadn't completely lost it? Maybe she'd cracked mentally and wouldn't realize it until after everyone else had. Maybe this whole thing had been nothing but a crazy dream, or a figment of her warped mind, and she would wake up, back in that cell with no hope.

Jax dead.

Bradley gone.

No hope. No future.

She hadn't realized she said his name aloud until Jax sniffed. Kenna turned, facing backward on the seat so her upper body faced him even though it was uncomfortable. She touched both hands to his cheeks and leaned her face close. "Tell me this is real."

His brow flickered.

"Tell me I'm not imagining you. That I'm not trapped back there still, and you're dead and I'm all alone. And no one is coming to rescue me."

His expression softened. He leaned down a fraction and kissed one cheek, then her other. "Feels pretty real to me."

She could only whimper and hang on. Tight.

"Are the two of you going to sit in there all night and make out?"

Ramon's voice brought her around so violently all the muscles in her abdomen wrenched. She wasn't even the injured one—okay fine, she was kind of bleeding. But compared to him? The guy was bent down and looking in the car with his arm in a sling.

She shoved open the door next to Jax and said, "Let's get out this way."

Jax said, "Because you're in danger of wringing his neck?" But didn't move to get out.

Ramon called out, "I didn't do anything! I just got shot helping you."

Right. It had been completely selfless. "I thought it shattered your shoulder or something."

Ramon shook his head. "Hurt like it had, but it wasn't that bad."

Kenna wasn't convinced that was true. He didn't look all right and probably still needed to be in the hospital.

Geez, they're all cut from the same cloth, aren't they?

"You worked for Navarro, though. So you aren't inno-cent." Kenna climbed out, visually checking Jax was all right. Not wanting to face Ramon, knowing she had zero ability to hide her emotions right now. She was broken, and anyone who looked at her would know it.

And yet, that was what God had accepted as His—all her mess.

"You work for Navarro." She faced Ramon, standing in a huddle with Jax by her side. "You're an accessory at best."

"We need to go inside and get your arm looked at." Jax spoke so softly she almost didn't hear it.

Ramon frowned. "You got hurt?"

She lifted her arm. "No thanks to your boss. He's dead now."

"And the FBI is no doubt going to want me here, with a finger on the pulse of who is taking over this vacuum." Ramon's expression flickered with something dark. "They'll probably have me be the new cartel boss just so they have an in. And they'll keep it top secret so no one ever knows the truth."

Kenna said, "Kart is dead, that operation is decimated. But how does you gladhanding with the feds and positioning yourself as the one in charge of Navarro's operation help me find Maizie?"

She was almost desperate with the need to run.

Yet, deep inside there was a calm—a sense of peace—she could draw from rather than the panic that swirled on the surface. Part of it had to do with Jax being here, alive. Stairns would fight for his life. She would leave that in God's hands. But she wanted Him to send her to rescue Maizie.

She'd rarely wanted anything in her life the way she wanted this. "I need to track where Elliot has Maizie."

Jax's hand curled around hers, but she couldn't relax. As much as she wanted to lean into his shoulder. There would be time for that when this was over.

Jax sighed. "We can't just go in guns blazing. We need to be smart, or he'll execute her."

Ramon said, "That sheriff took her?"

"That's what Stairns said." Kenna nodded even though she wanted to be sick. "Elliot probably heard us come in and made a detour. He decided to hit me where it hurts." Her voice cracked. She cleared her throat. That man wanted to destroy her.

The sheriff must have done his homework on Kenna. Learned where her vulnerabilities were, and how to hit back at her in revenge and do the most damage.

"Oh." Jax shifted. "Ramon, do you know the code to Navarro's phone?"

Ramon just waved his fingers. He tapped the screen. "I can get in."

"Good. Give me it." Kenna took the phone and got on the browser. She typed in what she thought the system was called. She had Maizie's email address—the anonymous one she used. "I don't know the password."

"I have an idea. Give me the phone."

Kenna frowned. "You need to make a call?"

"Yeah," Ramon said. "To that sheriff, so we can get your kid back."

She's not my kid. But in a lot of ways, Maizie was hers. "What do you mean?"

Ramon continued, "It's faster if I call Elliot. I tell him you guys killed Navarro. The operation is decimated. Does he want to do a deal with me and have a controlling share in the cartel operation going forward? A guy like that won't want to pass up the chance for power down here. The money? The access he gets to product?"

And he was worried people would think he wasn't an upright man. Kenna shook her head.

"He'll kill you and take it all," she said. "He won't do a deal for a share." Even Kenna could figure out that much about the guy. The only saving grace was that it would distract Elliot from whatever he was doing with Maizie.

"All we need is for him to tell us where he wants to meet," Ramon said. "If I can get eyes on your girl, you can move in and rescue her."

Kenna shuddered. Jax held tight to her hand.

"Your friends can track his phone, right?"

She frowned. "I can do that from Maizie's computer."

"The feds grabbed it when they were at the hotel, so no one else did. It should be in the trunk." Jax motioned to the car behind them.

Kenna handed the phone to Ramon. "Make the call. Get him distracted. Tell him you want to meet to discuss terms, and you'll make it worth his while."

The hurricane might have turned, but the wind remained out in full force along with the steady rain falling. She and Jax were both soaked through.

They had the beginning of a plan.

Would Elliot take the bait and hang around long enough for them to catch up?

Jax got the trunk open and dug out the computer from a backpack. Kenna opened it in the trunk, covered from the rain by the lid, and put in Maizie's pin.

The teen had forced her to memorize the code even though Kenna had pointed out that she'd probably never have occasion to use it. Now she would admit it had been a good idea. She didn't agree with everything Maizie wanted—like the chance to go out with Kenna and solve cases. But the girl had a lot of solid ideas.

Kenna wanted to get her back so they could argue some more about it. Even if it sounded funny, that was one of the things she missed right now.

"Thank you, Maizie." *And thank You.* "Now be somewhere I can find you and come get you."

Jax squeezed her shoulder.

Kenna got on the hospital Wi-Fi and logged onto the website. Maizie's password manager filled the log in information in for her, and she waited for the map to load. She glanced back at Ramon, on Navarro's cell phone. They should probably touch base with the agents.

"Is the FBI going to be mad that Ramon and I are taking point trying to get Elliot?" she asked. They could make it difficult if they had other ideas—if they wanted the sheriff in custody, answering for why he was here.

Jax shrugged. "I'll let them know. They didn't even have Elliot on their radar, so they don't have probable cause to go after him even if they wanted to. But if a certain private investigator wanted to pull her signature move and hand over both the criminal and all the evidence to law enforcement, I'm not sure they'd object."

"I'm gonna nail him to a wall for this."

He grinned. "You're so cute when you're vicious."

"I'm not trying to be cute!"

"I know. That's why it was cute."

He was only trying to get her to think about something other than the abject fear over Maizie's fate currently.

God, surround her with angels.

Kenna would pray for everything God could possibly use as a resource to keep the teen safe. All the things she could think of. God would take care of the how, but Kenna would have all her bases covered. She wasn't going to leave anything to chance.

Jax patted her shoulder. "It loaded."

Kenna zoomed in on the map. "That's not far from here, and she's not moving."

He pulled out his phone. "The agents are going to the compound where Kart kept us. They can't get in contact with the agent that went there."

"Well, that's not where Elliot is." She wrung her hands together, but that just made things hurt. "I'll need weapons. Maybe a vest." She could use a shower and a change of clothes, but that would take too long. "We don't know how long he's going to keep her there. Or where he's planning on taking her next. Probably out of the country."

"Maybe he's waiting out the storm."

She turned to Jax. "We can hit the motel, stock up with supplies. Stairns will have brought what we need."

"We?" Jax's brows rose. "You aren't going to go off alone?"

Kenna shook her head. "Why would I do that when you're here? Together is better than being alone. Even with the risk."

Something warm entered his expression.

"We don't have time for that. We need to go."

Jax barked a laugh. "I'll tell the agents I'm not going with them."

"Are they going to object?"

He shrugged. "I'm on medical leave. It's none of their business what I'm doing on personal time."

"I'm not sure that's *exactly* how it works."

Jax tugged her close and kissed the side of her temple. "Not sure I exactly care."

Ramon wrapped up his call and came back over.

Kenna checked the laptop and saw that Maizie hadn't moved.

Jax said, "Well?"

"He agreed to meet," Ramon said. "Did you find her?"

Kenna nodded. "There." She pointed to the map on the screen, which Ramon peered at.

"That's the place. He said an hour." Ramon looked almost excited.

"I'm not giving him that much time with her. He doesn't get an hour." Kenna grabbed the laptop. "Let's go."

Maizie had been broken far too many times. One more might not kill her—but that wasn't a chance Kenna wasn't willing to risk.

Ramon headed for the front passenger seat.

Jax cut him off. "Back seat, buddy."

Kenna slid in the driver's seat and pulled out, going to the motel. Pushing out every stray thought that threatened her composure. Nothing would jeopardize this. No way would God allow Maizie to be destroyed. Kenna just knew with everything in her that He had a plan for that teen girl.

Which meant she was going to live.

Chapter Thirty

Ramon pushed open the door and headed inside.

From across the street, Kenna could see the door close. A brand-new build that wasn't open yet. Someone's attempt to better the economy of this part of town. "Question is, did he drive back to town, or did he never leave?"

Jax shifted, sat in the passenger seat. "Maybe he had something to do."

She shuddered, not wanting to think what that might be with a teenage girl. "I'll kill him."

Jax said nothing, didn't give her any reassuring hand squeeze. He just let her be. Probably a good idea considering the knife edge her nerves were on right now.

"She's still here?"

He had the laptop on his knees, the brightness of the screen turned all the way down though it still amounted to a decent glow she hoped didn't draw the wrong attention. With the steady rainfall visibility was reduced enough they might be all right. "Yes, she's still here. Or the necklace is, at least."

Kenna bounced her knee.

"You know why we can't just bust in and search every room."

She kept bouncing it, trying to let out some of the pent-up frustration.

"He could have her with him."

"Then I'll kill him and take her." She clenched down on her molars.

Jax motioned to the building. "When he has armed guards?"

She hissed. "Ramon doesn't know that." But still, it lent credence to Jax's order that they sit here and let this play out. See what Ramon could accomplish with Elliot Preston. Give the FBI the evidence that would connect Elliot to the open case they were working.

Even if she didn't like it.

"Preston." Ramon's voice came through the phone speaker, the cell on the dash in front of them. They'd opted for a phone call they could record with the laptop.

It had better be worth it.

Maizie had to be in there—and she had to believe that Kenna would never let her be lost again.

"So you're him." Elliot's voice had a lethal tone to it.

Kenna leaned forward, itching to hear something from Maizie.

"And you're the guy who bailed on Navarro to take some girl from the ranch?" Ramon's tone dripped with disdain. "You could've saved his life, but you ran because you got what you wanted."

"My business."

Maizie wasn't in the room, and Elliot wasn't going to talk about where she was, or what he had planned for her? Kenna glanced at Jax. He held her gaze with that steady stare she needed to see.

Through the phone line, Ramon said, "You left so soon. Seems like you're not interested in salvaging what we can now that Navarro and Ian Kartom are both dead."

Elliot didn't answer right away. "I have my business. They have theirs."

"Not anymore. Your supply will run out, and you might not find whoever takes their place so amenable to provide what you...need." Ramon paused. "Your arrangement with Kart is over now he's dead."

"My cousin made his own way in the world." Elliot paused. "My brothers needed employees, and he provided. Who says that had anything to do with me?"

"This isn't a sting operation." Ramon chuckled. "You think American law enforcement would trust a turncoat like me to get you to admit what you've done?" He laughed louder. "That's rich. I couldn't care less where the feds are now. Who I surround myself with is a means to an end."

"And the same would be true with me?"

"I figure we can make it worth both our time," Ramon said. "Neither of us can afford to be on the radar of some Homeland Security Investigations' international taskforce. Or the FBI office across the border. You've done a stellar job being a silent partner so far. Why not keep the good stuff coming?"

"While you take care of everything here?"

"The goal is a good life, right?" Ramon paused. "You visit on the regular, I'll make it worth your while. Plenty of fish in the sea where that girl you've got came from. If that's your thing. Or you tell me what interests you. I can fill orders. You and I can divvy up what Kart had going on, and Navarro's operation."

"Drugs?"

"So you don't know." Ramon's voice took on a smarmy

tone—so fake and sleazy she could almost feel it. "Hopefully, you have a better handle on what Kart was doing."

"What was Navarro into?"

Ramon chuckled. "You ever heard of lithium mines?"

"Like the battery?"

"It's the fastest growing black-market industry south of the border. But if you're gonna be shortsighted...like this revenge plan...too easy to make a mistake and get yourself noticed." Ramon paused. "Maybe this was a mistake."

"Hold up," Elliot said. "I got in with them because they're family. They made it good for me, and I kept the US operation off the radar of everyone in Colorado until Kenna Banbury came along." His voice dripped with disdain. "But that doesn't mean I can't see a good business opportunity when it presents itself."

Jax touched the back of her hand, then pointed. He lowered the lid of the laptop to lessen the glow, and she watched over where he'd indicated. Two men. Not locals, they were dressed more like the guys who had been with Kart at the harbor when that delivery had come in—now getting soaked by the rain. They knew it had been a sting operation. Some of their friends had gone with Kart and encountered the FBI.

Kart had abandoned them to their fate.

Were these a different group, or more of the same—with a chip on their shoulder over how tonight had gone down?

Jax had been right that they shouldn't run into this building headlong, with no plan for how they would fight. She'd wrapped her arm, but the cut hurt. Ramon had been shot twice. He couldn't defend himself. No one was going to ask Jax to do so when he had been unconscious for days. Internal injuries. Surgery. A concussion, though he hadn't admitted it. She could see it at the edges of his expression—

the slightly distant look in his eyes, and the little slur in some of his words.

They were all running on empty at this point.

But until Maizie was free, no one was giving up.

The two men both carried guns and walked around the building on alert, like a patrol.

Kenna said, "He has protection."

That meant it would be harder to get Maizie out.

Jax squeezed her hand.

"I'm interested in a long-term partnership," Ramon said through the phone. "I have all Navarro's contacts. All his holdings. All his property and resources. If we combine what Kart built with that, we'll control this part of Mexico...and what your family had established in the US."

"So we work together." Elliot paused. "But I'm not giving you what's mine now."

"A partnership. This isn't about stealing. It's about how big we can be with both of us pulling in the same direction versus fighting each other." Ramon paused. "They did nothing but spend money and resources trying to get one up on the other. It was such a waste."

"And you're above such things. A fed who walked away from the Bureau for a bigger paycheck?"

Ramon chuckled. "The retirement plan is a whole lot better. Bigger risk. Bigger reward."

"I can see that."

"Once we get the feds and that woman you want revenge against *out of here*, then we can talk about building something real. But if you're gonna delay, I'll have to start working. I can't afford for some local to get big ideas and make a play for controlling stakes in what Navarro had."

"So you need protection from my friends, is that it?"

"Hardly. But I'll have things to deal with here," Ramon

said. "I won't be free to follow whatever personal agenda I might have."

"I can multitask. And if you knew what this woman did to my brothers, you'd be cheering me on."

Kenna huffed out a breath. *As if.* Men who kept people locked up, used them as laborers, and treated them despicably didn't get a free pass. She hadn't lifted a hand to either of Elliot's brothers. But she also hadn't forcibly stopped it when their victims took the situation into their own hands.

It might look a whole lot more like street justice than Kenna's specific brand of justice. But she'd tried to handle the situation and the actions of those people. In the end, she'd saved more than had lost their lives.

She could sleep at night.

How Elliot managed it, she had no idea.

Ramon said, "Sounds like maybe you don't have as much of a handle on your business as you think. But we can make both our lives easier, if we agree to work together. Pool resources. Like a partnership."

"It's an interesting offer." Elliot paused. "Perhaps you should deal with your situation here, with the federal agents you've got running around...and the usurpers who will no doubt try to steal Navarro's power. I'll take care of my business. And then we'll talk."

"If that's the way you want to play this." It sounded like Ramon wanted Elliot to believe he might've moved on from interest in a partnership by the time Elliot came back around.

"We'll see how it plays out," Elliot said. "If it's meant to be, it'll work for both of us."

Ramon huffed. "Whatever, bro. If you believe in all that." Footsteps echoed across the phone line. "Best of luck and all that, I guess."

"You don't gotta worry about me."

A door closed.

She watched the front of the building and spotted Ramon exit. He turned away from them and continued down the street, where the wind bent the trees over. Two men they'd seen on patrol followed after him, leaving enough distance he might not realize they were there with the noise of the storm.

Kenna grabbed the phone. "They're in pursuit."

"Copy that," Ramon said. "I didn't see her."

Jax leaned toward the phone. "We got enough from his statement for the FBI to get a warrant to dig into Elliot Preston's life. We'll take him down one way or another."

"And my name will be on that report, right?" Ramon sounded almost hopeful.

Kenna said, "If that's what you want."

"I'll let you know." Ramon hung up and didn't reappear.

The two men following him stopped at a corner and didn't go any farther. A few seconds later, they turned back to the building.

An SUV pulled around the structure.

"She's on the move." Jax had the laptop open again. The GPS signal emanating from the necklace Maizie had made for Kenna followed the path of the SUV, though the signal looked more like she was still inside one of the buildings.

Kenna's stomach lurched. "She's in the SUV?"

"That's what we'll find out."

The vehicle stopped, and the two men who'd followed Ramon climbed in. It sped away. The signal for the necklace raced along the buildings beside the street, then slipped onto the road as though whatever it connected to had recalculated her location with greater accuracy.

"She's with them. Not here."

"And they're headed toward the storm by the look of it."

Kenna pulled out behind them but kept her lights off. "As

long as we're in pursuit."

"What's the plan for when you catch us up to them?" Jax asked. "We can't take on multiple gunmen the state we're in."

Before she could answer, his phone rang.

"Special Agent Jaxton." He listened. Then said, "Copy that," his tone almost sad. "I'm sorry to hear that. Is everyone else good?" After another pause, he continued, "West, toward the highway. I can share my phone's location, and you can catch up. Track us. We could use the backup."

He told the caller—presumably one of the other agents here—what Ramon had gathered for them from Elliot Preston. How they now had evidence that he was involved with Kart's operation. Or, had been, before Kart was killed by one of those very agents he was talking to.

"Thanks." Jax hung up. "They'll be along shortly. Wherever we end up, there will be agents with us. But they have to call in first. The guy they had go to the compound to check it out was still there. Dead in the dirt with no shirt on and a W carved into his back."

She flinched. "What?"

"I know." Jax blew out a breath. "Someone involved with this killed him before he could call for help. All because he went there to see what we could salvage."

This was unbelievable. "They should know better than to let someone go alone somewhere around here with no backup."

Jax glanced at her. "Don't you do it all the time?"

"Am I alone right now?"

He said nothing for a second.

"I'm being smart."

"Right." He paused again. "And now an agent is dead on foreign soil, no one is gonna rest until they find whoever did it."

"I hope they do. He has a list of victims, and I didn't have enough to figure out who it was."

"I guess we can rule out Elliot Preston."

She gripped the wheel and stared at the SUV up ahead. His crimes weren't that, but they were sufficient for her. "And Ramon Santiago."

"You really thought it might be him?"

She lifted one shoulder. "I was more interested in getting out of there, and getting all of us home."

"We'll get there," he said.

"It's taken too long already." She flipped on the windshield wipers. "And this guy is driving right into a hurricane. Who does that?"

"Is the weather gonna make you stop, or will you get her back anyway?"

"I don't need a pep talk!" She stomped harder on the gas pedal.

"Try not to crash us."

"I've had enough car accidents for a month. I'm not running him off the road. It could kill her." She sucked in a breath and tried to tamp down the panic.

Lord, help us.

She continued, "Once they stop, we find a place to intercept. And I hope those FBI agents drive fast, because I'm not hanging around waiting for backup if I have the chance to get her back."

"Good thing you have backup right here."

And an arsenal of weapons, thanks to Stairns. How he'd managed to transport them across the border—or pick them up locally—was a question she wanted an answer to. When he got out of surgery.

Kenna let go of the wheel with one hand. "Start praying."

Jax clasped her hand. "I haven't stopped."

Chapter Thirty-One

Rain battered against the windshield. Kenna had long since cleared her mind, focusing on nothing but each breath. Each foot of asphalt under the car. Each mile they traversed along the highway toward the harbor.

Where the shipment had come in.

And now Elliot was taking Maizie there? "He's making a run for it."

She tapped her index finger on the steering wheel while the wipers beat back the rain. Or, at least, they attempted it. The hurricane was back in full force. Not because it changed directions but because they'd driven right back into it.

"You think he's gonna take her back to the US?" Jax said.

Kenna stared at the taillights up ahead. "Boat. He's leaving this area, maybe the country. But why does keeping her hit back at me if he doesn't contact me to gloat?"

"He could be gathering materials. Whatever he's going to send you to torture you with what he did to her."

Kenna sucked in a breath through her nose, held it, and swallowed. "Can't do much in a packed SUV on the road."

"So that's what the boat is for."

The vehicle up ahead turned off the highway. "This is the worst kind of déjà vu. Being back here. We've seriously spent all night going back and forth to the coast, and now we're here again."

He'd offered to drive a couple of times, but adrenaline kept her alert. Eventually it would burn out. But for right now she was running on anger and prayers.

He typed on his computer. Making notes that would become reports later. When she'd asked why he was continually typing on the road when they had no internet connection, he'd told her that he was typing up everything he could remember and all that'd happened that evening while it was fresh.

If he wanted to do something rather than simply sit there doing nothing, she wasn't going to begrudge him it.

Same reason she was driving.

Except if the worst happened and for some reason the two of them didn't live past tonight, Jax had left record of who they were and what went down here. Not to mention who was responsible for the crimes committed in this part of Mexico that they were aware of.

She wasn't going to leave a last-will-and-testament-type statement. With Maizie and Stairns in her life, there would always be someone who knew what she had been doing right before she died.

Lord, protect us. And protect Maizie—mentally and physically.

Kenna sniffed.

She followed the SUV and found a spot not too obvious but from which they could watch Elliot's vehicle. "We need to get closer."

Jax shook his head. "Not without weapons."

They climbed out. She hit the button to lift the trunk lid,

and Jax handed her a pistol and suppressor while the rain battered down on them. She got it secured on the end of the barrel. Protective vests. Stairns had been prepared, and she would forever be grateful for the people in her life.

Not something she'd asked for, but which God had provided to her regardless.

Jax jogged ahead of her. Kenna took cover with him, at the corner of a shed while rain poured down the back of her neck.

The SUV doors opened, and several figures in dark clothes headed along the pier.

Which boat was theirs? And would Kenna and Jax get the chance to climb aboard without being spotted before the captors left with Maizie?

Their only other option was to force a fight right now rather than face the choppy waves.

"I count six. Not including Elliot," Jax said. "No. More like ten."

Kenna grasped the T-shirt at his side, careful of what wounds she knew he had. But she needed to anchor herself or she was going to dissolve. "There she is."

Both of them held still.

Her blond hair seemed to catch the moonlight. Maizie looked around. Expecting a rescue?

We're here.

The teen had her hands bound in front of her, and walked with a slight limp.

"They hurt her," Kenna said.

"You know she would've fought back," Jax said. "She wouldn't go down without a fight."

"I was more afraid she would freeze and be able to do nothing while they..." Her voice caught. "Let's go."

Jax didn't move. He held up a hand stalling her forward

momentum. "We can't get close enough without being seen. And it's too risky us against so many."

"I'm not letting them take her."

A car squealed into the parking lot at high speed, taking the turn fast and drawing the attention of the men on the pier. They started to run as the car barreled across the empty lot toward them.

Two of the men broke away from the group, moving back toward the SUV. They opened fire on the car as it sped to the front end of the SUV. The windshield splintered. Bullets hit the side of the car.

"They're going to get killed." Jax started forward.

Kenna held his elbow and went with him, unwilling to stop him from doing what he needed to do even if it was just a knee-jerk reaction. Then watched the boat as they moved. "She's on board. They're going to leave, and we won't be able to stop them."

The agents in the car opened fire on the gunmen, and both went down.

Three doors opened, and they climbed out, the body language of each man indicating they were at the end of their ropes. She didn't blame them. They'd come to protect an agent, one of their own had been killed, and they'd wound up in the middle of more than one crazy situation tonight.

And they weren't done.

The boat pulled away from the dock.

Kenna broke away from Jax and ran past the car. Someone spoke to her, but she ignored them and kept running, down the pier to the slip, even though the boat was long gone.

Maizie was out there.

Her breaths came fast. The water rippled, split by the trail that dissolved into the choppy water as they boat sped away. Out of reach.

Gone.

"Come on." Jax tugged at her.

She couldn't look away.

He tugged again. "Kenna, come *on*. We're going after her."

Those words got her moving. She nearly stumbled but followed him onto a smaller boat. One of the agents stood behind the wheel. The engine caught and came to life. Another agent jumped on board behind them and tossed down a rope. Soaked. "Got it. Let's go."

"Come on." Jax tugged her to a seat.

They were all soaked.

She realized why he wanted her to sit when the boat set off away from the pier and she stumbled to the seat. They'd just hotwired a boat and were stealing it. Because these FBI agents believed the person responsible for their colleague's death was on the boat ahead of them? Since it could absolutely be the case, she didn't begrudge their determination.

Jax spoke in her ear, over the pounding rain and the noise of the boat engine. "She knows how to survive."

Kenna stared at the boat ahead, unwilling to let Stairns wake up from surgery and not have word that they'd got Maizie back. She was going to spend every ounce of her energy protecting this child. Even if Maizie would never refer to herself as that. The girl never had a childhood and was never given the chance to be a kid.

If they didn't succeed tonight, she would never be able to see what Maizie could become. The girl would never know what real peace felt like—the kind Kenna had found just tonight. The kind of soul deep reassurance that tethered her when every bit of her wanted to spin out of control.

She grasped Jax's hand and held on.

There was so much that made up Maizie which Kenna couldn't wait to see. The teen was *so* smart. And that wasn't just a doting hero talking. Maizie was off-the-charts smart, and she wanted to do good in the world. Kenna couldn't wait to see what became of her.

She turned now and saw Jax's lips moving, though she couldn't hear what he was saying.

Praying.

He was praying.

She wanted to pull his face down and kiss him, but they'd been interrupted last time, and right now they had an audience of three angry FBI agents.

One stormed over to them. "Come with me."

He didn't wait to see if they agreed, just headed for a hatch and climbed down into it. Kenna followed. Jax came with her. Below the deck was a small enclosure, but it seemed someone lived in here from time to time. It smelled like salt and dead fish. Maybe the owner liked what those scents represented.

Freedom.

The thing they wanted to give back to Maizie tonight.

For some people, freedom wasn't a right. It was a gift that had to be given to them.

"Okay," the agent began. He faced them both, one of his hands braced on the low ceiling. "There's nowhere to sit, so we'll just have to do this standing."

"I'd rather be on the deck watching the boat." Kenna wanted Maizie in sight—as much as that was possible.

"Be that as it may..." He paused to catch his balance as the boat swayed. "We need answers from you as to what's about to happen."

Jax said, "We're about to rescue a seventeen-year-old female trafficking victim."

Kenna's stomach lurched, and it had nothing to do with the rocking of the ocean under them.

The agent looked at her. "Do you always bring minors on cases with you?"

She didn't know how to answer that.

"Once this is complete, you will accompany the other agents and I back to *our* plane to return to the US, where you will be fully debriefed at our FBI field office in San Diego."

Go back to the FBI to make a statement? She glanced at Jax, not sure her heart could handle him in any more danger.

He nodded. "It's the right thing."

"I can't even think right now," she said. "We just need to get Maizie back."

"And then you'll be returning to the US with us. And your friends will be coming as well." The agent shrugged. "You can stay together while you explain who you all are and why you're down here."

Jax shifted. "I told you when I woke up in the hospital how we got here, Farnes. We aren't part of your case."

"Right, you're just material witnesses," Agent Farnes said. Then he glanced at Kenna. "And you roll with a former ASAC who dropped off the grid after he retired. What about your teenage friend? Who is she?"

Kenna didn't want to say if she didn't have to. "I'm assuming you looked her up?"

"You have few known associates." Farnes stared at her. "Of those listed, a teen isn't one of them. So who is she, and where did she come from?"

They really needed her to answer? Couldn't they just focus on saving Maizie and then figure it out? The girl could procure a fake ID by then that would be convincing enough.

She could be Kenna's cousin, and then the FBI would never know where she'd come from.

Jax shifted slightly. "How about the truth?"

She didn't look at Jax. The insinuation in that question indicated yet again his ability to read her. It was a little disconcerting. Or right now she was simply not doing so well hiding her feelings from her expression.

"Fine," she said. *The truth.* "I'm sure you have people who can access those databases of seized material labeled 'child exploitation.' You know, the ones where the children have never even been identified and no one has any idea who they are, or where to find them."

The agent stared at her.

"Why don't you run her image through a search of those. When we get her back. Because unlike social media, or any educational institution, doctor's office, family album or sport... she might actually show up there."

Only because Kenna was pretty sure Maizie had deleted any record of herself from the servers at the company run by the man who had held her for years.

"So she's nobody."

Kenna bristled. "She's very definitely *somebody*."

"You know what I mean."

"Honestly, I'm not sure I do, Farnes. But that girl is family, and the only thing I care about right now is getting her back." She headed for the open hatch, where the rain fell inside. It misted against her face like tears running down her cheeks.

He stepped after her. "If I'm risking the lives of my agents, I have a right to ask for intel."

She glanced over her shoulder. "I didn't ask for your help."

And she didn't look at Jax. He knew how she felt, and he

was as determined as her to get Maizie back. What was there to say? Except to pray over this whole situation—and Stairns' surgery.

Kenna climbed the ladder. It took a few seconds longer than she would've liked, but she found the boat in the distance. Below the deck, she could hear Jax and the agent arguing.

They followed the boat nearly all night.

Hours and hours of swelling ocean. The clouds dissipated until she could see stars. Then the first glow of sunrise coming up from below the horizon...and she spotted an island.

No doubt Elliot Preston knew they were behind him.

But still, she refused to do anything but press on. She had a gun. She had a vest, even though she couldn't have cared less about personal safety right now. It was a means to an end—a way to keep going even if she was hit. A chance to tip the odds in her favor if she could take one more step. Cover one more bit of ground.

And get Maizie back.

"You really care about this girl."

Kenna didn't bother to look at the agent, whichever one of them it was. "Like I said. She's family."

The boat ahead of them stopped at a dock. Agent Farnes handed her binoculars, and she saw Maizie being led from the boat—carried, not walking on her own.

Kenna's stomach clenched.

Two of the gunmen moved onto the deck of their boat and opened fire with rifles. A steady rattle of rounds spent in their direction. All that deadly intention backed up by firepower.

The agent piloting their boat made a sharp turn, and they all hunkered down. Bullets hit the water in front of them. "Get us closer!"

She wasn't willing to give up. Not when they were so close.

Kenna looked up.

Jax pulled her back down. "Don't!"

"We need to get to her."

"I know that." Jax turned. "Find a place we can swim to shore."

The agents on board opened fire on the gunmen, giving enough cover for them to pilot away from them going parallel to shore.

Kenna couldn't not look. She had to know what was happening. Her young friend was alive, wasn't she?

Please tell me her life doesn't end this way.

Kenna stood again and spotted her. "Maizie."

Her heart caught in her throat as she saw the girl tumble out of the man's arms. The guy carrying her reached for his gun. Elliot shoved him away and ran after Maizie himself.

"Run." The word escaped her lips.

The boat rocked, caught up on a shallow sandbar.

Kenna launched up and jumped over the side. She splashed into knee-high water. "Maizie!"

The girl was too far to hear. She'd disappeared into the trees, racing out of sight. Running for her life.

Run.

Elliot Preston saw Kenna and didn't slow. Instead, he went after the girl.

Chapter Thirty-Two

A bullet whizzed past Kenna's head.

She ducked reflexively, but no way would she slow down. She raced out of the water onto the shore and pounded sand as fast as she could to the path where Maizie had disappeared, followed by Elliot. She had no weapon. All she had was the strength in her legs she'd been building before she was kidnapped in Washington.

And the trust in God that He hadn't brought her this far only to let her fail now.

She ran so hard that one boot came off. The other followed behind not more than a couple of steps later, leaving her no other option but to run in her socks. Kicking up sand. Her vision so focused on that path—rather than the gun battle going on around her—that pain sliced into her head.

She blinked. Gasped a breath.

Caught herself before she could stumble.

There was someone running behind her, not too far back. Jax. She hoped it was him, anyway, and there was no time to check.

She tore down the path, the nascent morning giving her enough light to see. At the end there was a white structure.

Between her and the building Elliot had caught Maizie.

The girl made no sound. She didn't fight. She didn't scream.

Kenna ran to them. She spotted the gun Elliot had pressed to the underside of Maizie's neck. "Don't! Don't shoot her!"

She had nothing to threaten him with. No weapons to take him out if he decided to kill the teen.

"Let...her...go." Kenna could only gasp out the words, desperate to get Maizie safe.

She took another step closer. Elliot seemed to relish it, intently watching her approach.

"Please." If that was what he wanted, she would give it to him. She would trade herself back into her nightmare to save Maizie.

God would go with her into the darkness.

She wouldn't be alone.

Whoever was behind her shifted slightly. Elliot didn't notice, intently watching Kenna. She should keep his focus on her.

Kenna took another half step. "Let her go. Please. I'll go with you. Whatever you want."

Maizie flinched. The first and only reaction she'd seen from the girl.

A gunshot exploded close behind her. Kenna flinched, caught off guard by the loud crack. Elliot stiffened, then went down, taking Maizie with him.

Kenna ran to them. She dragged Elliot's gun from where he dropped it and tossed it away.

Then she gathered Maizie up. Her legs gave out, and she whimpered, holding the girl close to her as they stumbled onto the ground together. She tucked Maizie's head in her neck. "I've got you." Tears rolled down Kenna's cheeks. "It's over."

The girl didn't reach for her. Didn't hold on.

"Maze." Kenna squeezed her shoulder. Maybe she wasn't ready to engage. Maybe she never would be, and this experience was the thing that finally broke what little hold she had on her psyche.

Kenna couldn't help the tears that escaped over that thought.

Jax felt Elliot's neck for a pulse. "He's gone."

"But he got what he wanted."

Maizie flinched.

Kenna didn't let go. "He wanted to see me destroyed, and he did it." Plus whatever else he'd taken from Maizie that had her like this. "We need to go."

Maizie shifted.

Kenna spoke the words she imagined her young friend wanted to say. "I don't want to be here anymore." They needed to get Maizie to Stairns' wife, Elizabeth, so they could talk it through, and hopefully soon Maizie would be on the path to being the young woman she had started to become over the past few months.

There were so many other things she wanted to say.

Maizie should never have come down here. Stairns should never have brought her, or allowed her to come. Her young friend should've been smarter than to come to Mexico, regardless of their need to find and rescue Kenna.

She wasn't worth all this.

Jax injured, hospitalized. Stairns now in surgery. Maizie broken...again.

They'd all given so much just to help her.

Too much.

She almost couldn't handle it. She wanted to tell them all

that it hadn't been worth it. The cost was too high. *She* wasn't worth it.

But the fact they'd taken the risk regardless meant they thought she was, something that turned out to be a kind of grace. A reflection of how God felt about her, and the gift He had given her.

Thank You.

Jax came over and crouched in Maizie's line of sight. The last thing Kenna wanted was for the girl to be scared of him. But she stiffened on Kenna's lap and didn't move. She needed to learn the difference between a good man, and the kind who only wanted to victimize her.

Kenna said, "Thank you for saving both of us."

Jax leaned down slowly and touched his lips to hers. Just a simple, soft touch. Brief but with a wealth of statement even in something so small. "Always."

He stood, the stance a whole lot like he was keeping guard.

The gunfire on the shore had ceased.

It took a few minutes, but eventually she heard one of the agents approaching—it had to be a friendly because their sentry didn't shoot the person. The agent moved to Jax's side so she could see him without turning around.

The one who had confronted her below deck on the ship crouched. Special Agent Farnes. "Are you ladies all right?"

Kenna nodded. "Yes, thank you."

"We're going to search the island. My agents are already going to the structure up there." He motioned over his shoulder. "So hopefully we can find something that ties the man that took you to a bigger operation."

She knew it was about the scope of the case, and how wide they could cast the net. That way they might be able to find someone involved that wasn't dead as of tonight.

They would also want to find the person who'd killed their agent at the compound.

Though, right now Kenna couldn't figure out who that might be.

"We would like to get out of here," Kenna said. "We can take one of the boats."

The skin around Farnes' eyes flexed. "I will need statements from both of you, and you should get checked out by a doctor. But unless you've got a line to a private company that can send a helicopter to pick you up, I'm afraid you'll be leaving when we do."

Kenna stared at him. Then she glanced at Jax. "Can I borrow your phone?"

Four hours later, the rented black SUV pulled up outside the hospital in Cielo Ardiente. Not because either of them wanted to see a doctor. Maizie still hadn't said a word, but Kenna could guess she didn't want to be seen by a medical professional. Poked and prodded.

Except it was likely necessary.

The driver didn't get out. She'd given them explicit instructions after she had the private security company fly from Miami to the island, then to the east coast of Mexico where three rented armored SUVs met them. They'd hustled —and she'd paid extra for it. But all Kenna wanted to do was get Maizie and Stairns, then get out of Mexico.

Jax had stayed behind with the FBI even though she'd argued that he should come with her and get medical treatment. No way should the guy be out of the hospital.

Did he listen? No.

I'll find you. Let me wrap this up.

Maybe he thought he was doing her and Maizie a favor, making sure it was actually over. Or he figured the less the FBI had eyes on her, the better. Or he needed space. Or...

She should quit worrying about it.

"Maizie." She touched the girl's hand. The teen stared at the tinted window, her eyes unseeing. Kenna tugged on her hand. "Maizie, I need to know if...you were raped. Because if you were, I'd like you to see a doctor. You don't want...injuries that go untreated."

Maizie said nothing.

"Honey, if I find a doctor you can be comfortable with, can you let her take a look at you?"

Maizie's fingers flexed. Just the barest movement.

"I'm going to take that as a yes." Kenna held herself very still. "I'm going to be with you every step, and we're going to make sure you aren't in pain. Then we're going to get Stairns and go home. Okay?"

Just then, Stairns' wife stepped outside the hospital, wringing her hands in front of her.

Kenna's stomach clenched. *Please tell me he's all right.* "Look." She tugged on Maizie's hand and used her other to push open the door. "Elizabeth is here." Not giving Maizie much choice but to go with her, Kenna climbed out.

Elizabeth gave her a hug.

"We're in one piece," Kenna said. "How is Stairns?"

Maizie sat in the open door.

"He's awake," Elizabeth said. "I had to convince him you were on your way, or he'd have unhooked himself and come after you."

"I couldn't believe it when you said you were already on your way." Kenna had called Stairns' wife right after she'd booked the private security company.

Elizabeth shrugged. "I knew when they didn't check in that something had happened, and a member of staff from the hospital called me when he went into surgery. I haven't been here long."

"It's really good to see you." Kenna didn't want this to just be about Maizie when Elizabeth was also here for her husband, but the teen needed to be carefully guided through this.

"There's a crowd gathering." Elizabeth leaned close and said to Maizie, "Let's get inside before it gets busy out here."

Kenna helped the girl stand.

Elizabeth said, "I've got her," and walked with Maizie into the hospital.

The front passenger unfolded himself from the SUV and stood. Kenna blinked. He was at least six four, and that suit had to have been fitted to NFL player size. Hair shaved close to his head, and a tiny scar in his left eyebrow. Midthirties and the size of a bear.

Of the three SUVs, now causing quite the spectacle, she spotted at least five men, one woman. Kenna had no idea if this was the whole team. She'd called the first number for a private security company in Miami with their own helicopter, and it had said on the website they covered Mexico as a specialty.

Money took care of the rest.

She might have to buy last year's model RV for her next home, but it was worth it to make sure Maizie felt safe. Honestly, she was glad they were here as well.

The legacy of royalties from her father's book sales finally put to good use.

Maybe she should donate some to the church here—or the local school.

"You look exhausted, but you're safe." The man strode toward her, towering over her. "We're good to hang here as long as you're inside. If this goes overnight, I'll have to rotate my people out so they can get some sleep."

Kenna nodded. "I'll keep you apprised." She pushed out a

long breath, hardly believing this thing was over. "Thank you for coming so fast. I really appreciate how professional you guys have been."

He nodded. "Client satisfaction is what we're about."

Kenna stuck her hand out. "Thank you."

He shook it, thankfully not crushing the bones in her hand. "Take care of your girl. We'll be here when you need us."

Kenna headed inside and found the priest waiting in the lobby. He turned to her as she approached, even though she was only headed to the elevator so she could go check on Stairns.

"Ms. Kenna."

She stopped in front of the priest.

"There are people in town who wish to express their gratitude for your ridding us of El Falcón. You must understand. My friend in Albuquerque who died, he..." His voice broke.

"I understand how hard it is to lose someone you care for a great deal." Kenna took a deep breath. "I will pray for Cielo Ardiente that the town can be at peace, and the people here can be free of men like Navarro."

His brows rose, and he gave her a short nod. "Thank you."

Kenna squeezed his hand and went to find her family.

Chapter Thirty-Three

Kenna hit Send on the email to the CEO of the Miami private security company, thanking them for their help, even though she'd been generous with her tip. She planned to call them again if she ever needed a rescue like that. Or bodyguards.

Having them take care of making sure she—along with Stairns, Elizabeth, and Maizie—got back to Colorado had been worth every penny.

She set the phone on the arm of the plastic Adirondak chair. There might be a foot of snow on the ground, but she'd slept out here in front of the fire. Covered in blankets. Right now her dog lay curled up between her feet and the chair, though Cabot spent most of her time in the trailer with Maizie.

The old mutt had a dog door in the screen. Maizie had opened the door early, though Kenna hadn't even caught sight of her, and Cabot had hopped outside. She'd been with Kenna since, but it wouldn't be long before she went back to the teen's side.

Stairns was on the mend, but still resting a lot. Elizabeth had been up giving Stairns medication, and she'd brought Kenna hot chocolate in the early hours of the morning. Then Kenna had spent half an hour web searching for tiny homes since one of those would be warmer than sleeping outside in November in the Colorado mountains.

She could put one next to the Airstream and be Maizie's neighbor when she stopped by the Stairns' residence between cases. Or just a new rig to park by Maizie.

Kenna hadn't worked since she left Mexico, but she'd talked to the Rysons often the last couple of weeks.

Jax had called every day, asking for updates on Maizie and Stairns. His current assignment in San Diego was keeping him busy searching for the killer who had slipped by them. He was also living at his parents' house while he found a condo and had his stuff shipped over. He'd invited her down for the holidays. She hadn't answered about that yet.

No one had mentioned Ramon Santiago, and she hadn't heard from him since he walked away that night after meeting with Elliot. She had no idea where he'd gone, or what he was doing.

Maybe she never would.

Her phone beeped. Maizie had sent her a news article about a gruesome murder in Scottsdale, Arizona.

The MO matched their killer.

Kenna should send the FBI everything she knew about Kart's associate who had taken those girls north. They could find him and track him down, right? She could stay here for the holidays and make sure Maizie eventually emerged from the trailer.

Every day Elizabeth went inside for an hour.

When she came out, her face would be gray. Kenna wanted to know what they spoke about but wasn't going to pry between a counselor and her patient. She just wanted to be here for both of them. For Maizie to know she was being watched over and protected, and sleep with the reassurance she was safe here.

Kenna needed a new home, an RV or motorhome of some kind that would give her a home base on the road since she'd have a tiny home in Colorado. And she needed a case to work...preferably somewhere nowhere near Jax's mother's Christmas dinner table.

They were close, but she wasn't sure she was quite ready for that step.

So far since they got back here, she'd been reading her Bible. Listening to teachings online. She'd bought a car, finally getting something newer rather than a nondescript old car liable to overheat at any moment. Calling that company in Miami had made her realize that she could use her money for positive things, and she didn't need to feel guilty about inheriting income from her dad's sensational stories.

She messaged Maizie back.

How about something northeast of here?

Not that she usually chose cases based on location, but she could use a change of scenery. Maizie would be able to work and hopefully keep her mind from going back to what those men had done while they held her.

There were only so many ways for Kenna to tell her that she would heal. That sometime in the future she'd realize she'd gone a whole day without thinking about it.

Another beep.

An article about a decades old unsolved mystery. Washington Island. Kenna had to look it up. The Wisconsin penin-sula, and it was only accessible by ferry? One constable. A small population.

I like it.

Another beep.

A link to a website that sold Class C motor homes. *I guess it's time to get moving.*

Kenna messaged back,

You think it's time for me to go?

Maybe she was hovering. Or Maizie wanted some kind of normalcy. Whichever it was, Kenna would be happy to take a case that might prove interesting, and certainly wouldn't involve a cartel or drug dealers, or human trafficking.

She hoped.

Maizie replied,

It's time for someone to find out what
happened to Meri Santiago.

Kenna frowned. She tapped the screen and swiped through until she had the answer to what she was looking for.

Ramon Santiago had a sister. Twenty-five years ago she had gone missing during a family vacation to Washington Island from their home in Chicago. Six years old, and she had been missing one morning. Bed empty, window open. No suspects. No leads.

No one had ever found her.

Kenna pushed out of the chair. Cabot groaned and stood, shaking off before she licked Kenna's hand, and then trotted back through the dog door into the Airstream. Maizie stayed out of sight but managed to shut the door.

She sent another message.

Take care of her.

The reply:

> I always do.

Three separate articles dropped as links after Maizie's message. Research for the case, and a place to start looking into what had happened to Ramon's sister. Wherever he was in the world she'd be able to give him closure.

It was time for Kenna to get back to work.

Also by Lisa Phillips

Find out more about Brand of Justice at my website:

https://authorlisaphillips.com/brand-of-justice

Book 1: Cold Dead Night (Aug 2022)

Book 2: Burn the Dawn (Nov 2022)

Book 3: Quick and Dead (Feb 2023)

Book 4: Over the Limit (June 2023)

Book 5: Skin and Bone (August 2023)

Book 6: Dust and Ashes (November 2023)

Book 7: Long Way Home (January 2024)

———

For Lovers of Romantic Suspense check out

-Benson First Responders-

———

Other series by Lisa:

Last Chance Downrange

Chevalier Protection Specialists

Last Chance County

Northwest Counter-Terrorism Taskforce

Double Down

WITSEC Town (Sanctuary)

———

For other titles including several with Love Inspired Suspense, you can find the complete list here:

https://authorlisaphillips.com/full-book-list

About the Author

Find out more about Lisa Phillips, and other books she has written, by visiting her website: https://authorlisaphillips.com

Follow Lisa on Facebook and Instagram, and subscribe to her newsletter to stay up to date and be the first to find out about raffles and giveaways! https://authorlisaphillips.com/subscribe

facebook.com/authorlisaphillips

instagram.com/lisaphillipsbks

bookbub.com/authors/lisa-phillips

www.ingramcontent.com/pod-product-compliance
Lightning Source LLC
Chambersburg PA
CBHW020055310726
48970CB00002B/325